PASSAGE TO BELLE FOURCHE

John A Lamb

Barnstead Press

ISBN 978-0-615-81211-3

Also available
at
www.barnsteadpress.com

Cover artwork and book design by Melissa Darnell
Project Managed by Allison D'Amato

For my children

Andy
Chris
C.J.
John
Liz

With my deepest respect, gratitude and love
for brightening my life

About the Author

Born in 1921, Lamb has lived during the time of the most social extremes in the twentieth century. Intermittent wars, depressions and prosperity have temporarily retarded or stimulated advances in scientific, economic and equal rights and along the way provided Lamb with perspectives and participation in endeavors ranging over the years from errand boy to corporate counselor. Since retirement, Lamb has counseled college graduates seeking employment, volunteered in prisoner rehabilitation and worked with street people. After several years of painting he concentrated on writing and completed his autobiography and three novels – the last, Strange Bedfellows, Foul Play – Fair Play – Foreplay, was published in 2010.

Chapter 1

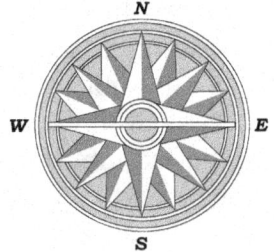

For centuries, confined to limited functions in designated territories known as shtetls, Russian Jews served surrounding inhabitants as millers, inn-keepers, metal-workers, cobblers, weavers, tanners, bakers and peddlers, only to be displaced with the emancipation of the serfs. No longer nobility's sole sources of service, shtetls found their recompense so seriously undercut by the new competitors, large numbers of Jews were forced to beg for survival or move to industrialized Warsaw and Grodno. Others migrated to a more distant America, a working people's haven with religious freedom. At seventeen, Moses Morgenstern embraced his misty-eyed father and less adventuresome seven brothers and sisters, slung a peddler's pack over his shoulder and never looked back, knowing to do so would imprison him forever.

The walk to Bremen, port of embarkation for New York, was much longer than it appeared on the map, requiring intermittent delays for Moses to help farmers along the way with their harvests in exchange for a meal and a night's sleep in their haylofts. Too proud to beg, he went hungry when there was no work. On the worst days he ate cabbages overlooked in the harvested fields, suffering bloat and diarrhea, but he never faltered in his exodus, reassuring himself that the land he was going to offered a better life than the place he'd left. With the hardship of a freezing winter overtaking him, Moses slowed his pace to Bremen, stopping at more villages and towns along the way to work indoors at odd jobs in exchange for food and shelter. His offer to barter, initially turned down by some innkeepers, won out when he volunteered to clean toilets. Advancing along a thoroughfare to Bremen, paths, lanes and secondary roads converged like tributaries to a river carrying a swelling flow of refugees to the German port.

As the migrant masses increased, Moses hoped to find companionship to end the long, solitary trek on which he'd been accompanied only by the persistent threat of extinction. All those he approached for friendship rebuffed him, fearing affability committed them to share their dwindling resources. Like others displaced, Moses became the target for shysters scheming to separate him from his pittance no matter how small. Sickness and death also traveled the road to Bremen and Jews, upon the demise of a family member, were obligated to observe Hebrew law in secluded mourning, causing some to miss the boat to America. Many of the old and frail, obsessed with the fear of being left behind, drove themselves to exhaustion, hastening the end of life in a grotesque paradox.

One day of winter's leaden skies, when the émigrés were pressed against the twenty-feet high, chain-linked fence restraining them from entering the Bremen docks, an argument erupted over which of the more than eight hundred applicants for the New York voyage should be chosen to fill the four hundred passenger quota. Yelling and shoving escalated in the absence of an authority prepared to restore order. Quick to sense the potential havoc of an unruly mob, Moses climbed the wire fence in order to be visible to the crowd.

"Stop! Stop before harm is done. Stop before the authorities refuse to take any of us," he yelled. "Stop before you harm loved ones."

The women grew quiet and reproached the men for not listening. Moses continued speaking in a loud voice, then lowered it as the crowd calmed so they might not miss anything he said.

"We all cannot go on this ship, but there will be other ships. If I am chosen for this ship, I will give the space to someone more deserving and take the next ship. Let us choose our candidates for this ship or the authorities' choices may tear families apart."

"How would you figure out who goes and who stays for the next boat, whenever that is, Young Mister Know-It-All? There are more than eight hundred of us here and only room for four hundred on the boat."

Words came freely to Moses, and he called out, "Form twenty groups of forty people each and appoint a leader. When that is done I will tell you what do to next."

The agitated crowd, curious to know his plan, became orderly and followed his instructions. Twenty groups were formed haphazardly and a representative chosen for each.

Then Moses explained further. "Now each leader, starting with any but his own group, chooses one person from each of the twenty groups, saving your own group for last. Then do this over and over until you have ten groups of forty each. These are the four hundred who take this boat. The others take the next boat to America."

The crowd grew quiet, the burden of what they were about to do weighing heavily on each.

"What if a family is split with some going and others staying?" an old man asked in a tearful voice.

"Then someone chosen can give up his place to another. I've already promised my place if this should happen to me." Moses was aware of hearing a few discontents question the lottery, their voices growing fainter till all was quiet.

Moses blinked his eyes several times to be rid of the heavy stupor settled on him, erasing the division between sleep and wakefulness, between imagination and reality, or was it the other way around. Attempting to orient himself in unidentifiable surroundings, he forcibly focused on the shadowless, white room of undetermined dimension except where empty, double-decker bunks interrupted the monotony of the walls. He sat up, forgetting he was on the top bunk. Swinging his legs over the side of the mattress, he almost fell five feet to the floor below.

Presiding over this sterile domain sat a woman, not yet wrinkled from age, sheathed in white except for her face and hands, scrubbed red as a sunburn. The woman wagged her head, her white, sail-like headdress flapping as though she might soon be airborne.

"You had quite a fall," she said in a detached, clinical manner. "When you didn't gain consciousness after five days, we held a Mass for you."

"Oh yes, I remember a disturbing heretical chant with bells punctuating a departure from our Patriarch's Law," Moses said, never thinking his reply might be offensive or at least unappreciated.

"When you stand up, hold onto something stable," the sister directed, forgiving the patient's blaspheme with a prayer.

"Where am I?" Moses asked, unsure if he was awake or dreaming and apprehensive about whatever answer she might give.

"You are in the Sisters of Good Intentions Infirmary in Bremen."

"The boat to America...what about the boat?" Moses asked anxiously.

"It left on our last feast day with four hundred remarkably orderly Jews aboard - no interrupting, one more polite than the next and looking out for each other. We were told this change in behavior happened about the time you fell off the fence. Now, can you give me your next of kin's name and address in case you suffer a relapse?"

"I can remember falling. I don't know why I was on the fence as you say I was."

"It wasn't I who saw the incident. That's what was reported." The sister chose her words carefully. "You may never have been on the fence. You know how busybodies like to exaggerate, especially with bad news. I suppose that's a sin of vanity," she added, shaking her winged headdress as though to soar with the angels.

"Where are my clothes?" Moses asked, aware for the first time he wore an unfamiliar gown.

"They've been laundered and put in the chest at the foot of your bunk. We removed them when you needed to be bathed."

"Did you notice it?" he asked, worried his secret money pocket had been discovered.

"Oh, yes," the sister answered, "but the sisters, respecting your circumcision covenant with God, looked the other way. We also found the alms pocket in your waistband and added a shekel."

From the day 'Moses fell from the sky,' as the nuns told it, they scrutinized Catholic text for its significance. From his arrival on the feast day of the current sacred celebration, the sisters observed no sorcery in the patient, nor had he confessed to any raptures. For weeks the nuns had employed stratagems to expose demons lurking in the patient, but finding nothing for the priest in residence to exorcise, gave up. It appeared his only transgressions were failing to fast and depleting the sisters' larder by indulging an enormous appetite not denied by the satisfaction of knackwurst. The nuns thought he must be a secular Jew.

Honest to the core, Moses worked on the convent grounds to pay for his room and board twice over before he felt it was time to leave. On the day following the celebration of St. Francis, whether Assisi or Xavier was not determined, the doctor arrived to discharge Moses. Comfortable with the constraints of a convent, he was chosen for his asexuality rather than his medical proficiency. The third ring of the infirmary bell was answered to admit a rotund, florid-faced man smelling of cologne. As in previous visits, with no attempt to establish patient/doctor rapport, he extracted an instrument from his bag and peered into Moses' ears, chuckling and murmuring that he couldn't see daylight. After tapping the patient's humerus with a rubber hammer and getting the desired reflex, he timed the pulse rate. Pronouncing Moses free of any temporal frailty, he collected his fee, tipped his hat to the Mother Superior and departed.

Chapter 2

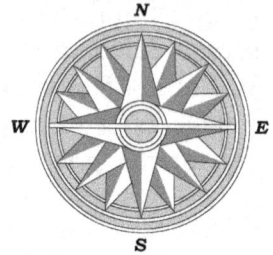

The ship on which Moses booked passage to New York City was scheduled to arrive on the winter's Solstice. Its crossing time was extended to avoid melting icebergs drifting into regular shipping lanes. Preparing to embark on the unfamiliar, he experienced unexpected marvels and minor annoyances.

Having arrived at the port two hours before departure, his first glimpse of transport to the New World was suddenly framed as he passed an open space in the wall of the pier's shed. Drawing closer to the opening for an unobstructed view, the enormity of an ocean liner loomed up and stretched beyond his peripheral vision. Twice Moses walked out of the shed's end along the pier parallel to the ship to be certain he'd accurately measured its length. It was the largest structure he'd ever seen. Men, small as toys, worked on the decks above; countless portholes, black upon the white hull, followed him like eyes in his paced measurement.

When he returned amidships, a small booth containing a sullen purser stood on the pier by the gangplank leading to the main deck. Moses joined the lengthening line of immigrants being validated for departure to America. Finally reaching the purser who was checking passports and collecting fares, Moses realized he'd not withdrawn fare-money from his waistband. Unwilling to reveal its hiding place, he told the official he needed a toilet and would be right back. The purser cleared documents for the next in line, all the time muttering how much trouble these people were - damned foreigners not worth his bother. In a few minutes Moses returned with the correct fare and walked up the gangplank undeterred by the disagreeable man's curses.

He was going to America.

After circling the main deck Moses, inquisitive about all new things, was about to climb to the one above when he found his way barred by a ship's officer in a more ornate uniform than the purser's. Polite but firm, the officer explained that steerage class was only allowed access to the main deck, the dining saloon and sleeping quarters. He pointed to a sign marked 'steerage class,' gestured downward, saluted and walked away.

Disappointed by this restraint, Moses started down the gangway to look for his cabin. Reaching the first deck below the main, he wandered the passageways until he found a door with a number that matched the one on his ticket. As he tried to open the lock, the door was thrown open with such force it nearly came off its hinges. Barring the entrance, a muscular man, stripped to the waist, his jet-black pomaded hair combed straight back, peered through a monocle over a cavalryman's mustache. Contemptuously sneering, he grabbed the ticket from Moses and pointed to the words 'steerage class' while yelling in some foreign language, as though the louder his voice the better he'd be understood. Then he yelled 'dummkopf' and slammed the door in the face of a bewildered Moses.

Moses continued his descent, his peddler's pack scraping along the narrow bulkheads, convinced at each level he could go no lower, but always finding another deck below, till he reached steerage class in the bowels of the boat. Even at idle, the engines of the great transport sent shudders through the ship's lower hull - an inescapable irritant to the unfortunate steerage class.

After several minutes of meandering among the honeycombs of passenger quarters, Moses found his cabin and noted at ten feet below ocean level the cabin's slatted entry door was the sole source of ventilation. First of the occupants to arrive, Moses had his choice of the four bunk-like berths and, remembering the infirmary furnishings, concluded they must be the preferred accommodation for sleeping everywhere but his country. Mindful of the cabin's poor ventilation, Moses chose a lower bunk opposite the door, placed his pack at its foot and lay down to establish the time-honored tradition of squatter's sovereignty.

Moments later a cherubic, middle-aged man entered, announcing in a mechanical monotone that he was Ludwig König, a deaf piano tuner. He explained he was named König Ludwig at birth, but British students at the conservatory learned the English translation of König is 'king,' added 'mad' to his appellation, and he became their very own mad King Ludwig until he reversed his first and last names.

He handed Moses a slate and chalk, eager for a reply from his new acquaintance. Puzzled how such a disabled person could successfully tune pianos, Moses encouraged their novel but tedious communication, although there were times when even the man's unique adaptation of his faculties seemed inadequate for his vocation. Occasionally their mode of communication was so laborious, Moses, impatient and forgetful of Ludwig's affliction, talked instead of writing to the man.

Pleased to have an amiable cabinmate, Ludwig related how he'd trained to be a concert pianist, but a severe illness in his early teens left him incurably deaf. For a while he found no pleasure in life. Then one day in reading about Beethoven, who wrote some of his greatest works as he lost his hearing, König discovered the composer placed one end of a wooden peg in his ear and the other end on a piano's sounding board to transmit vibrations of each note. It worked for Ludwig König, and though he was denied the concert stage as a soloist, he was part of many outstanding ensembles' performances.

Fifteen minutes before the ship's three p.m. departure a young man, sweating under his load, butted the cabin door open and backed in with all his earthly possessions piled high in his arms. He staggered towards an upper bunk and dumped a mountain of assorted articles on it before turning to engage Ludwig and Moses with a broad smile. With no immediate success testing his cabinmates' Italian, and speaking neither German nor English, he departed for the main deck to pursue his second favorite occupation - girl watching. It was some time later before Moses and Ludwig learned from a sailor fluent in languages that the handsome man was Alfredo Chianti.

Alfredo Chianti, from a village in the Apennines, was a maker of stone statues for veneration by the faithful. Migrating north from Italy as the fascination with icons fell precipitously, as it does with all things when supply exceeds diminishing demand even in the case of adornments in the name of piety, he searched Germany for sculptural commissions. Unable to make a living with his art, he compromised his skill by cutting gravestones at pauper's wages until he heard there was a growing conceit among Americans with great fortunes who wished to be memorialized, dead or alive, with statues. Without hesitation Alfredo packed his hammer and chisel and boarded the ship for New York to feed this hunger of the needy rich.

At exactly three p.m., with German precision, the ship simultaneously gave a violent shudder as though shaking off land's grip, sounded three horn blasts and pulled into the harbor with no apparent occupant for the fourth berth.

Long after the sun set and winter's chill over the North Sea had driven most passengers to their cabins, Lightning Lance uncrossed his legs and rose from where he'd squatted on the fore deck since departure. Driving westward through the great waters, he conjured up a vision of his family keeping a fire burning in the lodge until he returned. Lightning Lance had taken but one wife, a faithful and agreeable woman, to make three sons. In the hardest of winters his two oldest, forced to seek game beyond their tribe's hunting grounds now depleted by the settlers, lost their way in a great blizzard and froze to death. For months, no augury would light upon the father telling where to look for his sons. Then at the first thaw, Black Feather returning from the trading post found their ice-encased bodies and brought them home on his travois to be buried near the wickerwork saplings. For the time prescribed by the Great Spirit, Lightning Lance practiced the sacred rites of mourning to drive out the devils, but a piece of his heart lay forever out among the willows on the rise to the West, and he would never be whole again.

Each new season brought more disintegration of his tribe's fragile fabric as their lands were wounded by white trespassers and their people reduced to withered chaff by drunkenness and disease. In the fourth year of broken treaties and continuing deprivation, Lightning Lance emerged from the sweat lodge, his head full of answers from the Great Spirit, choked down his pride and joined a Wild West show. He toured American and Europe, suffering the indignity of being displayed like some animal before disrespectful people, but it paid for his family's survival.

One day, after three years of constantly moving from place to place and never seeing his family, he was told because he was not as well-known by the public as Sitting Bull and no longer had a young man's body to perform feats, he should go home to his lodge.

And so he had begun his journey toward the setting sun to rejoin his people. He entered the cabin as noiselessly as his shadow to pick his way among the strewn odds and ends of three unrelated lives. One berth remained unoccupied, and finding no success in forcing his long bony body within its confines, he moved all the sleeping occupants' belongings onto the next bunk and fell asleep on the floor instead. Before the first light of the next day, Lightning Lance awoke, replaced the baggage in the same disorder he'd found it, and left the cabin again to look westward from the ship's fore deck.

Lightning Lance repeated this routine until the fifth night when a blinding fog reduced the ship to quarter-speed and set the warning horn to blaring, disorienting Ludwig, Moses and Alfredo. As in a trance, all three were startled by an apparition.

"Who are you?" each asked all at once in his own tongue, creating an unintelligible mixture. Lightning Lance drew the shadows around him and waited for the hypnotic motion of the ship and the muffled drone of the foghorn to return the three to sleep. Then, in harmony with the order of the earth, Lightning Lance anticipated dawn and left the cabin to watch night's darkness give way to an ashen day.

One by one each of the three awoke to an annoyingly fragmented dream of an Indian-like figure who had disappeared before his existence could be proven. None spoke of this confusion, but each resolved to stay awake during the coming night. However, only Moses remained alert to witness the reality of Lightning Lance, the majestic chief.

"Shalom!" Moses said, because it was a soft, non-threatening sound and he thought the Bible's global reach might make known to all it meant 'peace.'

The Indian stood immobile, only his bright eyes alive in the dark. Then he slowly moved his right arm over his heart and made a fist before extending it palm upright to Moses. He spoke in a language Moses had never heard before but understood perfectly.

"I'm Moses, descendent of Father Abraham," Moses replied.

"My people are from the old woman who never dies but replenishes our tribe with babies as she brings back each year's harvest," Lightning Lance replied. "Before I became a warrior I had a child's name, but after my first battle a shaman consulted the Great Spirit and I was given the name of Lightning Lance."

"Do you have a last name?" Moses asked naively.

"My people have the number of names to picture who they are. That's all that is necessary. There are enough different names to go around."

"We used to be like that a long time ago, but there became so many of us they had to think up second names to tell us apart. What if somebody was also named Lightning Lance?"

"I suppose one of us would have to kill the other," Lightning Lance said, leaving Moses wondering if he was being ridiculed.

"Wouldn't it be less trouble to flip a coin and see who won the toss to keep the name?"

"But then there would be a loser who couldn't save face by dying," Lightning Lance replied, seeming to continue the farce.

"I'm not sure that's the best way to settle disputes," Moses said at a loss with the impasse.

Acting to revive the conversation with subjects of common interest, Lightning Lance said, "You are going to a strange land. I'm returning from one."

"I hope to make money to send to my family for food," Moses said.

"And I left America for your land to earn money to feed the people of my lodge."
"We are not so different," Moses observed.

"How can such contradictions to solve the same problem exist?"

"For centuries my ancestors fled from one country to another, always beleaguered by an enemy, always seeking their promised land."

"My people have been driven from their eastern hunting grounds on the edge of the great waters halfway across the land toward the sea where the sun sets. Each time they moved they were promised it would be the last, but promises were lies and every new land was stolen from them. There is evil in the hearts of those who take more from nature than their bodies need while they watch neighbors starve."

At pauses in the conversation when the two reflected on the similarity of their ancestral holocausts, Moses once again wondered if he was dreaming, but the ship's thumping engines, overlaid with the heavy breathing of Ludwig and Alfredo, suggested he was awake and the Indian chief was real. Still uncertain, Moses searched for a respectful way to verify the material being of Lightning Lance.

Finding no perfect phrasing, Moses blurted out, "Do you ever dream?"

Lightning Lance, wise in the ways of reading minds, particularly those of the young not yet bent by guile, answered with a question. "Do you have visions?"

"I'm not sure," Moses answered. "I have dreams. Are they the same?"

"I have visions that guide me," Lightning Lance replied. "The Great Spirit comes to me in visions and speaks to me in ways one cannot remember in dreams. Visions are real."

"How can I tell if I'm having a vision or a dream right now? How can I know if you are real?" Moses persisted.

"You must believe I'm real right now as you are real. If you doubt it, look for me tomorrow when you know you're awake. Discover if we can speak of these things we speak of now. Dreams are like clouds that make pictures that are gone the next day."

Moses said, "I will try to remember everything we've talked of tonight."

"I'll leave now, for it is a good omen to be looking homeward at daybreak." And before the chief had closed the cabin door, Moses was asleep.

Ludwig was the first to wake. While he could not hear the ship's engines, he could feel their rapid vibrations traveling through the wood of his berth, confirming they were moving at full speed. He rolled over to find Alfredo in the opposite berth sleeping with a pillow clutched to his belly, a lascivious smile forming to suggest a dream of past or anticipated conquests. Ludwig rebuked himself for complicit voyeurism, but my God, the Italian pantomiming intercourse was only nine feet away. The German decided to roll over with his back to the orgy while he reordered his thoughts about the Italian. From the first day, Alfredo had shown no interest in communicating with either Ludwig or Moses – even at the most primitive level of signs or symbols - nor any curiosity in learning the identity of the fourth occupant of the cabin, if there was one.

As the ship moved west through different time zones, miraculous adjustments to Alfredo's anatomical clock continued to awaken him for breakfast just minutes before the dining quarters closed. Last minute admissions to dinner and supper, though not as challenging, were accomplished with equal ease. In the intervals separating the inflexible dining schedule, Alfredo either slept or prowled the main deck ever lusting for a liaison. Fortunately or unfortunately, depending on the view of the hunter and the hunted, only one woman acquiesced. Driven by ardor rather than reason, Alfredo had failed to find a place in advance for consummation, and on the night of triumph desperation forced the couple to loosen the tarpaulin covering on a lifeboat and climb into their improvised bedchamber. A sailor with but one mind to keep things shipshape noticed the unsecured canvas and relashed it, thereby animating the axiom 'a place for everything and everything in its place.'

Ludwig rose, washed, dressed and waited for Moses to finish shaving and join him at breakfast. As the steward prepared to bar the dining area to late-comers for breakfast, Alfredo made his spectacular sprint to the finish line with thirty seconds to spare. His repeated successes nettled the steward to an apoplectic red, tempting him to set the dining area clock ahead by a minute. However, he rejected the deceit, knowing when the bridge bells rang out the official hour he'd be censured for a failure in synchronization.

After breakfast, Alfredo resumed his tireless stalking while Ludwig and Moses returned to their cabin. Having finished his only book by the middle of the second day at sea, Ludwig hoped to become better acquainted with the young man but on terms he controlled with the slate. Moses, however, spent much of the day in prayer or meditation. Ludwig wasn't sure there was a difference but decided prayers probably included meditation but not the other way around.

That was one of the many matters Ludwig wanted to explore with Moses, and perhaps this was as good a time as any. He waited for Moses to move and stretch before settling back into a posture of quiet reflection, then asked in a mechanical monotone, "Would you like to learn how to read lips?"

To Ludwig's delight Moses, without waiting to write 'yes' on the slate, nodded his head in the affirmative.

He motioned to Moses to stand in front of the mirror with the slate and chalk handy. "Now watch my mouth and cheeks very closely when I say a word. Then you repeat the word and remember how similar or different you and I look when we speak. Ha ha. See how my lips spread and my cheeks pull back. Now you say 'ha ha.'"

"Ha ha," Moses repeated.

"No, no, you must always look at the mirror to watch your mouth."

"No, no," Moses repeated.

"I meant you must always say 'ha ha' to the mirror," Ludwig corrected.

"I meant you must always say 'ha ha' to the mirror," Moses mimicked and burst out laughing.

"You're not watching yourself in the mirror. You must always look in the mirror when you're practicing. Try 'ho, ho, ho.' Notice how your lips form a circle and don't move much."

"Ho ho," the young man said, studying his face in the glass. "You're right."

"Try 'ha, ha, ho, ho' and see the difference."

"My mouth is shaped very differently with each of these similar words, not at all like yours," Moses commented on the slate.

"That's because I've been deaf for so long, I've lost tonal harmony and pitch variations without knowing it."

"Now what?" Moses asked.

"Top, pop, stop. Notice how much your tongue extends and your lips close when you say them softly? Yell the words and your mouth bites out the sound. Music is a soft word that hardly moves your mouth."

"Let me try that in the mirror," Moses wrote on the slate and turned away from Ludwig.

"And 'sleep.' Then 'sleepy' and your lips open and close as your tongue turns up to finish the word. Both are different from 'asleep.' Say all three and notice the difference in your mouth."

"Where did you learn this?" Moses wrote.

"I invented it from watching people read aloud, mostly at worship where I could follow in the Bible."

"Are you a Jew or a German Catholic?" Moses asked, turning toward him.

"Neither, but I am a believer."

Unexpectedly Moses realized he'd been hoodwinked by Ludwig who understood most people if he could see their mouths. "Why do you bother with the slate and chalk?" he asked.

"Because most people talk too much and say too little. With the slate I quickly learn when something has worth and who will take the time to communicate with the disabled. Remember, I'm totally deaf but not stupid, and I converse with people if I can see their mouths. You have your hearing, but don't let it interfere with your lip reading practice. Plug your ears or stay outside the range of the speaker's voice. Look at a person's mouth who's speaking. Note the words not only for their meaning, but the way they're formed with the mouth. Now let's get back to our lesson?"

With Ludwig's tutoring Moses learned to read lips with increasing skill and found watching people at meals especially helpful for practice. When someone at dinner detected what Ludwig and Moses were doing, they were annoyed by the invasion of their privacy. Some resented their loss of aural superiority, and a paranoid few suspected they might be caught in a sinister plot. Within days, the most insecure passengers tried to insulate themselves from the lip readers by taking their meals early and filling all seats at the table where Ludwig and Moses regularly sat. Then the tide of irrational behavior turned and diners decided they'd rather be seated with Ludwig and Moses to hear all that was discussed.

The powerful surveillance of combined sound and sight excited Alfredo's keen animal instincts, and he immediately petitioned Ludwig for an accelerated course in this promising snare. Offended that he was being asked to be a procurer Ludwig refused, but always encouraging self improvement, proposed the stone mason learn this skill to awaken his better nature. The piano tuner's appeal was unsuccessful, but Alfredo quickly joined Moses in learning English from Ludwig - the prospects of gratifying one's carnal impulses in America now seemed limitless.

Early one morning while others slept Moses, walking the main deck for exercise, approached the bow to find a ship's officer bristling over a person facing forward, squatting against a warm air exhaust funnel. As Moses neared them he heard the officer's voice rise in anger while the other remained impassive.

"You don't belong here. People do not sit here all night wrapped in a blanket. You'll have to leave. Do you understand? You'll have to leave or I'll have you forcibly removed."

Moses' unexpected presence interrupted the officer's harangue.

"Good morning, sir," Moses said. "Perhaps this noble chief from America does not understand you. Could it be because he doesn't speak German? If you would try to explain to him in his native tongue you might come to some agreement. Of course, you'd need to speak in the right tongue. From the thousand existing dialects you'd have to choose the chief's to be effective."

The officer was aghast that a young immigrant could know these things much less dare to address him in this manner.

"On the other hand, you could continue to yell at him believing louder is the key to comprehension," Moses continued. "Such a hullabaloo would undoubtedly attract a crowd who might think you stupid if not abusive; not to mention you'd be violating passenger rights to be above decks except in inclement weather. As you can see, it's going to be a lovely day. Good morning, sir." Moses turned to stride around the ship.

In the night following the day of the incident with the ship's officer, Lightning Lance came noiselessly as a deer mouse to awaken Moses while Ludwig and Alfredo remained asleep.

"Moses, it is good that we talk with so much to say in the few days left on this ship. It was a shrewd reprimand you delivered this day. You show the promise of being a great chief, and I will not forget it as long as I can remember my name. You speak powerful sense like our grey-haired men of wisdom who say only truth endures."

"I believe there is no justice without respect," Moses replied.

"For you wisdom is as natural as breathing."

"Our creeds are very much alike. That's why they are enduring," Moses said.

Both were silenced by the significance of the exchange.

"What will you do when your feet first tread American soil?" Lighting Lance asked.

"I will bow down and kiss the earth in thanks to my maker," Moses replied. "Then I will give my daily meal and some of my coins to a hungry soul and fast for guidance."

"But you are not a rich man," Lightning Lance reminded Moses.

"That is not so, I just don't have much money. On the second day, I will study people to learn if all are treated as equals. On the third day, I will observe how Indians and other Americans live together in New York City."

"There are no Indians. They were all slaughtered in the time of my ancestor," Lightning Lance stated in distress.

"Then I will seek those stained with the shame of their ancestors' evil to know how they atoned for their crime. On the fourth day, I will go to the place where those of my heritage have settled. On the fifth day, I will seek work in one of the many trades my family has practiced. On the sixth day, I will find shelter, and on the seventh day, I will go to temple to hear how the most oppressed reach out to others in affliction."

The fervor of his pledge caused a great surge of energy to rise through his body and pour out his skull, leaving him weakened in a drenching sweat. Both men closed their eyes, tilting towards each other in connected prayer. The supplications were not of hypocrites but revolutionists fused like the blood-mixing rite of Indian brotherhood.

As one they roused from their meditations to talk of many differences - their bloods, their ancestors and customs - but always returned to the force of their sameness.

Moses spoke of the oppression of his people for thousands of years. "From enslavement in Egypt when Pharaoh issued three separate edicts to kill our newborns to exterminate the race, the Philistines, Babylonians, Assyrians and others have threatened us with genocide. Even today, the Catholic Church in Spain subjects Jews to subtle inquisition."

"Our southeastern brothers, the Cherokees, were driven from their hunting grounds, never finding a home or peace," Lightning Lance said.

"The Israelites wandered homeless in a wasteland for forty years," Moses interjected.

"And ours was the 'Trail of Tears' - after a half-century of white-man persecution a nation of Indian families, dragged from their homes with only the clothes they wore, were forced by the U. S. Army to walk a thousand miles to their deaths."

Made mute by the enormity of these inhumanities, both stopped talking.

"Can you hear what we're doing?" Moses asked.

"Our tongues have choked our hearts by trying to make one wickedness bigger than the other."

"One should do more than feel only the wounds of his ancestors," Moses said.

Lightning Lance talked about the members of his lodge, describing each in minute detail. Then a deep melancholy seized him, his voice growing huskier, eyes closing with the pain as he described how the scalps of enemies defeated long ago hung decaying on the lodge-poles like the treaties with the Great White Father. Now their hunting grounds were overrun with whites, their livestock driving game farther away, the tribe's sources of nuts, roots and berries plundered, the great herds of buffalo reduced to extinction. Now his people grew gaunt from hunger or wretched from whiskey.

The chief's story led him deeper into his pain - his good and constant wife, Stirring Kettles, descended into madness with the loss of their two sons. Lightning Lance named his sons in descending order of age; Trailing Deer, Wind Runner and Red Fox - all destined to be great chiefs before a killing blizzard spared two of them the indignity of submitting to the white man's degradation. Red Fox, the youngest surviving child, preparing at sixteen for the ordeals and tests to sit with the council, seemed in every way born for leading the tribe, but the devils had stolen his soul and cast him into the waters of oblivion.

Chapter 3

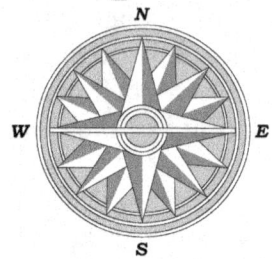

There were but two days and two nights till the ship docked in New York City. As disembarkation grew near, a sort of frenzy seized first class passengers who began tourists' age-old ritual of exchanging addresses with newly made acquaintances, knowing well the luster would dull with the return to the commonplace distractions at home. Weather surprises, weight gains, indecisiveness and ship festivities also set in motion a major undertaking to retrieve prematurely packed garments.

Each nautical mile nearer the New World, some of the crew became more obsequious to the gratuity-capable, first-class passengers and less civil with steerage, characterizing the latter as bilge to be flushed upon arrival in port. On one occasion Ludwig, singled out by a bully seeking amusement or venting frustration, was ordered to submit his immigration papers for inspection several times on the same day. Noting his victim's deafness, he began to berate Ludwig with vile language. With each attack, Ludwig only smiled like a simpleton, further enraging the tormentor who punctuated his assault by sticking his finger in his victim's belly.

Passive no longer, Ludwig grabbed the sailor's wrist and broke the offending finger, saying, "I could have broken your arm as easily, but I might need you to carry my luggage off the ship when we land."

The bully, crying out in pain, retreated in amazement at the agility and strength of a seemingly sedentary man, while searching for a plausible excuse if asked about his injury.

In the dark of the previous two nights, Lightning Lance with eerie prescience had entered the cabin the instant Ludwig and Alfredo fell into deep sleep, their snoring forming tenor and baritone parts of a nocturnal duet. Now, two nights before making port, the same extraordinary suspension of consciousness came upon them with the chief's arrival while Moses remained alert.

This time as the Indian and the Jew talked, both sensed their shared path would soon split into separate journeys and they should waste no time in celebrating the blessing of linking according to their individual traditions. Lightning Lance, the elder and entitled to conduct his ritual first, yielded to Moses as a token of esteem for his young friend.

"We will celebrate a Passover Seder for which I will attempt to be the Haggadah to guide us through, although I have never led one before," Moses explained.

"A boy becomes a man by breaking new trails," Lightning Lance replied.

"I believe it is no coincidence you will attend your first Seder with me and it is significant we celebrate it on the anniversary of Passover, the 14th day of the Hebrew month of Nisan, marking the liberation of my people from slavery in Egypt three thousand years ago."

"We pray many times to Omahank-Numakshi for delivery from subjugation," the Indian explained to emphasize his people were still being persecuted.

"Because there were no Seder foods aboard this ship, we will use the best substitutes I could think of, which I hope is acceptable to God. Let me try to explain the Jewish name of each item and the food that it represents.

Maror and Chazeret - two types of bitter herbs symbolizing
the harshness of slavery - we'll use mustard and beet roots.

Charoset - a sweet, brown pebbly mixture representing mortar
used by slaves in buildings - brown sugar for this.

Karpas - a vegetable such as celery - we have this.

Salt Water- we certainly have plenty of that.

Z'roar- roasted shank bone of lamb suggesting lamb sacrificed
at Temple in Jerusalem - we have lamb chop bones.

Beitzah- roasted egg - we have hard-boiled eggs."

Let us begin. Each fills a cup of wine for the other while I recite
the Kadeish, which is a blessing on those who fill each other's cups."

"I cannot drink firewater, it makes Indians crazy."

Moses thought for a moment. "Each time the Seder directs the
drinking of wine, I'll pass the bottle over your glass without pouring
any, and you can fill mine while I relate the Exodus from Egypt."

Nodding his agreement, Lightning Lance said, "It is like passing
the pipe as our wise men tell stories of long ago."

Both Indian and Jew observed a moment of respectful silence.

"Now I wash my hands, which is a Jewish custom called Urchatz
required before eating each meal. Next is Karpas, the vegetable we
dip in salt water to remind us of the tears shed by our enslaved
ancestors."

"Feasts are one of our favorite celebrations. Guests must eat
everything, except snakes, set before them so as not to offend the
host. If one is unable to finish the food received, he gives it to another
with a small, wooden stick, signifying he will give the other a horse
the next day for his assistance," Lightning Lance related.

"Yachatz, breaking the bread of affliction," Moses announced,
breaking the middle matzo. "This is the stage in the Seder when the
celebrants are asked questions. Why is this night different from
others? Why do we dip our food twice this night? Why is it we eat
only unleavened bread this night? Why is it we eat only bitter herbs
this night and dine reclining?"

Occasionally, Ludwig or Alfredo rolled over in his berth or
yawned but never awoke to witness this ancient rite.

"Three verses in the Torah record the answers given by the sons of the father who asks these questions. They are the wise son, the wicked son and a simple son who doesn't understand. Each is asked to explain the meaning of the Seder by answering these questions. The wise son's answer indicates that because he knows the meaning of each part of the ritual; he is impatient but recognizes it is critical to retell the story publicly for the edification of all. The wicked son replies by asking his father 'What is this service to you?' His father, rebuking him, replies, 'It's because God acted for my sake when I left Egypt,' implying the Seder was not for the wicked son who did not deserve to be freed from Egyptian slavery. The simple son, unsure of how to respond, asks, 'What is this?' and his father answers, 'With a strong hand the Almighty led us out from Egypt.' The son who does not know how to ask is told, 'It is what the Almighty did for me when I left Egypt.'"

Lightning Lance was puzzled by how the story of an ancestor's release from enslavement could be revered with rambling questions and answers. As he searched for an explanation, he was mindful of Indians' respect for legends that were simple and unambiguous. The Jews' inconclusive meandering made the chief wonder if Jews didn't listen, were forgetful or maybe not as smart as Indians, but he thought it would be rude to interrupt Moses with questions.

Moses next told the story of his Biblical namesake's ten separate petitions to the Pharaoh to release the Israelites. Each time Pharaoh refused, God punished the Egyptians with a different plague. Finally, God told the Israelites to cook a lamb and mark their doorways with the animal's blood so when God sent another plague to kill all first-born children, it would pass over the Israelites' marked homes and strike only the Egyptians. Then Pharaoh released the slaves.

In accordance with Jewish tradition, Moses scrupulously observed each act of cleanliness and dedication of the food and drink to the conclusion of the Seder. After blessing the last cup of wine with a prayer, he lay back against his berth spent by the celebration's demands, but at peace.

Having observed the post Seder moment of quiet, the chief rose
to help Moses stand. "Tomorrow is our last night on the water. We
will meet again so I may honor you in our manner."

Not a sound registered the Indian's departure, nor any evidence
of his presence.

A sickly, yellowish haze enveloped the ship at first light of its
last full day at sea. Oily, grey swells slapped the prow, parting and
flattening with no hint of chlorine usually released by the disturbance
of ozone-laden sea water. Passengers normally invigorated by ocean
breezes were phlegmatic, possibly subdued by the responsibilities
awaiting them at debarkation or the anxieties for some that
accompany a ship's farewell gala. With the commencement of the
festivities but twelve hours away, crew members tried to restore shop-
worn decorations to their pristine origins, while female passengers
repeatedly appraised their wardrobes for fashion's perfection, all the
time rationalizing if their elegance was eclipsed this party, after all,
was not that important.

At mid-afternoon when the purser and head steward were
reviewing the evening's program, it was discovered the makeshift
orchestra was without a piano player, the absentee berth-bound with a
violent case of diarrhea. The purser, a man with limited ability to
improvise and an abundance of apprehension, was sure the Captain
would blame him for anything that compromised his ship's traditional
farewell celebration. By chance the sailor whose finger Ludwig had
broken heard of the dilemma and, always ready to ingratiate himself
with superiors, suggested the purser search the passengers' records for
another pianist, knowing in advance this was impractical. When the
purser dismissed this idea, the sailor said he might know somebody
who could locate a piano player. He was wished God speed and sent
on his way with no mention of a reward for success.

The mindless, would-be-manipulative seaman whistled his way
down two decks toward steerage before it occurred to him that the
piano tuner would reject substituting for the sick musician or worse,
become violent. Reaching the tuner's cabin, he heard through the

partially open doorway three people speaking a language he knew to be English. At his knock, admittance was granted and he entered the cramped quarters the tuner shared with two unfamiliar passengers pointing to objects they identified in their new language.

"Excuse me, sir," the seaman addressed Ludwig in German.

"What is it?"

"Do you by any chance play the piano?"

"I'm a piano tuner. Why do you ask if I played?"

"Because if you played you might want to make some money at tonight's party. The regular piano player is sick and they're looking for someone to fill in."

Ludwig, not a man to drop his guard with abusive people, demanded, "How do I know this is not another of your underhanded harassments?"

"Oh no, sir," the seaman pleaded, becoming more certain he had trapped himself between the purser's expectations and the piano tuner's revenge.

"You said I'd be paid for playing? How much? How many marks?"

"I don't know that, sir. It will have to be decided by the purser."

"By the purser and me, you mean," Ludwig replied. "You'd better bring the purser down here and we'll get this straight."

"Oh, I can't do that, sir, he never goes below tourist level."

"No meeting, no playing," Ludwig said, returning to the English lesson with Moses and Alfredo.

The seaman slunk away, only to return a few minutes later with the purser.

Ludwig studiously appraised the newcomer who entered, his insecurity as conspicuous as the elaborate disguise he'd constructed to hide it. His navy blue uniform, pressed to knife-edge precision with brass buttons burnished to a blinding brilliance, served as a pillar to a flushed face unsettled by darting, colorless eyes. Prussian haircut and mustache, barbered to a millimeter, completed the inadequate disguise of an inferiority complex. He fanned himself with his visor-peaked cap, waiting uncomfortably to be introduced. Taking the initiative, Ludwig stated his name, listed his repertoire and named his fee.

Sensing there was no room for negotiation, the purser accepted Ludwig's terms, glad to be free from the oppressive, stale air and convinced his problem was solved.

Then, as an afterthought, he returned to the cabin and asked, "How do I know you can play at the level appropriate for tonight?"

"You don't," Ludwig replied, slipping into a shirt. "Let's go up to the piano and find out."

For half an hour Ludwig played contemporary and classical selections, gathering a large crowd of passengers who called "Encore" each time he stopped. The purser beamed, Ludwig bowed, and the seaman, unrewarded, concluded ship's officers were as contemptible as immigrants.

Long after the gala was over, the wine cabinet emptied, party favors swept up, salvaged decorations stored for the next voyage and tables set for breakfast, the red-eyed dining saloon staff groped wearily to bed. Revelers committed infidelities to later be regretted as the celebration swept first-time lovers to abandon their inhibitions.

"You did not join the celebration?" Lightning Lance said as he came into the cabin to find Moses waiting.

"No. I'm observing the second and last night of Passover. The reverential seclusion saved me the embarrassment of appearing inappropriately dressed."

"Day is not far over the horizon and we must not waste our last time together. Listen, for I will tell you but once and there is much for you to remember. Are you ready?"

"Yes," Moses answered solemnly, preparing for the unknown about to be received.

"I will teach you ways few but Indians have been trusted to know. All tribes tell different versions when they look back to their creation, but their beginnings all start with a supreme power. Like you we have prophets and wise men, but our Lord of Life is Omahank-Numakshi, the most exalted and powerful, who created the earth, man and every existing object. Sometimes our Lord appears as an aged man with a tail, sometimes as a youthful man. The first man,

Numank-Machana was created by our Lord of Life and is second only to him. He is filled with great power, to be worshipped and offered sacrifices. Omahank-Chika, the third most powerful, has much influence over men and is a malignant and evil spirit."

"Satan tested our forefathers with corruption, but each time our God rebuked the treacherous spirit," Moses interjected.

"The fourth being, Rohanka-Tanihanka dwells in the bright light you call Venus and protects us from extinction. The fifth who has no power is ever in motion wandering the world over and called the lying wolf."

"Like your legends of such beings there are many stories in the Bible. Some tell of a man like Rohanka-Tanihanka who was present at Jesus' crucifixion. He's identified with Judas, Pilot, the man in the moon and many others. When he reaches the age of 100, he's supposed to return to his 30th year; the age when he sinned. Some see him as the personification of the painful exile of the Israelites; many from different countries call him the Wandering Jew," Moses explained.

"The sixth and last of the superior beings is named Ochkih-Hadda, a bad omen in our tradition of dreams because the one who sees him will die. Like your devils, he comes to our villages and teaches many things that make people fearful, always requiring sacrifices be made to him."

"Many ages ago the Jews worshipped several deities they believed responsible for different influences in their lives and then the Lord God Almighty punished them every time they forgot the one and only God was Lord over everything," Moses added.

"We worship the sun because it is the residence of our Lord of Life. All our sacrifices and medicines are offered to the Lord of Life, Omahank-Numakshi, who gives us our guardian spirit. After many days of fasting, we withdraw to a solitary place to do penance and beseech his guidance."

"On the Sabbath," Moses said, simplifying his explanation for Lightning Lance, "every seven days we rest from preoccupation with worldly things and give thanks to our Lord."

"The Indian has special ceremonies whenever they're needed to worship the supreme being for everything we do. We pray for his favor for good hunting, full harvests and victory over our enemies. Now you know enough of our ways, it is best you practice some of our customs. Let me lead you through a renewal for the body and spirit in a sweat lodge. Our people build a special place that unites two of our sacred gifts, water and fire, and turns them into steam so that one may purify himself with nature's purges."

"Surely there is not such a place on this ship," Moses said.

"Not as our tradition intended, but there is a practical substitute. Follow me and you will find the fulfillment of your needs often hides in the most improbable places."

Lightning Lance and Moses left Ludwig and Alfredo in oblivious slumber, and with the chief leading, crept noiselessly along the passageways past cabins with some doors ajar for ventilation and other doors closed for sweaty privacy.

At the end of the gangway they halted before a heavy metal hatchway marked in German and English red letters "Stop! Danger! Crew only!" Lightning Lance opened the hatchway and a surge of steamy, oil-fouled air engulfed them, burning their eyes and smarting their lungs. Steam-driven pistons in the black pit far below clanked like the hammers of hell. On the edge of darkness, two naked-to-the-waist, sweaty creatures fed ravenous boilers like the damned of the inferno. A sudden roll of the ship swung the hatch shut behind them, announcing there was no turning back and making their descent on the oily steel stairs precarious.

"Don't look at the open doors to the furnaces; the fires will rob you of your night eyes," Lightning Lance instructed.

Moses, never before in a ship's engine compartment, found the chief's advice only made him more curious. But he resisted, recalling the Biblical story of Lot's wife who ignored the warning to look back at the destruction of Sodom and turned into a pillar of salt.

"Follow me," Lightning Lance repeated.

"But I can't see anything. We Jews don't have eyesight as good as you people."

"That's because the white man is not satisfied with what light has revealed. He thinks there is more hidden from the source of light so he gives up everything shown for something that doesn't exist and becomes blind to everything."

Lightning Lance continued down the steep, narrow metal stairs to the ship's bilge with Moses gingerly following. Step by step the sure-footed Indian led the cautious Jew down the precipitous incline to a landing where Moses asked, "Won't the firemen find us down here where we're not allowed?"

"No. They've been looking at the fire so long they're blind in the dark and the engines drown out our noise."

Several times Moses missed a step and almost fell into the black void, but through some agility he felt he received from Lightning Lance, recovered and reached the bottom unscathed. Now within the metal cavity of the ship's hull the engines' reverberations sounded like being encased in a huge heart. Distracted, it wasn't until Moses completed his perilous descent that he noticed the ship had reached heavier seas and its rolling motion together with the putrid air threatened nausea or fainting. In his distress he tried to minimize his plight by concentrating on Jonah's ordeal in the whale's belly, but finding no relief prayed for his very own Passover.

Lightning Lance tugged Moses' sleeve, gained his attention and led him forward to stacked cargo in the bow. Pointing to a place tunneled between the crates, the chief crawled in and beckoned Moses to follow.

"This is where we'll share our sweat purification. This place is never inspected during the voyage. Sit down," Lightning Lance encouraged, crossing his legs and gracefully lowering himself to a sitting position, preparing to begin the sacrament.

Moses tried to sit in the manner of the chief and activated rebellious nerves, tendons and muscles from his back to his feet. Unwilling to reveal he could not tolerate the discomfort of seasickness or the unnatural posture, but seeking an outlet to complain about his misery, Moses cried out, "That maddening noise makes it impossible to think."

"You are right, the outside world is deafening," Lightning Lance said, rousing from his contemplation. "Listen to your inner spirit and unwelcome trespassers will be turned away. Now rid yourself of disturbances with patience and prayer."

Moses, after several attempts to emulate the chief's enlightenment, abandoned his meditation and was immediately seized with muscle cramps, but determined not to disturb Lightning Lance a second time. He endured the pain to his limit and beyond till he was bathed in sweat before breaking his pledge to himself to not give in. Then he uncrossed his legs and felt the suffering flow out of his back and calves.

"How long does expiation take in the sweat lodge ceremony?" Moses asked.

"Until you don't need to ask that question," the chief replied, returning to quiet supplication.

"You know we Jews started asking interminable questions long before the Greeks got the idea," Moses said, his words trailing his entry to the Spirit World.

He withdrew slowly from his otherworld displacement, breaking his link with the supernatural. He was first conscious of light and breathing, then sound and touch, only to discover he was alone. Regaining his balance, he climbed out from the cargo cave space into the main of the hull, suffering no lingering aches or distraction from the engine noise. He effortlessly mounted the steep, steel stairs to the steerage deck, quickly located his cabin and entered without disturbing Ludwig's and Alfredo's contrapuntal snoring.

"Your long time at the sweat healing told me you had much prayer and many visions," Lightning Lance greeted him upon his return. "I would not enter your place without permission and came here to wait. Let us celebrate the passing of the pipe while others sleep."

From an elk hide, sleeve-like pouch intricately decorated in dyed porcupine quills and tufts of colored horse hair, Lightning Lance withdrew in two separate pieces the bowl and stem of a medicine pipe. With deep respect he laid them on the blanket before where they sat in contemplation, as though it was the first time the power of such a beautiful and delicate talisman had been recognized.

"Few have bonded as brothers with such a pipe as this," he boasted. "Most pipes are common and cannot make medicine as powerful as mine. The bowls of all but a few are made from clay. This bowl is made from rare redstone found only in the Dakota Sioux's secret quarry, highly prized and in harmony with the legendary characters carved on the side," he explained, holding it for Moses to see but not touch. "Much time was given to creating such a sacred pipe."

"Why is the pipe kept in two separate pieces?"

"Because the bowl is woman and the stem is man, and joining them is a ceremony celebrating an act of completeness," the chief replied, picking up the long, broad, tubular stem covered with red, yellow and green porcupine quills and horse hair. With appropriate solemnity, he fitted the stem into the bowl and filled its hollow with Kini-Kenich, a smoking material made from the inner green bark of the red willow dried and powdered for smoking.

"In the pipe ceremony, there is a bearer who, after the pieces are joined, holds it and with the stem pointing away from his body, turns always from north to east, south and west before offering it to the oldest man. The pipe is always passed to the right, and each man inhales exactly three puffs, only three."

"Why is the pipe passed always to the right?" Moses asked. "Because the world turns right to left?"

The chief at first ignored the question as though it was trivia that didn't deserve an answer, but then reconsidering said, "I don't know, but you can think that if it makes you feel better."

"Are women included in the ceremony?" Moses asked.

"No," Lightning Lance replied gruffly, seeking to dismiss these silly questions. "We are but two and I am the elder, so I will pass the pipe to myself for three puffs only."

Holding the long-stemmed pipe at arm's length, he paused for a moment in deference before opening his lips to accept the mouthpiece. He inhaled three times then with an incantation for brotherhood passed it to Moses.

With Moses' third puff the acrid smoke scorched his throat and he was seized with uncontrollable coughing. Humiliated by his unmanly interruption of the sacred ceremony, Moses cast down his eyes and returned the pipe to the chief.

"You are not yet an Indian," the chief said with a smile, "but you have seen the spirit of my people and I give you my medicine bundle to guide you in the days ahead."

The chief passed a tightly bound elk hide wrapper filled with what Moses, too polite to inspect, assumed were amulets, herbs and bones.

"And I give you my most precious possession, the Star of David, as a tribute to our amity," Moses said, lifting the silver chain with inverse triangles over his head and placing them in the chief's palm with a handshake. "David was the greatest warrior and King of the Israelites. I know this emblem belongs to one who'll honor it."

In unity the Jew and the Indian squatted facing each other, knee to knee, wrists clasped, forehead to forehead, pondering the permanence of their pledges.

"There is a storm coming," Lightning Lance said after a while.

"I hear nothing."

"Nor can I, but I feel it. I must be ready to welcome its purifications of my crystals. I go now."

"It will be dangerous for you on deck in a thunderstorm," Moses protested.

"Only lightning can restore the energy in my crystals, which carry me on my way," the chief said and vanished, leaving Moses to sleep unmindful of the rumble of thunder bouncing down the hatchways to the decks below.

Within minutes the storm, full of blinding lightning and thunder's terror, struck the ship's forward funnel, sending a shudder through the vessel's steel hull. Unnerved passengers rushed about yelling for assurance the ship was still seaworthy or fell to their knees asking for deliverance.

Moses, instantly awake, worked his way through the mob clogging the stairs to the main deck where a seaman was turning people back into the lounge and dining rooms. Ignoring the seaman's instruction to stay inside, Moses pushed him aside and fought the wind to the foredeck where the chief always went to meditate.

The acrid stink of lightning's discharge fouled the air, and as a reminder of Nature's fickle furry, a bolt had cauterized a gash down the funnel to burn a zigzag scar around the place where the chief prayed before disappearing in a scupper.

Moses searched the foredeck, grateful for failing to find any trace of the chief's corporeal existence, which suggested his Indian companion was some sort of revenant. Emotionally exhausted by a night of being tossed back and forth from the surrealistic to the actual, he sought revival in the drenching rain and stood guard until dawn.

Chapter 4

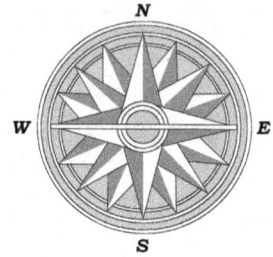

T he storm ended so abruptly it could have been an illusion except for the gentle roll of the ship, setting puddles to play hide and seek under the lifeboats, as yet to be found by the ascending sun. Atlantic water, jade green, rolled off the prow of the ship like verdant fields filled with white blossoms opened by spring light. Gulls, a welcoming committee from the land not yet in sight, squealed for the remains of breakfast even before passengers had been served. Returning to business as usual, peace having been restored, a flurry of activity was energized with little relevance to disembarkation. In the disorder of thoughtlessness or impetuous whims, children and luggage were lost, found and lost again. The kaleidoscopic confusion of misunderstandings and short tempers of passengers and crew alike created adversaries with the latter hopelessly outgunned. East-bound vessels saluted the immigrants' transport nearing New York City with horns, bells and whistles - a carnival-like stimuli missing only a barker to call out, "Step right up ladies and gents, there's enough for everyone where we just came from."

As midmorning revealed the American coast line, the prize of a new life seemed at hand, but as often is the case, reality's obstacles arose and a speedy completion of the trip was to be denied by quarantine inspection. Six miles outside New York's narrows, the ship dropped anchor and a medical team boarded to examine crew and passengers for communicable diseases. Competent diagnoses and treatment were limited by the mediocrity of physicians willing to accept this assignment. In the absence of professional supervision, quarantine duty also became a haven for corruption when some passengers received clearance from quarantine by bribing an examiner or were quarantined because they refused to be blackmailed. The extortionist was rarely exposed, for if challenged, he could simply say he'd misdiagnosed the passenger. The threat of forty days in quarantine made the stakes high, and many immigrants were beginning to change their opinion about the land of opportunity before they ever stepped ashore.

In spite of suspicion of any latent disease, the ship and all aboard were released from quarantine after twenty-four tantalizing hours anchored six miles from the prize of the New World. As the ship slowly moved from the foggy narrows to the harbor, the sky suddenly cleared to reveal the awe-inspiring Statue of Liberty enlightening the world. Towering one hundred and fifty-one feet above the water, cradling a book of law with one arm and holding up the Torch of Enlightenment with the other, she welcomed all with hope. It is a rarity when an individual is silenced by glimpsing greatness, an inexplicable phenomenon when an agitated crowd is struck dumb by the revelation of their destiny. While hundreds held their breath, paying respects, gulls quieted and the sea smoothed, then simultaneously a loud cheer arose from the immigrants.

Magically the harbor came alive with vessels of all classes crisscrossing in intricately timed courses that daringly defied collision. Ketches, sloops and yawls repeatedly raced roundtrip from Manhattan to New Jersey, Long Island and Staten Island, leaving the ports' deep water channels free for intercontinental vessels. Ocean transports lay at anchor waiting to dock or at piers loading or unloading passengers and cargo. Some of the older craft still carried masts to provide sail power in case the unreliable steam engines failed.

Moses studied Manhattan's skyline, noting all the buildings seemed bigger, taller and newer than any back home. Still captive to the Statue of Liberty's grandeur, he looked back to again study the statue's benevolent dominance of the port, unlike the crude braggadocio he imagined had inspired the statues of Jupiter, Nero and the Colossus at Rhodes.

After enduring the frustrating delays of bureaucratic inefficiencies aboard the ship, the immigrants were barged to the Emigrant Landing Depot set on a small island a hundred yards offshore from New York City's Battery Park. This strategically located cay, early on the site of gun emplacement, artisans' shops, exhibition halls and entertainment rooms, was joined to the mainland by a rickety bridge that had once collapsed under the weight of President Andrew Jackson and a group of sedentary politicians on an inspection tour. Now immigrants crossed this unimpressive entry to take their first step on American soil.

The Emigrant Landing's reception center provided a wide range of assistance for the ever-growing flood of Europeans. Government clerks processed final papers for admission, supervised baggage handling, monitored porter fees and maintained an official cashier service to prevent gouging, extortion and fraud. A labor bureau, working with contractors and manufacturers, directed job applicants to farms, mines, construction, domestic and other employment sources.

Unlike their previous encounters with immigration officials, Moses, Ludwig and Alfredo found the competency of the reception center personnel exceeded all expectations, and they were soon cleared to join the shouting, shoving, smiling line waiting to push through the turnstile to freedom. Remembering his pledge before Lightning Lance about his first act on American soil, Moses dropped to his knees to thank his Maker and was almost trampled by the unruly mob.

Chapter 5

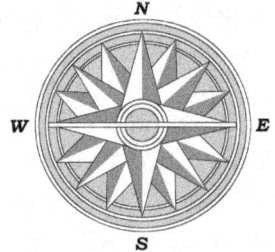

oses was unprepared for the disquiet that seized him as he crossed the bridge from the Emigrant Landing Depot to Battery Park's new world, leaving behind the ways he'd found manageable. Anxious about an unknown future, he forced himself to remember realization was seldom as bad as anticipation. It was difficult to determine if Ludwig was experiencing the same feelings, but Alfredo was fully occupied hauling his oversized bundle and leering at the ladies.

Released at last from authoritative constraints, Moses, Ludwig and Alfredo left the Battery to walk into an alien place of contradictions - the power of wealth's buildings, bridges and boulevards; the indifference to poverty, filth and usury. So entranced with discoveries, they were unaware of ever-present hoodlums speculating on how to part the immigrants from their money or the piles of garbage strewn along the streets of the land of promised opportunity.

Moses was baffled that with so much to see New Yorkers hurried wherever they went, looking straight ahead and down. Deciding to experiment, he walked directly to a well-dressed man coming towards him and when a few feet away smiled his best and said, "Good day, sir." The oncoming pedestrian, startled and annoyed, muttered something unpleasant as he stepped around Moses.

Walking north Trinity Church's dominant steeple pointed heavenward, unmistakably proclaiming that Episcopal faith was a mighty force for salvation. The trio changed course to the northeast, leaving the center of commerce and Christianity to search for a room, and immediately entered progressively rundown neighborhoods. Irish, German, Italian and Eastern Europeans, so destitute they were rejected by their own kind, huddled together in squalor and suspicion.

Trying to hold off nausea, Moses almost missed seeing the grey-haired, bony, black man sitting on the curb of the filthy street. He extended a trembling hand, his mouth slack, lusterless eyes asking for help, reminding Moses of his second vow to give his daily meal to a hungry soul and know where he comes from.

Moses studied the beggar's purplish/black shiny skin, matted beard and unmatched coat and pants, their difference almost erased by dirt and wear. A striped shirt turning yellow from constant use and laceless boots completed the picture of hopeless poverty.

Controlling the urge to escape from this repulsive derelict, Moses pulled a portion of wurstsausage, cheese and black bread from his knapsack and handed them to the beggar.

The black man took the meal and sniffed it.

"Ah don wan nonna yah stinkin' Jew junk," he yelled. "Ah wan money."

Moses, stunned by the hostile response, was tempted to yell, "You don't deserve any charity."

But before he could form the words, the derelict said, "Ya done know nothin' 'bout bein' a poah nigga and livin' on handouts. Ya ain't never been put outa work by ferenas like ya. Why diden ya stay home so us poah folks could earn a wage? I wan the money back ya took from us folk."

Ludwig and Alfredo urged Moses to forget the man and come along with them, but the desperation in the outcast's eyes would not release the Jew until he bent down, took a penny from his pocket and gave it away as he'd pledged.

Moses awakened the second day remembering his promise to meet diverse peoples and observe if all were treated equally. After the previous day's incident, it seemed unnecessary to look further, but the apparent division between the poor and the rich in this land of plenty demanded his attention to avoid faulty premature conclusions.

Having found no lodging, the previous night had been spent under the balcony of a public building, which was tolerable in the uncommon spring warmth. However, knowing weather could become freezing in a few hours at this time of year, Ludwig and Alfredo set out to look for rooms while Moses fulfilled his second day's obligation.

Ludwig and Alfredo walked north on a street parallel to Broadway, populated by Gaelic-speaking Irish unable to understand German or Italian. At last the impasse was resolved when a Creole prostitute, multilingual by the demands of her trade, pointed north and told them there were mixed accommodations in the Grand Canal area.

Within minutes of their parting, Alfredo reasoned the prostitute judged he was an Italian womanizer offering her no business and spitefully misled them with visions of a grand canal rivaling Venice's renowned waterway. After traveling some distance in the direction given by the streetwalker, they agreed they might have been tricked and stopped a pedestrian to confirm the existence of a grand canal in New York City and the probability of finding lodging.

The man finally deciphered Alfredo's inadequate English. "Oh! You must mean Grand and Canal Streets. There is no grand canal or mediocre or even insignificant canal," he said, hurrying away.

Believing they'd been tricked again, Ludwig and Alfredo changed their course to take them to the East River, which they supposed would be the probable source of the canal's water. Furthermore, they reasoned no one had ever heard of a canal without water or a Canal Street without a canal.

Reaching Fulton Street's end at the East River, they discovered the streets were so narrow even a four-storied building could block the view of much taller structures but a short distance away. It was no wonder then that as they rounded the corner of the last building on the street before the river they were awestruck by the panorama of the majestic Brooklyn Bridge. Towering stone pillars on each side of the river anchored dozens of shiny cables draped over three separate pillars like strings on the gods' harps.

Without warning, Ludwig's reverie was disturbed with a barrage of empty clam shells fired by Irish laborers protecting their Fulton Fish Market employment monopoly from intruders.

One of the most vocal yelled, "We don't want no gibberish-talkin' fereners comin' here to take our jobs. Go back where ya come from. Get on with ya now 'fore we throw pavin' blocks."

Ludwig, less used to street toughs than Alfredo, found the Irishman's insults outrageous, especially coming from one whose people had migrated to America only thirty-five years earlier. Knowing it was best to avoid confrontation, Alfredo steered Ludwig away from the Irish brawlers.

At their black bread and borscht supper that evening, Moses told his friends he'd also been treated rudely by many that day, some even threatening violence, but he realized no matter how great the risk he was bound to fulfill his covenant's third day of befriending the Indians.

Moses awoke on the day of his third quest, recalling Lightning Lance's vague account of the Indian decline in Manhattan nearly two centuries before. Since then, countless immigrants of various races arrived to settle in neighborhoods of their own kind or mix with different bloods to lose their original identity. Wasn't it possible most Indians had been absorbed into an unrecognizable mutation or had withdrawn to inaccessible obscurity? He concluded his only chance of finding Indians was to search the less populated settlements beyond the affluents' community constantly moving north to escape the riffraff's expansion. With little but common sense and the hope someone along the way might have information to simplify his task, he quickened his pace optimistic about the prospects for success.

Horse-drawn wagons and elegant carriages sped by, but a half hour passed before Moses met a pedestrian he could ask for information. A wiry, bearded man in a modestly-decorated military uniform descended the stairs of a town house, apparently absorbed in his own thoughts, unaware he was heading straight towards Moses. Though the soldier showed no sign of friendliness, he appeared intelligent and knowledgeable and might give directions to simplify the search.

"Excuse me, sir," Moses said softly in halting English, intending to solicit sympathetic help.

"Speak up, man," the uniformed one barked in a commanding style.

"Sir, can you tell me where the Indians live around here?"

"Indians? Blazes, man, there aren't any of them varmints around here any longer. Cleaned them out years ago and good riddance, too. Like I always say, 'a good Indian is a dead Indian' or my name's not General Phil Sherman."

Meaning to leave the exchange on a friendly note, Moses said, "shalom," wondering why some were obsessed with corrupting the American ethos in the name of patriotism by persecuting unlike cultures instead of practicing the country's pledge of brotherhood and opportunity for all. Hopeful others he'd meet would not be so unpleasant, he continued to look for a more helpful guide. Now paying more attention to the expressions of those he encountered, he waited until he saw an agreeable looking young man coming his way.

"Excuse me, sir," Moses said, his accented English bringing a smile to the stranger's face, which was welcomed as a sign of friendliness. "Can you direct me to where I might find an Indian?"

"Sure," the young man said after thinking for a minute. "Walk two blocks north, turn left and go till you see a church, turn left and walk south till you see a fountain. There is an Indian in the building on the corner." The young man, presumably happy he'd helped Moses, left chuckling.

"Thank you," Moses said, tipping his Polish knit cap, elated he'd been able to locate an Indian who'd surely know the place of others. Within minutes Moses made his left-hand turn and realized he'd been tricked into a wild-goose chase as the building he was seeking stood only two blocks from where he'd started, not the seven the young man had sent him along. But excited by the prospects of reaching his goal, he felt no malice toward the prankster.

The object of Moses' search seemed no different from the monotonous row of other buildings with which it stood, suggesting this might be another hoax of the young man or perhaps proof of Indians assimilating whites' ways. In either case, he would learn the answer to the riddle as soon as he opened the door of the nondescript establishment. His entry tripped a merry tinkle from a bell hung on the door waiting to greet visitors. The interior into which he stepped was so dark his eyes at first failed to see the disarray of boxes, bins, tins and parcels defying easy retrieval of any object by any but the creator of such havoc. Presiding over the clutter was a jolly-faced, rotund man astride a stool, scanning a newspaper in the dim light from a naked bulb suspended from a tin ceiling.

With Moses' arrival the man peered over his pince-nez spectacles and delivered a courtly welcome. "The House of Van Dyke at your service. Now, young fellow, I calculate by your age you're going to tell me you came to pick up cheroots for your father, and that would not be entirely untruthful even if you added to the purchase some smokes for yourself, which I reckon is the reason you came here in the first place. But Adrian Van Dyke is not here to pass judgment on every soul who passes his way or crosses his threshold. No, no, what my customers do is up to them and the Lord in heaven. I just aim to deliver the best quality tobacco at the most reasonable price. Take this tin of snuff, for example, a favorite of gents of high quality and manners; or this package of chews, especially handy for a young fellow who doesn't want the parson to catch him with smoke pouring out of his mouth like Dante's inferno. See, he can chew this tobacco plug and who's to know the difference, or if he's in polite company he can just spit it out and claim he choked on the pit of a plum."

Moses, careful not to seem rude, waited till the House of Van Dyke's proprietor paused for a breath then interrupted him.

"I was told this is the home of one of the few Indians in New York. If that is true, I'd like to talk to him."

"That's not entirely untrue and meet him you will, but it will be a one-sided conversation. He's been here with me for sixteen years and

I never heard him utter one word. If you'll turn around and look in the corner under that big cigar sign, you'll meet Chief Hearnoseenospeaknoevil."

In the darkest corner out of the way stood a seven-foot, carved wooden Indian in full war party regalia. The stoic figure poised as though in mid-stride, gazing despondently into an unknown future. Battle ready, a lance in one hand, a tomahawk in the other, he'd become the object of a cruel joke when someone stuck a cigar in his mouth and hung a sign on a string of beads around his neck reading, "Have island, will trade for $24.00 worth of beads."

Moses, deeply distressed, checked his anger before asking, "Are no Indians living in New York now?"

"None. Two hundred years ago there were many tribes in the area, but they died out from disease, and those left moved away or were absorbed by other peoples."

"Why do tobacco stores have wooden Indians?" he asked.

"If I were a learned anthropologist or historian, I might give you the real answer, but as a humble tobacconist I can only guess it's because the Indians taught us to smoke."

"I thank you, Mr. Van Dyke, but before I go, may I take the cigar and sign off the Indian?"

"Yes, young fellow, but in a week's time some prankster will put something back on my mascot."

"But you're the proprietor; this is your store."

"Just the same, you can't insult the customers now, can you?"

"Goodbye, sir," Moses said, leaving the shop, angered that human dignity could be so easily bartered for customer loyalty.

Determined to pursue his search in a more organized manner, Moses set out to utilize the sources in the newly completely Astor Library on 14th Street. Aware his limited English skills could hinder optimum use of the archives, Moses asked for aid at the main desk and was passed in turn by two attendants to a shriveled myopic librarian in a floor-length, black cotter. It wasn't until Moses with difficulty categorized his request for data on racial dispersement that the attendant condescended to examine the files and quickly returned to report their resources did not include any material on America's aboriginal savages.

On his return to join Ludwig and Alfredo for supper, Moses passed the office of New York's largest newspaper and, ever hopeful, entered to explain his errand to a receptionist.

"Oh, you must want the morgue," he said, confusing Moses until it was explained the term was used for the stored back issues of the paper.

The publication's documentation of the New York Indians' demise was as nonexistent as the library's, but their civility made the disappointment less frustrating.

A short detour off his homeward route took Moses to a synagogue, which he entered thinking these extraordinary chroniclers would be enlightening. To his disappointment, he learned the rabbis confined their scholarship to Talmud's and Mishma's 300 - 700 interpretation of Jewish religion. Nothing more, not even the seventeenth century slaughter of Manhattan humans.

As though extending his inquiry of any religion's practice in relieving human suffering, Moses headed directly to New York's St. Peter's Church, a Roman Catholic denomination of which he knew little beyond the kindness of the nuns in a Bremen convent infirmary. He entered the cavernous sanctuary, his hobnailed boots striking the stone floor to violate the stillness of the nave. Speculating on why gloomy interiors were necessary to command reverence, he worked his way forward to the first pew and sat in the emptiness of late afternoon, thinking on how to find a cleric to help him. For an instant, blinding light flooded through an opened door to the street, interrupting Moses' inspection of the darkness among the shadowy pillars for a priest. Solitude's intruder soon revealed herself as an old, raggedly dressed woman. She hobbled up the aisle past him, kneeled with difficulty, crossed herself, rose, dropped money in a box and entered an inconspicuous cubicle.

In a short time, the old lady reappeared and knelt at the altar rail, mumbling a prayer in repetitive cadence. Presumably knowing when the full effect of her devotion had been achieved, she rose and was absorbed into the darkness. Moses watched three other communicants perform the same ritual before concluding the only connection of the church with the outside world was through the little door on which he knocked three times for admission.

"Come in. You don't need to announce your arrival, the Lord knows of your presence," a voice from within said.

The cubicle Moses entered, small yet large enough to hold two persons, was walled into two parts with a small slot in the divider for communication while preserving the identify of communicant and priest.

"Kneel and tell me what brings you here?"

"I'm searching for any descendants of the Indians who survived the massacre two hundred years ago."

The priest hesitated before replying, "The Church has no official position on any matter not stated in the Pope's encyclicals," and as an afterthought added, "only that those peoples were heathens. Now, my son, tell me of your sins."

"No, only the sins of others," Moses said as he rose and left.

As was the custom in early settlements, houses of worship tended to cluster within the concentration of the populations and like some force that wouldn't let go, the site of a Quaker Meeting stood between Moses and the end of his search. As he came along the front of the house of worship, an older woman was closing up for the night. It was notable that of the sanctuaries of three different faiths, the Quaker Meeting was the only one entrusted to a woman's responsibility.

She showed no impatience with the time of his arrival and sat on the steps beside him responding as best she could to his questions about the annihilation of the New York Indians. Composed and candid, she put Moses at ease, finding nothing unusual about a Jew's interest in Indian genocide. She related that as a small girl her grandmother told her there was still a lot of talk among the Friends of the horrible atrocity to the red man, but she knew nothing of any survivors.

"I can assure you Quakers would not have ignored such wickedness and would have taken all action short of violence to prevent that calamity. Remember in 1662 William Penn made a compact with the Indians which honored peaceful coexistence. We are a peaceful faith that believes violence begets violence."

She paused for a moment, shutting her eyes as though to block all outside disturbance. "Funny you're asking me about this. The custodian who preceded me in this duty told me about four years ago some man she thought was an Indian, in one of these Wild West shows, asked her the same questions you've been asking."

Chapter 6

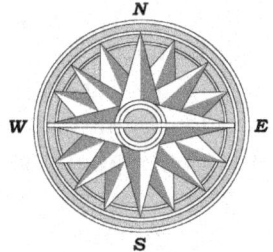

Moses, returning from an unsuccessful day of locating Indians, learned Ludwig and Alfredo had found temporary housing with two men, a wholesale hardware clerk and a night watchman in a dry goods store. The space for rent included a medium and a small bedroom-kitchen-dining room-living room combination and bathroom to be shared with the clerk and the watchman. The hallway connecting the rooms was so narrow one needed to step into a doorway to let another pass, and the dining table seated only three at a time, but they were off the street with a place to bathe and store their belongings.

The night watchman, older of the two, was reluctant at first to take in immigrants, but his partner reminded him his share of the rent would be cut from fifty to twenty percent and his nighttime job would allow him to be home all day to keep an eye on things. Later in recalling the episode, Ludwig liked to tell how the young man convinced the night watchman by using a negative/positive approach to win the xenophobic issue and a positive/positive approach with the rent reduction.

That night, in a bed for the first time since he'd left the ship, Moses, either awake or asleep but never knowing which, heard a familiar voice reminding him that tomorrow was the fourth day of his quest. Disappointed only hours earlier by the rabbis' indifference to the extermination of local Indians, he saw little purpose in visiting the place where people of his heritage congregated. However, as the Sabbath was a few days away, those not working might be receptive to his visit at their homes, and though unlikely it pleased him to think he might be reunited with an old friend or meet a person with common acquaintances.

A policeman's directions and a twenty minute brisk walk led him to a Jewish ghetto in an area bounded by Grant, Stanton and Ludlow Streets where a shopkeeper told Moses this was a new Jewish neighborhood, its residents having moved two miles north from the site near their entry to New York. Contiguous to this Jewish section were separate neighborhoods of Irish, Germans and Italians, all distinctly segregated from each other, but none as intolerant as the Jews amongst themselves.

The Germans, earliest migrants of the Jews, looked on those from Russia and Poland as inferior, ridiculing their Yiddish language and relegating them to a servile status. At first unaware of this bigotry, Moses entered a kosher slaughterhouse to meet the workers and received curses, jeers and threats of violence. He quickly departed, assuming as a class butchers were a rude exception to the majority, but no matter where he went in the neighborhood from the moment he spoke Yiddish, he was vilified. Not easily deterred, Moses continued to search for civility in the ghetto, believing he should not make a judgment based on one experience. However, with each attempt to make acquaintances, old and young ridiculed him. Worst of all, young children had been taught to hate strangers because they sounded different.

Sadly Moses exchanged his native tongue for English, limited but with perfect pronunciation as learned from Ludwig, his ever-surprisingly talented friend. People, no longer hostile, tried to copy him, admiring the clarity of his speech, repeating his pronunciation as though in a language class. This was certainly not the outcome he'd expected from the fourth day's quest, and he returned to his lodging unsure he understood his mission.

At supper that evening, Moses' day of disappointments seemed less discouraging after hearing Ludwig had a job with America's premier piano manufacturer.

By chance his search for work had taken him past a building displaying a "Help Wanted" sign and on applying for the job learned it was a musical instrument company. Impressed with his extensive musicology, his first interviewer recommended to several department managers he be hired immediately. Employment terms mutually acceptable to Ludwig and the company were reached, and then to Ludwig's surprise the owner asked him to play a piano about to be shipped. After a quick visual inspection of the piano's interior, Ludwig sat down, held his head to the music rack and performed a flawless rendition of Chopin's 'Minute Waltz' in exactly fifty-eight seconds, reserving the remaining two for bows.

Acknowledging the applause from the workers gathered around him, Ludwig suggested the piano needed minor tuning adjustments before being shipped. The owner, irritated by Ludwig's suggestion the piano had an imperfection, asked for a tuning fork.

"May I suggest you listen to a note and compare it against the sound of the tuning fork?" Ludwig said. "If there is a difference, let me make an adjustment of the note without using the tuning fork, then compare it to the sound with the fork."

The owner, impatient to settle the matter, performed the first step of the test. "Now it's your turn," he said, confident he'd soon prove the piano was in tune.

Ludwig took a wooden peg from his pocket and, with one end in his ear and the other on the piano's keyboard cover, adjusted the note. Then using the fork he again tested the pitch, confirming Ludwig's opinion.

"We're not running a side show here, you know. Why did you go through all that tom foolery with the peg?" the owner asked.

"Because I'm deaf," Ludwig answered, becoming a legend.

While Alfredo's search for work continued to be unsuccessful, his attempt to communicate in English improved his fluency in the new tongue despite having his face slapped occasionally by women who misunderstood his faulty vocabulary.

"And on the fifth day I will seek work in one of the many trades of my family," Moses recited, returning to Manhattan's commercial district.

If nothing else, his previous four days of failed missions had acquainted him with the city and he wasted no time in locating the department stores and filing his application for work.

In turn, Macys, Stearns, Straus, Orbachs and Altmans, all major retail establishments owned by German Jews, refused to hire Moses when they learned he came from the Polish/Yiddish tradition, making him an objectionable "kike" in their eyes.

Moses, unfamiliar with the term, asked why the East European Yiddish-speaking Jews were called "kikes" and learned it was because so many of their names like Polaski and Stowkowski ended in -ki or -ski.

Whether hurtfully candid or blatantly intolerant, the rejection was destructive.

One interviewer explained the prejudice in detail, then concluded by saying if one spoke Yiddish they were simply unemployable, to which Moses replied, "But you can't treat Yiddish customers like that."

The store's employee looked around nervously and leaned close to Moses. "We don't serve Yiddish customers."

"I speak proper English," Moses explained, switching to his second language. "None would be the wiser."

"Store owners would understand you as they've already adapted the way of New York's social register, but you'd have to dilute your English with a German accent to make most of our customers comfortable."

"Where do the 'kikes' buy their goods?" Moses asked, testing the cruel slur that plagued the lives of those denigrated.

"I'm not sure, maybe out-of-the-way shops miles from home."

"Walking miles for a spool of thread?" Moses said, shaking his head as he left the employee.

I'll go to them, Moses thought as he walked back to meet Ludwig and Alfredo. *I've worked in shops, but I'm also a peddler. I'll take their necessities to them.*

At supper on the fifth evening, Moses, Ludwig and Alfredo were told by the night watchman that his brother, wife and baby were coming from Ireland in about three weeks and had no place to stay. Unable to find lodging for them and bound to honor his sub-let agreement with Moses, Ludwig and Alfredo, the watchman was in a visible state of turmoil.

Ludwig motioned to Moses and Alfredo for a head-to-head conference, which produced a consensus to give up the space to his brother's family.

"Let's just think of us as coming in to bathe. After all, we've lived on the street before. I guess we can return to it for a few more days," Ludwig told the watchman.

Later on, recounting the incident, Moses moralized that generosity begets generosity because within the week their other landlord, the hardware clerk, announced his company was supplying building materials to a warehouse being converted into living quarters.

"I heard this just as I was leaving work, so you're in on the ground floor," the clerk told them.

His expression proved to be prophetic because the ground floor renovation of the two-story building was just getting underway, and Alfredo negotiated an exchange of his masonry work for a free deposit and the first month's rent. For forty days the trio lived amidst sawdust, spilled nails and popping welding torches, but always joyously grateful for their good fortune.

On the seventh day, the Sabbath, I will go to temple to discover how history's most oppressed reach out to other downtrodden people, Moses thought.

"By this day's end you will have fulfilled your covenant made before me and you will not hear me remind you of the pilgrimage you've chosen for your life," a voice deep within declared. "I will leave you now, for you have learned how the knowledge of experience can direct you to the wisdom of truth."

On one of his many excursions through the city, Moses had passed the Shearith Israel Synagogue on Mill Street where he chose to worship on his first Sabbath in America.

Upon entering the temple, he noted none spoke Yiddish nor looked like any Polish Jews he'd ever seen, and the service conducted in the Sepharic tradition confirmed the Spanish-Portuguese roots of the congregation. To his dismay, Moses found the Sepharic dogma so at odds with Ashkenazim that it verged on being anti-Semitic. The following Sabbath, he attended services at B'nai Jeshurum Temple whose members were Ashkenazim Jews of Polish, Dutch and German descent. Before the service had ended, Moses concluded much of the Ashkenazim energy was used in retaliating against the Sepharic sect - reconciliation was not a priority for either persuasion.

The farther he searched, the more the Jewish Religion seemed to be fragmenting as the orderly orthodoxy of the shtetls with which he'd been raised gave way to synagogues in store fronts, tenements and abandoned churches. Internal turmoil and by splintering, zealot-style dismantling of the faith, allowed little time for outreach missions.

By late summer, the threesome was settled in their converted warehouse. Alfredo, in his typical, extravagant, Italian conception, pronounced their dwelling perfect in every respect. It was new, within walking distance to work and ideally located for shopping, social and security purposes, being but a few blocks from the fire department, police station and a whorehouse - the latter serving to divert felons from the long arm of the law.

Ludwig now had become a celebrity of sorts with his skillful, impromptu recitals, inspiring some wit to suggest the piano manufacturer advertise with the slogan, "You don't have to hear to play the piano."

Moses was now serving a receptive market with his door-to-door deliveries of small wares including pins, needles, threads, tapes, buttons, clothing patterns, shoe laces, pencils and other expendables. He soon learned the demand for home-to-home delivery would exceed his ability to serve a growing market and began looking for salesmen to assist him in expanding the business.

Alfredo was the last to find employment as the Roman Catholic's feverish pursuit of icons had yet to become a competitive phenomenon. For the time being, Alfredo was reduced to the apprentice level of carving epitaphs on tombstones. He'd been occupied in this humbling work less than an hour before being approached by an unsavory character in a swallowtail coat, wing collar and bowler hat, sucking on a toothpick. Without introduction, the stranger launched into a slick appeal claiming he represented a highly professional establishment pioneering in medical research who could not continue their humane calling without cadavers.

Eloquent in rationalizing the removal of human remains from interment for the betterment of mankind, he continued by describing how Leonardo da Vinci without a corpse could never have rendered his medically invaluable drawings of the human anatomy. He stressed over and over how these scientific advances depended on a constant supply of newly buried corpses and who better than Alfredo could provide the source. Of course, there would be remuneration for Alfredo's contribution to the advance of this noble cause, which would exceed his modest wages as a stonecutter. Relieving the earth, as the confidence-man referred to graverobbing to make the practice more palatable, had been practiced for centuries and in New York dated back to the 1700s with the distinction of counting some of the most distinguished communicants of the city's Trinity Church among the donors.

"Wella Mista, I not talka too good English," Alfredo said, understanding his new language much better than he let the swindler know. "You tella me more plaina what I do one more timea."

"The first night after the burial you dig up the casket, we take the body and you rebury the casket. Simple as that and nobody gets upset because nobody knows the difference."

"Okay. I thinka bout it tonight and tomorrow you coma backa and we talka."

Alfredo, flexible in his application of morality, nevertheless believed when a body was buried it should stay buried and found the practice of graverobbing loathsome. Assuming it was his responsibility to apprehend the scoundrel, Alfredo notified the police who arrested the man the next day on his return to the cemetery.

As the police sergeant took his prisoner away, he cynically remarked that within a day's time another would replace the prisoner and the families of the deceased would not have better protection for their loved ones.

"As long as someone can make a buck on a corpse, graves won't be robber-proof," were the policeman's parting words.

Each day following the revolting experience, Alfredo found his work more unappealing. One noon's lunch break, his mind took a recess from its preoccupation with women and drifted across the rows of tombstones to visualize a magnificent sepulcher, safe as a bank, sculpted by the incomparable Alfredo Chiati. When the cemetery's superintendent heard Alfredo's proposal of offering grandiose memorials to rich families for their deceased, he rejected it as highly irregular and tasteless, but Alfredo was already possessed by the architectural conception.

Circumventing tradition, Alfredo approached and was granted an audience with M. T. Everest, flamboyant tycoon, whose characteristic flair for setting trends was legend. Rich and romantic at heart, he'd ordered a replica of the Taj Mahal for his home, slightly smaller than the original but no less ornate.

When Alfredo's work for him was at last completed, galas offering full access to the press informed the rich and famous of M. T. Everest's latest coup, and the rush of scions to create edifices, each grander than the last, became frenzied as though the clients couldn't wait to die.

It had become a weekly custom for Moses, Ludwig and Alfredo to greet newly-arrived immigrants as they crossed the bridge from the Emigrant Landing Depot to America's mainland. One of their intentions was to protect unsuspecting newcomers from being cheated by swindlers, at best a limited success because the crooks returned as soon as Moses, Ludwig and Alfredo left.

Searching for a way to eliminate or substantially reduce the cheating, Moses discovered the thieves were ignorant unemployables dependant on this once-a-week fraud for a livelihood.

Optimistic the security of legitimate, full-time employment might persuade some to quit exploiting immigrants and offer a model for others to follow, Moses studied the shysters at work.

One more assertively slick than the others approached a middle-aged couple, tipped his hat and, all smiles, began his scam.

Suddenly the possible solution to the problem seemed at hand.

"My good man," Moses said to the cheat, "I see you are acting kindly to these strangers to our shores and you hold their attention with your persuasiveness. I'm also aware undercover police are monitoring this area more closely now and jailing those even suspected of dishonest dealings with the immigrants. I judge you to be a good citizen and caution you to give the police no false impression that would cause them to arrest you."

The swindler lost the momentum of his scam, but intrigued by Moses' non-accusatory yet perceptive greeting, dropped his guard.

"I am Moses Morgenstern. My growing door-to-door sales business requires I hire an assistant, and I'm looking for worthy candidates. You appear to be a good person with selling skills, trapped in your current circumstances by the need to put bread on the table. A job with me could mean if you worked hard, you'd have regular weekly wages and avoid any mistaken appearance of belonging to those who cheat innocent immigrants and risk jail. What do you say to that?"

"Guv'nor, I'd say you're pretty persuasive. How do we get started?"

"We start right now by assisting these confused souls as they come ashore, showing them how to protect their worldly goods," Moses said. "Help them look for shelter, tell them where their countrymen may have settled. Let's see right now how well you do helping these people, and then we'll talk about the job. Oh, yes, one more thing. You'll be paid each week right here with us as we aid newcomers so we never forget where we came from."

In the year that followed, business doubled and doubled again as Moses, with the help of his first convert, persuaded several charlatans to retire from their nefarious trade to become his salesmen. During this expansion, Moses added soaps, hair tonics, hair pins, combs, paraffin and work gloves to his existing line of products, priced for the low-income market unattractive to large department stores. Concerned with all things affecting his employees' welfare, Moses carefully matched the weight of the peddler's cart load to a route with suitable grades and length.

In the beginning when he peddled alone, reconciling sales, inventory and payments had been simple, but now the business growth generated by four salesmen required better controls to maintain customer service and solvency. Aware that an error in the records undiscovered for even a short time could be disastrous, Moses devised a check on weekly orders, deliveries and receipts with all the salesmen participating. At each weekly meeting all the data related to a salesman's account were reviewed by Moses and an employee of the week before presenting it to the group. If honest errors were made, they could be corrected by deducting a weekly amount from the salesman's pay to reconcile the monetary loss. Cheating was an unforgivable offense and resulted in an immediate discharge of the offender. Moses rejoiced that neither had ever happened almost more than the sanction awarded by port authorities to Ludwig, Alfredo and himself to supervise all counseling given to new immigrants. The experiment had worked; most of the cheating at the dock had ceased.

In the second year of his door-to-door business, Moses had customers in half of Manhattan's homes, but he wisely decided not to expand his line with items competitive to the large stores' merchandise and attract their attention. Instead, he began selling to a rapidly growing Brooklyn, where in eighteen months his business amounted to half of Manhattan's.

Although he tried to operate with a minimum, rapidly-turned inventory, the business growth demanded larger volumes of on-hand stock than could be contained in the space shared with Ludwig and Alfredo, so he rented the floor above their living quarters. Some of his suppliers urged him to open a mail order business, but he rejected the idea knowing his face-to-face relationships with customers and maintaining the confidentiality of their identities were invaluable assets.

Three years after leaving an old world culture that submitted to despair, Moses with minor adaptations duplicated his Manhattan business mode in Brooklyn, Boston and Philadelphia. As New England's largest metropolis evolved from Puritanism into Brahmin elitism and Philadelphia's growing mercantile dynasty ignored the Quaker ethic, pockets of lower-income families remained unserved. Now the well-established customer base in these cities offered the opportunity to expand his franchise to other yet-undetermined locales.

The unfinished letter on his table awaited the inclusion of this update and an offer to bring his family to America to share in his success. He would tell them there was now sufficient work in the company for four or five of his brothers and sisters, and if plans for further expansion succeeded, there could be enough work for the entire family.

He wondered if despite the company's success his siblings would find the family's youngest an unacceptable boss.

Long ago his father had irrationally sworn never to leave the town of his birth and his father's and his father's father. With the passing of his dear, departed wife, he amended his oath to assure his resting place would be beside her and implored his children not to deny this final solace. Jacob, oldest of the children, had obediently stated if their father remained imbedded in the futureless shtetl, he would stay for the remainder of the old man's years, which judging by the patriarch's vitality could be a long time.

Trinka, narrowly escaping the unkind slur of old-maidism, was soon to be married and planning to live with the groom's parents, which Moses regarded as incentive for early migration to America.

Hannah, the second oldest girl and almost as adventurous as Moses, might be the first to leave, her departure strongly influencing Rebecca to come with her. If neither was interested in the work supporting the door-to-door peddling, a job restricted to men, there was always a demand for women in the cut and sew trade.

Moses had created a bridge of opportunity for those who'd crossed over from hopelessness to a new life, but he reminded himself it must be the decision of each.

As he reflected on the business accomplishments described in his letter, they gave him less satisfaction than expected or experienced in earlier years. Increased success minus decreased challenge equaled declined satisfaction.

Now he would put away his metropolitan maps and government statistics, close his eyes and ears to the outer world, and search for an inner voice.

Chapter 7

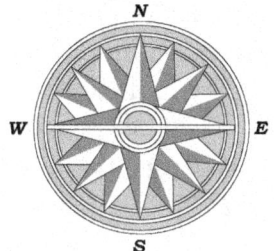

This Friday in the third year as the group gathered weekly to greet the foreign-born crossing the bridge to America, Moses was astounded by his record that they had welcomed nearly twelve thousand immigrants. The original committee of Ludwig, Alfredo and himself had grown to twenty-five, and a friendly smile, handshake and protection from swindlers of the early days had inspired multiple services including guidance on lodging, jobs, medical attention and locating friends and relatives. One hearty meal was also provided for each newcomer on arrival to provide a change from shipboard fare with a taste of American cooking.

On this day, nine hundred new arrivals jammed the Emigrant Landing Depot, straining the authorities' processing ability. Those cleared spilled over the bridge to the mainland in an endless stream. Moses tried to recapture his feelings when he was released to become an American, but his senses had been compromised. By one p.m. only half the applicants had been released, and Moses, Ludwig, Alfredo and the others prepared for the long day ahead.

As Ludwig straightened and leaned against a lamp post to relieve his tired back, he saw in the pack of bobbing heads a young woman noticeable because of her erect posture, coal-black hair and pale skin. At first glance she could have been mistaken for a chaperone to the girls who milled about her, but on closer inspection Ludwig detected she carried a guide staff and the youngsters were protecting her from being knocked over by the crowd. Approaching him, she deftly felt her way with a guide staff. An acute sense of surroundings, common to the sightless, warned her of something in her path. She halted in front of Ludwig as the young girls fanned out around the two adults. Despite an encumbrance of a battered suitcase, knapsack and guide staff, she had moved with extraordinary gracefulness. Her lineless face and fixed stare showed no emotion when Ludwig spoke to her.

"Good day, madam. My colleagues and I welcome you to America. We are authorized to act on behalf of the Immigration Service to offer our assistance to the newcomers wherever we can. We help find jobs, lodging, relatives and places of worship. Now what can we do to help you?"

"What on earth makes you think you can help me?" she replied rudely.

Moses, Ludwig and Alfredo stood speechless trying to think how to deal with such anger.

"What can you do that will ever help me?"

"I offered to assist you, not cure you," Ludwig said calmly, deciding to be patient but firm. "There's a difference."

"Who said anything about curing me?" the woman flashed back, apparently wanting to start an argument.

"You did in your tone, not your words," Ludwig replied, thinking she appeared more frail close by than in the crowd when he first saw her - or perhaps the bravado had used all her adrenalin.

"I can never be cured, I'm blind. Do you hear, I'm blind!"

"No, I don't hear. I'm deaf."

"If you're really deaf and just not listening, how can you know what I'm saying? How can you talk with me?" the woman asked, startled by Ludwig's answer.

"I can talk with you because I read lips to overcome my deafness."

"Are you lecturing me? If so, it won't do any good. What can you say that I haven't heard from others?" she challenged, moderating her cynicism.

Then, thinking candor might weaken her will, she hardened. "I don't need any more well-intended experts telling me how to live my life. I'll be on my way."

"Not an expert but a concerned stranger willing to offer you help not sympathy. Right now you need some food and assistance getting settled."

"I'm still capable of taking care of myself."

"Debatable, but why waste time exploring what's already been discovered?" Ludwig persisted.

The woman tried not to give in, but slumping from fatigue and malnourishment, almost fell to the ground before Ludwig caught and carried her to the First Aid tent.

When the woman awoke hours later she lay in a feather bed, one of Ludwig's few indulgences. Disoriented by unfamiliar sounds and aromas, she called to whoever might be listening to tell her where she was. Unanswered, she groped for her guide staff and unable to find the solid, smooth, reassuring pilot and protector, swung her legs from the covers and attempted to stand, but dizziness forced her retreat to the bed.

"Easy!" a voice she'd heard before but couldn't quickly identify warned her. "It's Ludwig, the man at the boat. I'll help you to the bathroom if you'd like, and then I'll get you some soup. You need to eat more than you have been."

"Get me my stick. I'll find the bathroom myself," she said, the rest having restored some of her snappishness.

Ludwig watched her navigate back to the safety of the bed, then with Moses and Alfredo trailing, he returned from the kitchen a few moments later carrying a bowl of soup, a glass of milk and rye bread.

"I don't want anything to eat."

"You may not want it, but the doctor says you need it, and now that we've had the questionable pleasure of meeting and you're sleeping in my bed, you're going to eat," Ludwig said with nonnegotiable authority.

Moses and Alfredo watched in silent amusement at the testing of wills.

Begrudging Ludwig's unassailable dominance, she sipped a spoonful of the savory soup, then having capitulated, picked up the bowl and would have gulped it all had Ludwig not cautioned her that too much at once could make her vomit.

"You're in my bed," Ludwig reminded her.

After finishing her meal more slowly, she lay back against the pillows in thought, then asked, "How do I know you're not white slavers?"

Alfredo, silent for as long a he could restrain himself, said, "Because men don't go to brothels to argue."

With the trio's thoughtful encouragement and Ludwig's persuasive challenges, the woman began to recover. Their joking that none of them could decide if her malnutrition or stubbornness was the more difficult to remedy seemed to help her let down her guard and unquestionably trust the trio. Upon reaching the stage when those recovering from an illness often complain they're being pampered, she would demand more independence. The three men would then singly or in chorus cry out, "And we thought you'd act better when you became well," This would draw a smile or even a laugh from her.

During the recovery, none of the three inquired about, nor did she volunteer anything about her past, her destination or name. Thus she remained "the woman."

In those afternoons when Ludwig returned from work before Moses and Alfredo, he played intricate piano sonatas familiar to the woman's keen ear, and she marveled at his rapturous interpretations. The enthralling notes lifted her to a place beyond her handicap only till the composition ended, when she was then cruelly reminded of her imprisonment.

Early one afternoon, Alfredo returned to find the woman packing her clothes. His presence, muffled by street noise, made him feel like a voyeur, but he could not interrupt her touching ritual of holding each garment close to her heart before placing it in the battered suitcase.

"What are you doing?" he exclaimed, interrupting her reverie.

"I'm leaving," she answered undeterred.

"You can't leave now just as you're getting better. If you leave too soon you'll get sick again and who will take care of you?"

"I can't live on your charity, and I'm no use to anybody."

"That's not true, you just washed our clothes and...and you help out with many things," Alfredo said, unable at the moment to enumerate any more specifics. "You need more time to get well, then when you're ready you'll find a job and a place to live."

"That time will never come. I can't do anything. If I don't go now, I'll always be a burden living on someone's kindness the way I am here. I must make the break now before it's too late. I need to do it on my own. I must try," she sobbed.

"You'll find things to do on your own," Alfredo insisted again, though unable to name any actual occupation to prove his point.

"Like what?" she challenged.

"When we found this place being remodeled we were all broke. I did all the masonry in exchange for a down payment on the rent."

"But you were already a mason. You knew how to do something. I can't do what I used to do. You don't understand, I can't do anything," the woman cried out, using her helplessness to win the argument.

"Of course you can," Alfredo persisted and then blurted out, "You can be a model for a muse I'm carving." Sensing he'd interrupted her desperate fixation, he kept improvising. "You have just the right look, the way you hold your head and gaze past the world's trivia." The moment the words left his mouth he wished he'd not said 'gaze.' "You'd be just right," he repeated, hoping she'd missed his slip.

"What would I do?" she asked.

"You'd be the media for capturing the mystery of the muse in stone," Alfredo declared extravagantly.

"What do you mean?"

"You'd inspire me to find the person hidden in the marble. That's always the challenge in creating art. You'd pose every step of the way from my first sketches when I look for exactly the right stance, to the detailed drawing with the statue as part of the fountain. You'd give life to the sculpture," Alfredo continued, amazed at his eloquence.

"And I would never know what it looked like - if it looked like me."

"You could touch it and feel it. All along you could feel the muse being released from the stone."

The woman, caught up by Alfredo's imagination, unconsciously put her hand to her head and let it trail down her cheek over her chin to her throat. "Must I take my clothes off?"

"No, no. Muses were Greek women who always dressed in long nightgowns. It was the men who went around naked."

The woman smiled.

When the woman had gone to bed and the three men sat on the street curb in front of their tenement hoping for a cool breeze, Alfredo told Moses and Ludwig he'd come home that afternoon to find the woman distraught and determined to leave the next day. He related that with each attempt to convince her she was not useless, she became more upset, berating herself as worthless with no place in the world. As she had approached hysteria, he consoled the woman by offering her a job posing for a statue he was commissioned to sculpt.

"You did what?" Ludwig exclaimed, irritated with Alfredo's hasty action.

"It was the first thing that came into my head. It was something I thought she could do to feel useful."

"Why didn't you talk with us first?" Ludwig demanded.

"Because there wasn't time and something had to be done. She liked the idea. It seemed right."

"I'm the one who's taken the most care of her. She relates to me better because we're both handicapped. You should have come to me first," Ludwig said. "If this modeling is another of your ideas to make a conquest I'll ---"

"I don't like what you're suggesting," Alfredo interrupted, his tone hardening. "I'm trying not to lose my temper, but don't push any further."

Moses intervened, disheartened that in only a few minutes a quarrel threatened to destroy a friendship built over years of shared hardships and successes. "Stop! Ludwig, think of what you're saying, accusing Alfredo of poor intentions. What would you have done in the same situation? None of us owns the woman. We're supposed to be helping her become her own person, not ours. Now she needs to know she's important, and modeling for Alfredo may be the answer. She must first believe in her own worth before she'll believe she can care for herself. Chores here at home can be a start, as well as the modeling, to restore her confidence. We reached out because she couldn't survive alone. Let's help her find a trade. Then she can live alone. When she becomes self sufficient, she can respect herself. Pray we don't deny her that."

Ludwig, scolded more by an activated conscience than Moses, sought to end the controversy with some trivial anecdotes, but Alfredo was not to be appeased. Caught in an impasse, it would take some time before Ludwig put away his pride to confirm his apology by extending his hand, and Alfredo reached back in forgiveness.

The sculpture was begun with the woman twisting and turning into cramping poses while the artist stalked elusive perfection he couldn't describe but would know when he saw it. He launched unacceptable sketches from his pad to sail across the studio to drop to the floor littered with other frustrating failures. After each he rushed back to the model to request another pose soon doomed on his sketch pad. He talked ceaselessly in English and Italian, mostly to himself, occasionally addressing the woman with a comment or question. But before she could speak, he'd answer himself. Finally she stopped talking without him noticing she never replied. After a while, she realized he was subconsciously acting out the roles of student and teacher, apprentice and master, patron and critic to give her compensating sense for visionless eyes. He was affirming there is no art without a witness, and he was striving to make her a witness through oral communication.

After a dozen days of posing and drawing, drawing and posing, the initial excitement of the project dissipated and a lethargy overtook him as each attempt to capture his conception was foiled. Alfredo told the woman he couldn't produce a work worthy of her and they would not go to the studio that day.

"Let's go to the cemetery where you worked," she suggested. "The weather is good, you need to shape some stone, even if it's simple, and I need longer walks."

At first he wouldn't be coaxed from the self-pity of his pessimism. But she kept after him until he finally agreed, and they left carrying lunch and an umbrella for the dreary clouds that soon gave way.

Alfredo shaped the cemetery's unworked stones with skillful precision, describing each cutting and chipping of his output to the woman. Unlike his raving in the studio, he now spoke calmly with the confidence of an artist no longer fighting but embracing creativity's surprises, rewarding him with a sense of success and well-being.

The woman had given him a new beginning.

On their walk home Alfredo stopped, put his hands on her shoulders and turned her toward him. "Now I think I really understand how you felt when you told me you were useless. I trapped Alfredo the artist with self-pity. Do you know what you've done today?"

"What do you mean?" she asked.

"You've taught me how to free myself."

The day after Alfredo rediscovered himself they returned to the studio to clean up the wreckage of the counterfeit ideas, putting the misadventure behind him. Returning from removing the debris, he saw the woman sitting patiently, her body at ease, held in graceful serenity - a muse. Alfredo blinked away the outdoors glare he had returned from to find the image even more compelling. Moving to the easel, he rapidly sketched the personification of the muse that for so long had evaded him. When the marble released his inspiration and the sculpture was completed, the woman asked how he'd been able to cut the stone so rapidly.

"Seeing how ethereal you looked at rest, I realized that's the only pose a muse would hold for eternity. After all, she's just a little less than a goddess, not a contortionist."

Alfredo approached the completion of his work with elation and apprehension. He believed the metamorphosis of a timeless sculpture from the living woman was in conflict with the classic Greek fairytale Pygmalion.

For the woman there was an overpowering sense of relief from uselessness and despair - she could prevail.

Both kept counsel on the effect the sculpture's creation had on them, but each knew they could never return to that place.

At supper, the only meal when the four were usually gathered in the day, Alfredo remarked that the statue had met all his expectations and the patron would probably take possession of the work the next day.

"Moses and I have never seen it," Ludwig said, still sensitive he'd been excluded from the collaboration of the woman and Alfredo.

"If this is the last time we can visit her before she leaves, let's go to the studio and wish her goodbye," Moses suggested to cool tempers.

"And admire Alfredo's accomplishment," Ludwig added, trying to neutralize his earlier petty remark.

With supper finished and the house put in order, the four walked the mile to the studio through an overcast night. When Alfredo slid aside the warehouse door, squealing in protest for being disturbed at that hour, it opened on a studio large enough to admit a wagon load of marble blocks. At first it appeared the space was empty, except for two chairs and an easel on a small platform outlined above the floor in the dimness. Then as thinning clouds gradually released full moonlight to flood a corner of the studio, the glistening sculpture dominated the vision of the sighted - a muse contemplating the folly of humans.

"My God! My God!" Moses repeated as he stood captive to the Elysian masterpiece. "My God, I've glimpsed wisdom."

Ludwig, less verbal but equally astonished by the statue's peaceful power, silently transposed the work into music.

As the two men turned to congratulate Alfredo, he held his fingers to his lips and nodded toward the woman who'd stood alone so as not to disturb the sighted.

Confidently finding her way to the muse without the guide stick, she slowly palmed the statue's head, moving to the back of the skull, around and over the ears to the forehead, before returning upwards to the hairline, retracing the brow and eye sockets, splaying her fingers across the statue's cheekbones to the eyes, sliding down the nose, measuring the bridge and the nostrils' flair, tracing the lips, cupping the chin, locating the jawbone, inspecting the throat, dropping to the shoulders, breasts and hips to clutch the thighs and ankles before kissing the feet of the muse.

"Now I know how I look," she sobbed.

The woman, now more adept, ventured farther from the tenement to shop for the household, visit the post office and relieve the trio of other simple errands for which they had no time in their working days. Her improved cooking assured the men the stove held little danger for her, and she prepared the meals with stern rebukes for any who misplaced utensils or provisions. But despite the kudos received from the three well-cared-for bachelors, she was increasingly impatient to be independent, having become the target of some neighborhood gossips. When whispered inferences grew to malicious rumors that she was a common slut and the threat of violence might follow, she knew her departure was no longer an option but a necessity.

She began consciously preparing for self-sufficiency by conceding that modeling for the muse had been a once-in-a-lifetime experience, priceless but final, and progress might be found where least expected. Matching her limited skills with repetitious garment trade jobs could be a step forward, dissatisfying but necessary for setting a true compass, but she would not surrender her lively intellect forever.

One evening, the four lingered at the supper table enjoying each other's anecdotal accounts of the day. When the frothy small-talk lost its effervescence and the conversation turned serious, the woman reported she'd not yet found a job where her handicap would not disqualify her.

After some silence, Ludwig put a newspaper on the table before her and in a matter-of-fact tone asked, "Have you looked at the want ads today?"

"You know I can't read," she snapped back, for a moment forgetting he was provoking not demeaning her.

"But you could. A Frenchman named Louis Braille spent twenty years of his very short life educating the blind to read themselves out of their darkness. He embossed book pages with designs for every letter in the alphabet so the blind can read by feeling the text."

"How do you know this? I never heard of it," the woman replied in a tone suggesting it probably was bogus or she would have.

"I went to the library to learn how the blind lived with sightlessness and discovered an article on Louis Braille's invention of reading by feeling the text. He led an extraordinary life in only a few years - made me feel like a slacker."

The woman remained skeptical but listened to Ludwig's story.

"Sightless at age three, he was enrolled at ten in the Institute for the Blind in Paris and was educated in science and music. He became a distinguished organist and excelled with violoncello while conceiving a release from the isolation of blindness."

"Why are you telling me this? Why are you upsetting my acceptance of being blind and dealing with it in my own way?"

"Because you have the courage to live sightlessly in a world of the sighted. I have no doubt you can survive, but to reach your full capacity you must not just accept your condition when there are ways to rise above it," Ludwig challenged, the words coming more harshly than he intended.

For days a copy of Braille text, purchased by Ludwig, lay untouched on the table at the woman's place. Though nagged by her conscience, the woman deferred any decision on studying Braille, rationalizing she was too busy looking for work. Then annoyed that making no decision was a decision, she chided herself for allowing the refuge of the trio to make her timid.

Ultimately the discomfort of her ambivalence and the trio's detachment from the issue forced her hand, and crying out, she shoved the article in front of Ludwig.

"All right, I'll do it. You win."

"No, I think you win," he replied gently.

The next morning, Ludwig accompanied the woman to the school where Braille was taught.

Six months into her training in Braille, the woman showed such unusual aptitude she was offered a job assisting the school's director, a man who'd been a pupil at the Institute for the Blind in Paris.

Born to a widowed mother, the school director, when a child of three, had watched her become blinded by chemicals in an accident, committing her to darkness. With the introduction of the revolutionary Braille System, the indomitable mother and son enrolled in the reading by touch system, and for a year the child and parent triumphed over the mother's handicap. In the second year's first month of their studying Braille, the mother was killed while resisting a robbery and the son committed himself to a lifetime of spreading the empowering aid to the sightless. That boy, now a director of infinite patience, offered Braille instruction in New York and nearly starved to death waiting for customers.

The director's early detection of the woman's ability to link her dexterity and cognitive powers led him to monitor her progress to early completion of the course, and with enrollments at last increasing, the director invited the woman to be his assistant. She quickly accepted and returned home with the exciting news. The trio made a great display of praise, cheering, clapping and promising to attend her demonstration of the technique to the public a week off.

The day arrived, spectators sharing pupils' nervousness over their interpretations' accuracy causing them to shift in their seats while awaiting the first demonstration. The audience also fretted about how appreciation should be shown to each participant, novice and skilled, but reluctant to appear ignorant, they decided to clap if someone clapped first.

The director had anticipated this dilemma and in his introductory remarks suggested all applause be held till the end when the most advanced pupil had been heard, thereby relieving the audience and encouraging the beginner who would share the applause for the accomplished. Having explained that each touch-reading of the unfamiliar text would be spoken aloud by the pupil while a sighted monitor checked its accuracy, the demonstration began.

Despite some pupils' stumbles, the demonstration was a success and skeptics who'd come to deride the Braille System became converts or left disappointed their pessimism had not be validated. The audience, from the first pupil, ignored the director's suggestion and followed their animal instinct to applaud each reading in an unmistakable show of approval.

Ludwig, usually restrained, moved quickly to the woman and in an outpouring of congratulations embraced her to the surprise of both before drawing back to stammer, "You were extraordinary, the control and gracefulness of your hand movements were a perfect extension of the way you carry your body." He continued the flattery of her dexterity, but said little of her reading. "We've never pried into your past, but your skill shows professional training."

"My past is past, but I will tell you before my injury I studied ballet and piano," she replied and returned to the present.

Chapter 8

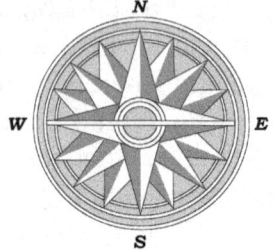

A t Moses' twenty-first birthday celebration, he listened to the other three chronicle the years since they'd landed in New York. Moses' continued expansion of his push-cart business, Alfredo's uninterrupted ascension as the memorializer of choice for the rich and famous, Ludwig's indispensible skill as piano perfecter, and the woman's transfiguration from passive sightlessness to teach the blind to read with Braille, had bound them to serve each other and the larger community.

It was inevitable that in rediscovering herself the subject of the woman's buried past would surface and she would reveal her name was Maud. But Moses, Ludwig and Alfredo found this inadequately described her presence and renamed her Muse. Prospering in health and spirit, she now regarded blindness as a nuisance, not a disablement, skillfully navigating her way to and fro.

She was aware that Ludwig's attention over the months had grown from regarding her as his ward to the object of his affection, and while nothing explicit prompted her to speak candidly to this shy man, it was clear the matter must soon be resolved. Truth be told, Muse had become attracted to Alfredo while she posed for the statue. If Alfredo sensed this, his latent code of honor awakened to restrain him in deference to Muse and Ludwig.

Meanwhile Moses, made increasingly restless by the monotony of his maturing business, suspected his dulling senses were obscuring his life's purpose. Attributing some of this to the unresolved issue of his successor, he wrote his family a forceful letter advising them he was going to expand the business into Chicago. The idea came to him as he wrote that he needed a manager in the New York warehouse while he was absent developing new markets. He had known he was on a journey and New York was only a temporary stop - that his direction was west to a place not yet revealed. With a clairvoyance so easily summoned, Moses didn't find it unusual to anticipate the family's reply would complicate, not simplify, his departure.

Papa's sturdy constitution at eighty-six, having survived the adversity of persecution, famine and pestilence, succumbed to the blandishments of an earthy matron but at the pivotal moment yielded to a heart attack. Jacob, the eldest child, having sworn and observed fealty to Papa, smelled the sweet, fresh air of freedom for a brief time until the old man's heart stabilized, snatching him from the jaws of death more optimistic than ever that he'd live another ten years. The letter concluded with the family's commitment to remain with Papa.

A letter following the first reported the earthy matron, learning there was no legacy for her in Papa's will, sued claiming as a common-law wife she was entitled to participate with the children in the division of the old man's worldly goods. Ever protective of his children's welfare and faithful to his deceased wife, the octogenarian gave up the ghost. The widow, never unrewarded in any previous liaisons and feeling little remorse except for her loss of a bequest, scanned the horizon for a more bountiful day.

The letter concluded by reporting the prescribed mourning ritual for Papa had been observed and arrangements were being made for Jacob's and Hannah's passage on the next available ship. The other children would follow in some mutually agreed order.

With the autumnal equinox, the first of the avian migrants began swarming for their intuitive departure south. The phenomena of their compass-accurate flight never failed to humble Moses, and though not an ornithologist or casual birder, the antics of a red-tailed hawk, unusual in a city habitat, were not to be ignored. At the most unexpected times the bird appeared and followed him a slight distance behind as a discreet parent watches a child cross the street for the first time. Then seemingly disapproving of Moses' choice of direction, the hawk climbed in circles overhead before diving west towards New Jersey, a most curious choice in view of the malodorous pig farms along the Hudson River's bank. It took several such exhibitions before Moses decoded the aerial acrobatics ending with a course to New Jersey by the self-appointed mentor indicated the direction to be followed.

Not yet, but soon, Moses thought after yet another such sighting.

On an October morning silvered by an early frost, Jacob and Hannah arrived wide-eyed as their youngest brother had been. Four years had not changed them as much as Moses, whose struggle for survival had required a kind but authoritative manner. Jacob, the eldest, turned over the traditional role of head of family as graciously as Moses assumed it. Space in the converted warehouse required some new allocation, worked out by Jacob doubling up with Moses in his bedroom and Hannah occupying Alfredo's, now freed with his recent departure to live in his studio.

With the country's recent centennial celebration arousing patriotic fervor, historical monuments were increasingly in demand of Alfredo's hammer and chisel. From there it was only a hop, skip and jump to vandal-proof marble immortalizations of powerful extroverts and, of course, once their place for eternity had been secured, temporal devotions might be paid to them in their conservatories and solariums. With his Italian good looks and liquid accent, cultivated to override Ludwig's English elocution, Alfredo became the darling of the notables' drawing rooms. Casting provocative glances at robber barons' daughters, who playing cat and mouse with him most often ended up the mouse before being shipped off to boarding school, Alfredo had reached the pinnacle of success.

To enhance his mystique and discourage uninvited visitors -- mainly inquisitive young women's guardians a few of whom went the way of all flesh -- Alfredo left the warehouse he'd shared with Moses, Ludwig and Muse to move into a building in the Bronx, combining living quarters and studio. He believed the new location separated from Manhattan by the Harlem River would be a deterrent to all but the invited or the persistent. Moses accepted his explanation that it was an ideal site for water transportation delivery of large slabs of sculpting stones. His new address, a success in making him less easily available, also put his attendance at socials at a premium for hostesses. Having cunningly rationed his acceptance of invitations to optimize his desirability, he was sought even more.

It was not unexpected that in time he would fall out of vogue with the fickle, young rich women searching for another thrill. But Alfredo, ever resourceful, made the adjustment by accommodating two mistresses, one in Manhattan and one in the Bronx, separated by the river, which he affectionately renamed Aphrodite's Moat.

But he never forgot Muse.

On his last day in Manhattan, Moses arose early while the flickering gas streetlights cast shadowy deceptions along the unbroken repetition of tenements filling the block. His view through the window had no sentimental relevance, as he'd seen it many times before at this hour. Was he not fully awake, or had he subconsciously excised it from the nostalgic lobe of his brain to ease the departure?

During his years in America, he'd often surprised himself with his business successes, but using the conventional measurements of wealth and power, they were nothing compared to those of the global changing Astors, Belmonts, Seligmans and Vanderbuilts. He hadn't thought of it before, but perhaps the decision to leave was his mind's sly trick of saving face because he hadn't attained the eminence of these immigrant merchants. He almost spilled his coffee with this distraction. Presumably the trip to Chicago was to explore that city's opportunities for expanding his business, yet even before going he knew he could profitably duplicate his sales formula as he had in

Boston and Philadelphia. Under the supervision he'd passed to Jacob and the first scoundrel he'd hired at the immigrant's reception site, the business prospered and offered employment for his siblings still in Poland as it had for those already come to the new world.

He need delay no longer.

Moses watched the lamp lighter pass along the street, reversing the course taken last night to illuminate the neighborhood, now snuffing out the gas lamps as day approached -- neither succeeding nor failing on his endless round, denied the satisfaction of making improvement or reaching a goal.

How bleak a life, Moses thought, trying to shake off the uncertainty that his undefined pull would turn out to be as vacuous.

He heard a board in the floor above creak under a person's weight. It was too early for any member of the household to be rising, but it warned him not to dawdle because lingering departures were enervating. Farewells should be said but once.

At supper the previous evening Ludwig, Muse and Alfredo had joined Moses, his family and employees to express their affection for this remarkable friend. To hide their sadness, they accused Moses of outrageous motives for leaving, but it did nothing to lighten their mood. As it grew later, none had made the move to depart as though their continued presence would prevent his going away.

Waiting until the conversations became fragmented, a time when many ill at ease know a gathering is ending but are too awkward to leave, Moses rose and stood before each to lay his left hand on their heads and his right index finger across their lips before leaving the room.

Now the barely audible bell in a distant steeple struck out the hour, reminding Moses to hurry as he slipped out the door to push his cart of peddler's goods over two miles of jolting cobblestones to the dock where the New York to Albany packet boat lay.

I wonder where I'm really going, he thought to himself and in answer heard the distinctive whistle of his red-tailed hawk as it flew in ever shorter loops to his boat on the Hudson River. In the sunless, humid morning, pushing the fully loaded cart was hard going, forcing him to shed sweat-soaked layers of clothing till he finally reached the boat, deflated by a less than grand exit from New York.

As Moses arrived the surprisingly young captain, a beneficiary of the emerging steamboat generation, was disciplining with fluent invectives two seamen who'd reported for work drunk. If the unruly sailors had been sober and minimally educated, the captain's abusive thrashing might have put his health at risk. As it was, they hung their heads in either child-like remorse or painful intoxication withdrawal.

Undeterred by Moses' presence, the captain drew a bucket of river water and doused them from head to toe, shouting, "If you ever step out of line again I'll deep-six you till the barnacles strip off your hide."

It remained a mystery how he might do that with only two other crew members to assist, but the threat browbeat the two into a hasty retreat, leaving the captain to turn to Moses with a most pleasant welcome.

"Captain Halliday at your service, sir. I take it you're the gent what's booked passage to Albany."

"To Watervliet, actually. I'm going west on the Erie Canal, and I understand that it joins the Hudson at Watervliet."

"We don't go to Watervliet, only as far as Albany. You'll need to hire a horse and wagon to carry your cart the rest of the way," the captain said.

"How far is it from your landing place to the start of the canal?" Moses asked.

"A good eight miles."

"I'll push my cart and save the expense," Moses replied, feeling his waistband money pocket against his belly.

"As you say, sir." The captain arched a large spittle of tobacco juice over the rail. "If you wait a few minutes I'll get Osgood to help you get your gear aboard. Osgood! Get your black ass up here and help this gent with his cart," he bellowed down a hatch.

A giant of a man, black as the coal he shoveled to fire the packet's boiler, emerged from below deck and gently lifted the push cart, as though crystal glass, a foot or more over the ship's gunnel to rest on the deck before sliding away toward the hatch.

"Thank you, Osgood," Moses said, astonished by the strength and gentle touch of the man. "Let's see where we should stow the cart and perhaps we can pick out something for your help."

"No, sir, you're not obliged to pay me for loading the cart," Osgood replied in a cultured English accent that surprised Moses.

"I know, but if you unload the cart in Albany, I have nothing to worry about. Let's see what we have here," Moses said, rolling the cover off the cart's top.

For twenty minutes they examined the tightly-packed merchandise, quickly eliminating most items, but as choices for Osgood's gift dwindled, Moses noticed the black man's eyes continue to wander towards a copy of the Holy Bible.

"Have you read the Bible?" Moses asked.

"No, sir. I just learned to read a little English a few years ago."

"But you speak English so well anyone would expect you could read."

"My mother was a slave who worked as a housemaid for an English gentleman. He made me his houseboy and was particular I spoke good English -- dressed me in livery and made me bathe once a week, winter and summer. One year he took us to England and Europe where he had business. Always told me, 'remember you're not a nigger, you're a black-a-moor.' Then he suddenly died and the estate sold us to another plantation just about the time my mother began to teach me to read. My new master wouldn't allow slaves to read or write because he thought it would make it easier for us to escape to the north.

"When the Union Army captured our town, Mother and I ran away from the plantation and started walking north with only the things we could carry -- the clothes we wore, a few Swahili trinkets and a French Bible from Zanzibar, the home of my ancestors. We walked for months to reach Pennsylvania, Mother doing odd jobs and I begging until the second winter when Mother died. I buried the trinkets and the French Bible with my mother because I thought they would speed her return to the Swahilis, a people she always talked about but never knew. I've been on my own ever since, working at any job I could find, hoping to save enough to buy a little piece of land to farm."

"But I still don't understand how you are so beautifully spoken and can't read."

"When I was a young boy, I was teased or beaten up when people heard me speak so I learned to keep my mouth shut and memorize things. When you're always moving from place to place it's hard to learn reading and writing, but you can listen and learn wherever you go."

"Can you speak any languages besides English?"

"Lingua franca, an eastern Mediterranean jargon my grandparents taught Mother, and a little French, Spanish and Italian, but I can't read any except a little English."

"How could you learn to speak all these languages without reading?"

"I keep my mind ready like a baby's. As the baby grows older the language becomes easy because that's all he ever heard. When I learn to read more English, I will understand the beautiful stories of the Bible."

"I think you understand many of them now," Moses replied, handing the Bible to Osgood. "Now let's stow the cart before I keep you away from your work any longer."

"Oh, sir, I can't take your Bible from you."

"You didn't. I gave it to you, and tonight we'll find a few minutes to read it together."

For several hours the drunken seamen endured the punishment of hard labor sobriety, moving cargo aboard the frigate while Osgood and another deckhand stowed the crates and boxes in place for the trip. Varying in size, weight and fragility, the cargo included window glass, fabrics, boilers, anvils, saws, axes, plows and pails and was placed for protection, proper distribution of the ship's load and efficient unpacking at destination.

At noon, the captain ordered the crew to cast off and get underway but not before a sharp looking man in tight pants, wing-

collared shirt and derby, carrying his coat and a Gladstone bag, leapt
five feet over water from dock to deck as the packet pulled away.

"Where are we going?" he inquired of the captain.

"Albany."

"Any stops along the way?"

"No."

"Good. How much for a gent with a slim appetite that stays out of
everyone's way?"

"The law after you?"

"No, a woman."

"That will be three and a half dollars for the boat ride and a dollar
for the meals, payable now," the captain said. "You can sleep in the
life boat aft, and no funny business or you'll have to swim to
wherever you're lucky to land."

When the newcomer realized there was no possibility of
negotiating with the captain, he settled his account then sidled over to
Moses to ingratiate himself with the young man.

Sticking his hand out to Moses, he said, "Jasper Goodbody is my
name, saving souls is my game. I'm an itinerant preacher known up
and down the Atlantic seaboard for bringing the good works of the
Lord into the lives of many. And may I inquire what your moniker
is?"

"Moses."

Temporarily stymied by Moses' answer Jasper, reasoning the
young man was too naïve to try and trick him, and pro,bably nobody's
fool obviously a man of the world, he resorted to flattery as the best
approach.

"You are blessed to be carrying the fine name of one who led his
people out of the wilderness much as I strive to do. And where are
you going, Moses?"

"I'm not sure."

"How will you ever know if you got there?"

"Oh, I'll know."

When the crew and the super cargo, as the captain liked to refer
to passengers in a somewhat derogatory manner, had finished their
midday meal of ham, bread and potatoes, all cooked in an oven

Osgood had ingeniously attached to the boat's boiler, Moses and the black giant sat aft on a coil of rope for a reading lesson. It wasn't long before Jasper, compulsively curious and intrusive, interrupted them.

"Ah! The Good Book, read it many times over from cover to cover," he said.

"We're reading it together," Moses replied, emphasizing 'together.'

"I'm learning how to read," Osgood volunteered proudly.

"Easy as falling off a log," Jasper replied. "When you find a new word, sound it out with your teacher several times, then draw a picture of the thing your teacher described with its name and write it over and over."

"What if you can't write?" Osgood asked.

"Draw a picture of the word and ask someone who reads to write the letters underneath it."

"Let me see how you'd teach Osgood," Moses said and withdrew to watch.

"Now, when you see a word beginning with a big letter, it's usually a place or someone's name," Jasper explained to Osgood, "like this word here is Moses' name. Now this is the most important name in the Bible because without God there wouldn't be any Bible."

Moses left the oddly-matched twosome and snaked his way through cargo to the foredeck to talk with the captain. All signs of New York remained behind, exchanged for intermittent sprinklings of tidy farms reaching from the hills to the houses and barns at the river's edge. And then, as though reminding the observer not everyone lived either in the country or New York City, a modestly populated town named Poughkeepsie appeared.

"We should be in Albany tomorrow mid-morning," the captain noted. "You'll have to wait a while for your pushcart to be unloaded. One of those drunken bums is quitting as soon as we tie up."

"Maybe I can help my cart off," Moses volunteered. "I'm in no hurry."

"I'd be obliged 'cause I have to find a deckhand replacement or I'll be delayed taking on cargo for the return trip, and that means lost revenue."

"Maybe I can help with that as well. I have an idea Jasper would like to disappear from the public eye for a few weeks, and I might just be able to persuade him to stay on until you find somebody permanent. He would be teaching Osgood to read when he's not on duty, so he's really not a bad sort."

"He'd have to be satisfied with beginner's pay."

"That's for you two to work out, but I believe he'd be reasonable. If you're interested, let me talk to him first."

"No harm in trying," the captain said, making a slight course correction while throwing Moses a grateful salute.

When Moses returned, teacher and student, captive to the opening verses of Genesis, paid him no heed.

"And God said 'let there be light' and there was light," Osgood said, repeating Jasper in a voice that rumbled like thunder.

"God saw that the light was good," Jasper continued.

"What kind of light?" the black giant asked. "There's daylight and moonlight and firelight and candlelight."

"Remember this is the beginning and God created the heavens and formed the earth from nothing," Jasper said. "Don't it seem sensible there should be more light during the day so you can work? And it don't need to say exactly what kind of light 'cause God expects people to have some brains and figure out what different lights are used for. Firelight's not good for reading and you can't dry hay with a candle. Besides, since God made all the lights or the things for us to make light, they all come from our Father."

"Oh," Osgood exclaimed over his revelation. "Maybe that's why when folks have figured out something, they say, 'I'm beginning to see the light.'"

At this break in what Moses silently observed as a novel and somewhat unorthodox but affective interpretation of scripture, Jasper and Osgood became aware of his presence.

"If anyone asked me I'd say you make a great teacher/student combination. Now I have a proposition for you both to think about. It's simple, and it will only work if you both want it to. The captain is going to lose a crew member as soon as he gets to Albany. Jasper, I suggested you might want the job at least temporarily until your personal problems are solved."

"What would I do? I don't know anything about boats."

"Osgood could teach you, same as you're teaching him. You'd have to work out your wages with the captain, but the meals wouldn't cost you anything. In your time off you could keep on teaching Osgood and I'd pay you three dollars a week for three weeks in advance. Then if Osgood can read the first twenty chapters of Exodus in a month to the manager of my company in New York he'll double the money. It will all be explained in one letter. Each of you will carry one-half the letter in a sealed envelope. If the seal is broken on either envelope, the deal is off. All this means you'll be traveling back and forth on this boat for a month. Think about it and let me know before we get to Albany.

"You're nobody's fool, Moses," Jasper said. "The twentieth chapter of Exodus includes the admonition 'thou shalt not steal' in the Ten Commandments."

"I try not to be," Moses said.

"I'll do it," Osgood volunteered.

"And so will I," Jasper added.

Chapter 9

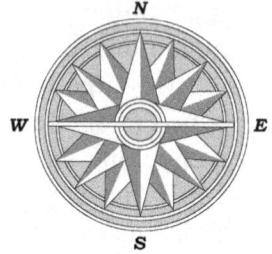

Midnight came with more than half the distance to Albany behind them when a sudden night-time squall swept down the Hudson River blotting out visibility to make continuous navigation the obstinacy of fools. The captain swung the ship into a protected, deep water cove, dropped anchor, tied fast to some trees and resigned himself to waiting out the storm.

With the cargo secured and other duty suspended, Osgood sought out Moses to return to their earlier conversation about medicines formulated and passed on from generation to generation by many primitive people. In childhood Osgood never tired of sponging up lore from an ancient black granny, too old to work the fields. He'd sit wide-eyed, memorizing the home cures she dispensed from her bottles, boxes and jars of animal, mineral and vegetable compounds.

Chew mint leaves for a toothache.
Drizzle wild honey down your throat for coughs.
Apply a paste of wet mud for insect bites, salt water for jelly-
  fish stings.
Mash aloe leaves in warm water for a lotion to cover skin
  eruptions, and poultices of soft, moist bread, meal, herbs
  and occasionally horse manure for a long list of muscle and
  joint distress.

Of the dozens of curatives Osgood described, Moses thought far and away the best was a skin graft. It began by skimming off in one piece the white membrane inside the shell of a hard-boiled egg to cover all the damaged flesh then covering the graft with moist, wild-grape leaves and immobilizing the area to speed regeneration of the skin. When Moses asked why these treatments weren't written down, Osgood replied that some people would ridicule anyone employing these remedies and others would exploit them for their own financial gain.

"Ah!" Moses exclaimed, "by restricting the knowledge help is being denied to those who need it."

"No. Being careful in choosing people who will use the healing wisely."

Moses, after keeping his promise to help unload the boat in Albany, said, "God be with you all" and set out for the eastern terminus of the Erie Canal. He whistled an old world folk-tune not because he was happy to have weathered the storm, nor because this leg of his journey was beginning on a sunny day, but because he was bored pushing an overloaded cart and needed diversion.

Having no previous knowledge of Albany's appearance, Moses arrived to be intrigued by the clear architectural demarcation of the city's ethnic evolution. From the Dutch founders' dwellings on the Hudson riverbank a hill swept upwards on which successive migrations marked their arrivals with building exemplifying their cultures. However, the founding fathers were not to be easily dislodged from the public memory by each generation's modernization, for streets bearing their Dutch names were as plentiful as the profusion of widespread plantings of perennial tulips.

The previous night's layover had added half a day's time to reaching Albany, and in three hours ashore, he'd covered less than half the distance to the canal's terminus at Watervliet. In fading daylight he left the main north/south river road to enter an industrial section with darkened factories interspersed among dimly lit homes and brilliantly illuminated taverns depicting the priorities of many laborers' affections. In need of food and rest he stopped at the first roadhouse; its signboard swinging in the wind over the door, bearing the curious picture of a woman's head on a bird's body below the name, 'The Happy Harpy.' Fancying a caprice to enliven his imagination, Moses invented an intellectual castaway, conversant in Greek Mythology, tossed up on the shore of the Hudson River to live out her life uttering oracles.

Catering to the drinking customers, the establishment's most profitable trade, the ground floor except for a small storage space and a hall for the staircase leading to second floor bedrooms, consisted of a bizarre bar room. Tables scattered over the sawdust coated floor were occupied by patrons quaffing from large steins and playing checkers, becoming more boisterous with each move on the board. Across the entire width of the room a bar stretched from wall to wall leaving only enough space behind for beer barrels, bottles and bartenders to serve the fifteen or twenty men along the expanse of polished wood. These patrons stood single; vapid or in contemplation of things private. Others in twos or threesomes engaged in exaggerations believed by none.

Midway atop the bar on a throne-shaped perch a woman of impressive musculature presided over her submissive subjects. Long, curly, henna-red hair shot out like a myriad of lightning bolts from around her boney horse face. Slotted eyes scanned unceasingly for any premonitions of trouble. If the unlikely occurred, it was snuffed out with a twenty foot long bull whip lying beside her. She was capable of flicking the ace of spades from a card player's hand. Knowing every patron by name and reputation, the entrance of a stranger into her domain immediately put her on guard.

"And what might your name be?" the overbearing proprietress demanded of Moses, motioning him to come closer.

"Moses."

"Moses what? Moses in the bulrushes? Holy Moses? Ya must have another name besides Moses," she hissed, leaning forward to intimidate Moses with her cold eyes. "Ca-mon mister, spit out another name."

"I see no reason to until I'm satisfied I want to do business with you," Moses said, standing his ground and silencing the pub's occupants with his boldness.

"Wha-cha come here for?" the proprietress sneered.

"Certainly not hospitality," Moses replied. "Are you always this rude or just when you have splitting headaches?"

"There's nothin' wrong with me. I don't have headaches, I give headaches."

"Then why do you squint even in this low light? And why do you pucker your nose and forehead?"

"You some kinda patent medicine man? One came through here a time back and sold me some of his quack tonic, just made matters worse. I'll skin off his hide with this here bull whip if I ever catch him, not that's any of your business Mister Highfalutin."

Then noting that Moses' clothing was different from her customers' and realizing she could not bully him, her tone became more conciliatory.

"If I was to introduce you to the mayor, Mr. Moses, where would I tell him you was from?"

"New York City."

"And are you gainfully employed, Mr. Moses?"

"I sell notions and small dry goods from my push cart outside."

"Then how come you know so much about medicines and cures?" she asked again, putting her hand to her forehead.

"Because I do and if I can't make you feel better by morning, I'll give you a scarf from my cart."

"And if you do, what do I owe you?" she said, dropping her voice to a tone only audible to Moses, which signaled to the drinkers there would be no confrontation for their amusement.

"Supper and a free room for the night?"

"With or without one of the girls?"

"Without."

"If you don't beat all."

"Watervliet! There ain't no easy access to the Erie Canal in Watervliet, you gotta push that cart all the way to Waterford," the teamster said the next day as he came alongside Moses. That's another ten miles and the roads are terrible. Why don't you get on the barge to Waterford at the dock up ahead? It won't cost but a few cents."

"That's very helpful," Moses said. "It will save me another day."

The teamster on the large wooden wagon filled with farm equipment pulled his Clydesdales to the side of the road and jumped down to drop the tailgate.

"Here, let's jockey your cart around and lash the push bar to the tail couplings so we can tow it up to the dock. I'm going in that direction anyway."

"That's very neighborly," Moses replied.

In the forty-minute trip to the barge depot Moses and the teamster exchanged accounts of their lives as comfortably as old friends. Though each regretted the trip was not longer and knew they'd never meet again, both sensed the brief encounter was complete and valuable.

Looking up from the tailboard where he unhitched his push cart, Moses asked, "Friend, what do I owe you for your tow?"

"Nothing, I'm glad you passed my way."

"Are you married?"

"No."

"Well then, here's a packet of needles and a few spools of thread. Find some nice young woman to sew your suspender buttons tighter on your pants before they fall off. If that leads to setting up housekeeping and you need more, my company's address is on the package."

"Thanks and have a good trip to wherever you're going. Goodbye, goodbye whatever your name is."

"Moses," the pilgrim called over his shoulder while pushing his cart up the dock to wait for the barge to take on passengers.

"Jeremy Caleb Gooch at your service. Welcome aboard the Seneca Chief, the very barge Governor DeWitt Clinton boarded on October 26, 1825 at the opening of the Erie Canal to travel from Buffalo to New York City. Of course we make the trip faster now with tug boats than in the Governor's time. Back then it could take upward of six days if you barged day and night with only stops for a few river-port drops and the locks which on average took twenty minutes to enter and leave. A lot of things have changed since horse-drawn days when the barge man was in charge, now with tugs instead of horses doing the hauling the boat-jockeys run the show. Most folk never think of how progress affects other people. Other passengers will come on at Waterford, but being first aboard you get to choose the best accommodation. Some people like to ride on the tug but they're noisy and not as clean as back here where you can just glide on the river peaceful-like. It seems each year tugs get more powerful to go faster and haul a couple of much bigger barges at once, but it suits me and the Chief here to be a single haul."

Jeremy Caleb Gooch had proven to be among those rare few who could breathe while delivering a non-stop monologue, often a tolerance lesson for the impatient, Moses observed. The shrill whistle of a small tug arriving to take the barge in tow drowned out Gooch in mid-sentence as he launched into the remainder of his soliloquy.

"And another thing - - -."

By early afternoon the Seneca Chief left the Hudson River for the eastern portal of the Erie Canal to climb five locks in one and a third miles. Drawing the barge close to the open downstream gate of the lock, the tug coupled its tow and entered the water elevator. The downstream gate closed, the chamber was flooded until water reached the upper level of the canal and the second gate was opened, releasing the vessels. Intrigued by the primitive hydrology of locks to elevate or lower massive loads by flooding or draining water, Moses waited until the tug and barge were moving on a clear stretch of the waterway before approaching the voluble Gooch for more information on the canal.

"This here canal took eight years to build. My grand-daddy worked on it. We've been a canal family for three generations. There's a couple a hundred miles of pick and shovel work through woods that had to be lumbered with axes and two-man saws, rock that needed splitting with sledges and dynamite; in sun, rain, wind and cold. They don't make men like that today who could do this work."

Even Gooch's extravagant narrative could not exaggerate the astounding achievement of linking the Atlantic Ocean with the Great Lakes. The barge-man's words so possessed Moses he wondered if tested, where he'd stand with those intrepid men, now passed and today mostly unknown. Moses returned to the present to hear Gooch reciting the canal's architecture.

"At water line the banks are forty-two feet apart, at the bottom twenty-six feet and no less than four-and-a-half feet deep. Of course, these measurements all change wherever the canal is routed through the Mohawk River. Passenger fare used to be a cent a mile and freight costs have always been the cheapest type of transportation. Old barges like the Chief can haul 200 tons and even the business of the newer, faster canal boats has dropped off because the railroads are faster, but cost more, too. If a shipment isn't in a rush our cheaper haul wins every time."

Gooch paused to light his pipe and maybe catch his breath. "There are dozens of locks between here and Buffalo, don't know how many 'cause I never stopped to count them, but the biggest lift is in Little Falls, forty and one half feet. I heard that once a lake bigger than any of the Great Lakes backed up west from the hills around Little Falls, but the glaciers or the river wore a cut through the rock making an escarpment marvel."

Gooch concentrated on puffing his pipe to let his use of geological knowledge sink in. "In a good year we can work the canal eight to ten months, but once that ice starts to form we're finished. In the early days the canal carried up to forty-thousand pioneers a year, most going out to settle the west. Manifest Destiny; Senator Thomas Hart Benton called it a God given right."

Gooch also wanted to establish his expertise in American history, Moses noted.

"I wonder if he ever gave any thought about stealing the God-given rights of Indians?" Moses asked.

Gooch's look of astonishment at Moses' question was sad testimony that indifference or disregarding one's neighbor is the devil's partner.

By early morning of the second day, the barge now high above the entrance to the canal, cleared another lock to the Mohawk River, a beckoning ribbon of sunrise silver winding through fertile bottom land sloping upward to partially forested hills, occasionally glacially scarred to complete the perfection of nature. Small settlements on either bank soon gave way to crops, meadows and wood lots interrupted by solitary houses and barns in turn yielding to virgin land. Just when pastoral panoramas had seemed to triumph with infinite wilderness, a home or two would spring up and a settlement would be revealed at a bend in the river. After sixty years of living beside the canal, few locals, except for those expecting shipments, paid little heed to the passing craft, but schoolchildren fled their classrooms to the river to cheer and wave bonnets and caps, paying homage to the reminder of the early eighteen hundreds' wonder.

"Mr. Gooch! Mr. Gooch, where are you? I'd like a word with you," an assertive female voice commanded. "Oh there you are. I couldn't find hide nor hair of you."

"Well, I couldn't have strayed very far now, could I, Miss Farthingale," Gooch said as he climbed out from behind a stack of cast-iron stoves.

"Mr. Gooch, when I booked passage on this barge I expressly reserved a private accommodation with no other creatures."

"And that you have ma'am. You're not in the women's dormitory."

"No, Mr. Gooch. That I do not have. What I have are rats running everywhere all night long."

"I beg to differ with you Miss Farthingale, but them are mice."

"Rats, mice, rats, they're all the same to me. I don't want to quibble over Darwinian distinctions. I want them off this barge."

"Oh Miss Farthingale, I'm afraid I can't do that."

"Why not?"

"Because rats only leave a sinking ship," Gooch said, rolling his eyes back in his head impatient with her picayune complaint. Miss Farthingale, frustrated by Gooch's failure to take her seriously, moved forward to confront him with her six feet frame and overpowering bosoms.

"Mr. Gooch," she began, her forefinger stiff and extended towards his chest to punctuate her demands. "Mr. Gooch, is that distilled spirits I smell?" she asked in a tone of disgust reinforced with an expression to match. "Is that hard liquor I smell?"

"I'm afraid it is, ma'am. You see I was just about to have my morning medication when the tug jerked the tow line, making me spill the tonic all over my shirt. That don't come cheap, either."

"Well, Mr. Gooch, as a member in good standing of the Immaculate Sisters in Temperance, I must insist you desist from further indulgence or I'll report you to the terminal manager in Buffalo."

"That won't do no good, ma'am. He drinks worse than me."

In their introductory encounter, lasting less than fifteen minutes, both man and woman recognized they might have begun a potentially endless contest of thrust and parry. To her credit, Miss Farthingale conceded her frontal attack had failed in every way and immediately offered a more conciliatory approach.

In a voice more solicitous than usually attributed to Miss Farthingale, she whimpered, "Let's not spoil this beautiful day with such unpleasantness. I'm taking this trip on your barge because I just love the lore of the canal. I'm sure you must know all its wonderful history, Mr. Gooch."

Within seconds, the palliative effect of her soft voice requesting him to relate the history of the Mohawk valley set things right and Gooch began a marathon exposition, which he loved only second to his daily elixir. The two, looking more like long lost friends than recent acquaintances, sauntered around the barge, she inquiring about objects of presumed interest, he expounding longer than necessary to answer the question. A couple of times making their way through a jumble of cargo, he held her arm to steady her footing as a courtesy, which an hour earlier she would have rejected as a bold familiarity.

At supper in the common galley, they sat together to continue their chit chat, talking long after the other passengers had gone to their bunks. When Miss Farthingale rose to retire, Gooch asked her to remain a minute more while he fetched something from his quarters. He returned pleased with himself and cradling a full-grown tiger cat.

"This here's Tomahawk, the best mouser on the Erie Canal. He'll keep things real peaceful for you tonight. And here's a saucer and a drop or two of moonshine. If he whines that means you need to let him out for a few minutes to do his business. When he's finished, he'll come back if you put a little moonshine in a saucer. Good night, Miss Farthingale."

Leaving the recipient and site of his gallant gesture, Gooch joined Moses at the rail for a last pipe before turning in. The moon, so bright one could easily read by its light, convinced Gooch to signal the tug captain his agreement to tow the barge all night but be prepared for sudden weather changes. It was not uncommon for a storm off Lake Erie or Ontario to come thundering through the Mohawk Valley and drop visibility and temperature in less than an hour.

"Nice night," Gooch observed.

"A great night for celestial navigation," Moses replied. "Can you believe the Vikings sailed thousands of miles setting their course from the position of the sun and stars? Look up there, that's Cassiopeia's chair, the constellation on the opposite side of Polaris in the Big Dipper."

"Where?"

"Right there," Moses said, extending his arm for Gooch to sight along.

"Oh yeah. If you take your time and search long enough, you can usually find things different from how they first look. Same thing with people. Can you believe this morning Miss Farthingale and I was going at it hammer and tongs before we began to listen to each other?"

"I noticed a difference of opinion at first, but later you both seemed to enjoy talking about barging the canal."

"Yes, and she told me all about herself. She's from a New England mill town, one of six children. Her father was a boozer, used to beat her ma until one day her ma packed up and moved the family to Vermont and joined one of them strict revival communities. When she growed up she became one of the Immaculate Sisters of Temperance.

"Her father was from an important English family who disowned him when he married a Spanish woman, so to get even he gave a Spanish first name to each of his children. Andalusia Farthingale. Ain't that some moniker?"

Gooch blew a cloud of smoke, studied his pipe and asked, "What about you, Mr. Moses? What's your story?"

"To begin, my name is Moses Morgenstern. Morgenstern means morning-star in German. If you're up before daybreak look over here at the horizon. You'll see the morning star, which isn't really a star, it's a planet. If it blinks at you it's a star and you're looking in the wrong place. Just look steady at the horizon in this direction till you see a bright steady light, that's the morning star. I don't know why we were named Morganstern," Moses said wistfully.

"Ain't that interesting," Gooch remarked.

"You might have guessed I'm a Jew and as the day after tomorrow is the Jew's Sabbath - the day when we rest - I'll stay in my cubicle from Friday sundown to Saturday sundown, praying and fasting."

"What do you do on the days that ain't the Sabbath?" Gooch asked. "What's that cart for?"

"I'm a peddler. I go house to house selling razors and scissors and sewing materials - things people need which they have to get mail-order or in a big city store. If we have any long layovers at the towns on the canal, I might walk around with my pushcart. When I leave you at Buffalo, I'll keep going till I reach Chicago."

"Did yah ever wonder why so many people keep on the move all the time, Mr. Morgenstern?"

"Oh yes, I think a lot about that. I suppose some think things will be better over the next hill. Others are pushed out by people because they have good land. Some earn a living by moving all time like you, Mr. Gooch. What interests me about your travel is you're always moving but on the same route. Isn't that monotonous?"

"Not yet. I see something new every trip with my own eyes or with other people's eyes. That may sound crazy, but some people have such odd ways of looking at things, it makes you think about them all over again. You'd be surprised how regular people see different angles on things."

"Do you have a family, Mr. Gooch?"

"Had a wife in Buffalo, but she died a year after we married. Never was married long enough to have children, probably best thing, too, 'cause I missed her so bad I probably would have been a bum father. Within a week after I lay my darling to rest I hopped on a barge and never got off. I suppose like we was talking about that was to get away from the pain. You never really get rid of pain like that. It happened so sudden like, I couldn't even say 'goodbye'."

"We all say 'goodbye,' Mr. Gooch, but I don't believe it's necessary because there's no ending to love. To me 'goodbye' is the same as saying, 'I'll catch up with you later.' No more, no less. Most of the time when we're alive we say, 'goodbye' because we're leaving the house for a short time or going away on a trip. It would be foolish if we said 'that's the end of our experience together, the relationship is over and done,' so we say 'goodbye'."

"Are you a teacher or something, Mr. Morganstern?"

"No, I'm a student trying to learn what I should learn. I'm a seeker of truth, but first I must know what truth is."

"You're a deep one," Gooch said.

"I want to know how we all fit together," Moses said, pausing before he added, "Let's hope we get another wonderful day tomorrow, Mr. Gooch. Au revoir. The French knew what we were talking about when they gave us the expression, 'au revoir,' till we meet again."

No matter how craftily he enticed sleep, it escaped Moses that night. Just as he felt the warm drift into drowsiness, a hidden thought would return to startle him into wakefulness. He prayed, meditated, waited patiently for a wave of comfort to carry him into unconsciousness, but none rewarded him with sleep. Concerned his restlessness would disturb other men in the dormitory, he dressed and went out on deck to the shelter of a large crate of equipment from which he could watch the reliable tug plowing a V through the dark water to slap against the banks of the canal.

He looked for any light, indicating someone beside him kept watch of the night, but the absence of other mortals recalled the Greek's mythological River Styx across which the dead were ferried. The faint aroma of tobacco smoke unlike Gooch's drifted back to where Moses stood and, eager for companionship, he made his way forward through the crates. In the midst of boxes of cargo, he found Gooch sprawled on the deck snoring so loudly Moses was surprised he didn't wake himself. *Drunk,* Moses thought, until he bent over to smell his breath and detected no sign of alcohol. Satisfied that Gooch was not ill, he worked his way forward through the cargo to find a man sitting against a large coil of towrope smoking a long-stemmed pipe. As he approached the figure, a lone cloud blocked out the moonlight, leaving only the glow of the smoking pipe.

This can't be, Moses thought. *How can I still be on the boat from Europe? That's where I saw Lighting Lance the last time smoking his pipe, keeping watch on the skies like this sentry, but this boat I'm on is too small to cross the ocean. When the moon was shining, I could see river banks and I knew it was not the ocean, but now no shores are in sight. Am I really on the Atlantic? Was my working and living in New York just a dream? How could I know the streets and the people so well? How could I make a business if that was a dream? If that was not a dream, this must be. Where am I? What am I doing here?*

Moses searched the night for things familiar but was defeated by the void. He pinched his cheek, bit his lip, but his pain didn't clear his brain. He tested his memory, naming people he'd met starting with the most recent and working backwards -- Jeremy Cabel Gooch, Andalusia Farthingale. No it was the other way around, he'd met her after Gooch. The nameless teamster who'd towed his push cart. Had he forgotten the man's name? The Happy Harpy, Jasper, Osgood.

Could I be dreaming about these encounters, about Lightning Lance smoking his pipe? I'll find out if this is a dream if he will talk to me.

As the passing cloud released the moon to flood the barge in white, Moses picked his way through scattered objects to the coil of towrope, where only the fragrance of a pipe offering remained. Moses, caught in his chaos, leaned against the centerless four feet high coil of rope hallucinating it was a kiva in which Lightning Lance had disappeared.

Exhausted and distraught, he covered himself with a nearby tarpaulin against the chill and tried to methodically recall his experiences since coming on deck. Each time he reconstructed an incident it was different, eluding all rational meaning, finally toppling him into a surrealistic cascade.

"He moaned and tossed all night like he was having a fit," said the first to speak, trying to impress his fellow passengers with his diagnosis.

"And he talked strange-like," added another, wishing to get his share of credit. "Look how he's sweating. The blankets are soaked."

"Let's give the man some air," Gooch ordered, shooing away all the curious but the indomitable Miss Farthingale. "He's got the canal fever if you ask me. I only seed that once before in all my days as a barge captain. We had a 'saw bones' aboard returning to his home in Amsterdam so he never knew how this poor fella done, but he told us to keep him covered up. I figured he died in his own juice, but that was a long time ago. Some time after that, another barge man told me an old, old lady healer living in the woods around Canajuharie Creek says he should have been soaked in cool water to get the fever down."

"I think we ought to try that," Miss Farthingale urged.

"We don't know for sure it's canal fever," the first, self-appointed expert cautioned. "What if we do the wrong thing?"

"What we do know is if he doesn't stop sweating, he'll die for sure," Miss Farthingale said decisively.

"How are we going to soak him? There's no tub aboard," the second observer asked.

"We'll have to soak him in the canal," Miss Farthingale improvised. "If it made him sick, it can make him well."

"Just wrap a rope under his arms and tie it to his belt, then drag him behind the barge," Gooch said. "We'll drag him with his clothes on to wash out the stink. Someone get his blankets up here on deck to dry out and some of his clean clothes to put him in when we fish him out of the canal"

Slowly Gooch and Miss Farthingale lowered Moses off the stern of the barge into the water. With several dousings the patient's temperature began to lower and he shivered, so they drew him from the water, changed his clothes and put him in his bunk.

"Mr. Gooch," Miss Farthingale said, "I've never heard of a Baptist minister baptizing from a boat, but you make a pretty good substitute preacher."

"I wish I knew how to give this fella a real powerful prayer. I think that's enough soaking now. We need to get water into him. His guts must be dry as a bone."

"I'll spoon water into him and keep his head cool with wet towels. I've done this with the old folks in the community back home."

"We'll be in Canajoharie in a few hours, maybe we can find some proper care for him there," Gooch said. "I wonder if that old lady healer is still around? She'd know what to do for him."

"I'll find out because I'm getting off there to attend a meeting honoring Susan B. Anthony."

"Who's she?" Gooch asked, not knowing what else to say as he considered the loss of Miss Farthingale.

"She's the leader of the Women's Rights Movement."

"What's she doing in Canajoharie?"

"Gooch, I just told you a town where she taught school is honoring her."

"Well, who's going to carry Mr. Morganstern around town looking for a druggist or a doctor?" Gooch asked.

"Maybe I can be of service," a burley, red-faced man who'd just joined the conversation offered. "I'm the town smitty and I'll be unloading my new tools there. My name's Doxdater, Hiram Doxdater."

"That would be mighty neighborly of you, Mr. Doxdater, to help me find a doctor," Miss Farthingale said.

"I'll do you one better than that. Nitti, the old lady healer I heered you talkin' about is still alive, and I can take you and Mr. Morganstern to her. I suspicion Mr. Morganstern either don't have canal disease or whatever it is, and he ain't contagious 'cause none of the rest of us is ailin'.'"

The Seneca Chief reached Canajoharie right on time, and the barge hands quickly unloaded Doxdater's forge equipment before carrying Moses and his cart ashore. At the signal the tug was ready to pull the barge back into the current, Gooch shook hands with Doxdater, doffed his cap and impulsively pulled Miss Farthingale into an embrace. He seemed as startled as she, which mixed up his parting speech, but she appeared to understand he'd commended her for being a fine lady whom he hoped to meet again.

With two warning toots from the tug and a responding yell of 'all aboard' from Gooch, the Seneca Chief eased away from the dock to continue westward. For the time being, Doxdater decided to leave his forge equipment on the dock where it lay because it was too heavy to easily steal and no one wanted Canajoharie to be without a smith. Before the barge was out of sight, Doxdater and Miss Farthingale, working as one, had rearranged the contents in the pushcart to cradle an unconscious Moses over the bumpy road ahead. Doxdater's courteous attempt to relieve Miss Farthingale of her burdensome valise was resolutely declined with the response she'd made it a rule never to travel when she was unable to fend for herself.

And so the threesome made as unlikely a spectacle as Canajoharie's town fathers might ever witness. Moses, first, prone yet highly visible on the cart's merchandise; next Doxdater providing locomotion for the improvised litter, followed by Miss Farthingale in perfect posture and impassive expression. The bizarre cortege advanced along Main Street to be inspected by a growing crowd threatening to eclipse the turnout for Susan B. Anthony. The rumor mill, at work moments after the barge docked, spread the false story that a Jew had died aboard the barge and was brought ashore for burial; before sundown preferred. The town had never been host to a Jew, dead or alive, and tempers were already flaring over who should bury him and where he should rest. Emotions ranged from ghoulish to sympathetic to lewd. One buffoon ran to the cart to poke Moses for signs of life. In the town's sporting house, a young lady of the night pulled aside the lace curtains to witness the event and remarked to a fellow hostess that she'd never had a man who was scalped down there.

Making their way through town with only minor incidents, they arrived at a road poorly maintained and climbing south out of the Mohawk Valley to a considerable elevation.

"Now Miss Farthingale, from here on the going gets pretty rough and steep, why don't you go back to the center and make yourself comfortable in the hotel at the cross roads."

"Where are you going, Mr. Doxdater?"

"Up here to Nitti, the healer. She's got a place about four miles away and it ain't goin' to be easy in them high-button shoes."

"Nonsense, Mr. Doxdater. I've come this far and I'll continue until I'm sure Mr. Morganstern will be well cared for. Carry on, Mr. Doxdater."

Up and down the hillsides they trudged through muddy hollows and over rocky crests on a road barely passable. Doxdater annoyingly remembered he'd volunteered to take Moses to Nitti, and he cursed his decision not to carry the sick man in a horse-drawn litter instead of pushing the cart and the whole kit and caboodle miles over the countryside. But, he was a man of his word and had no intention of backing out of his promise.

Forty-five minutes from the village and the road growing rougher, Doxdater noticed Miss Farthingale's stride becoming less steady and her face pale with fatigue, but she never suggested they rest. Nature's intercession came in the form of a dead branch lying across the road and in the time it took Doxdater to clear the way, her vigor returned to match her determination. Another mile over rut and hummock, forced Doxdater to accept this errand was proving he was less the man than when he started the forge years before. In one more grueling mile the land flattened by a giant spruce where they left the road for a trail across a field lately timbered, but now an undulating blanket of fading daisies halted on the farside at the distinct demarcation of virgin forest.

The ancient tree stood among boulders, rocky ledges and choppy ground, defying the economics of easy clear cutting. Within feet of the trail's entrance to the heavy woods they entered another world of light, shapes and silence, disturbed only by the breaking of sticks under their feet or a bird flushed from its nest. The trail became less distinct the deeper they penetrated the labyrinth, with pine branches pushed aside springing back to hide the trail as soon as they passed. It occurred to Miss Farthingale, Doxdater had lost his way. She was about to subtly raise the issue when Doxdater said, "There it is. Can you hear it?"

"Hear what?" she asked.

"The Canajoharie."

"The what?"

"The Canajoharie. It's the Iroquois name for 'the pot that washes itself.' That's where the town gets its name. It's a deep pothole in the Canajoharie creek where the water rushes in and swirls around before spilling out to go downstream."

"Hold it right there," a worn voice wheezed from the thick underbrush. "I don't see good enough to know who I'm shooting till after I've shot 'em, but I can still get you with this blunderbuss."

"Nitti, it's Doxdater."

"I don't need no shoeing; my mule died a year ago."

"I didn't come for that. I got enough business so's I don't need to walk four miles and back to get shot at."

"What are you doing here then? You come up here to take a bath in the Canajoharie Pot? You probably need one," she cackled, her wheezing trailing off into a cough.

"I got a man here they say is suffering from canal fever and you're the only one can cure him."

"I ain't in the healing business no more. I'm about healed out. Can't even fix myself. Take him to a doctor."

"We don't trust him to no doctor. He's so weak they'd kill him."

"You know you're on my property? You better take him and get out of here," Nitti said as she stepped into the open for a closer look at Moses. "What's the cart for he's lying on?"

"He's a peddler, goes around to people in the country selling things they'd have to go to the city for; scissors, combs, needles, things like that."

"Well I don't need no scissor or combs so get off my property 'fore I get really riled up."

"Who do you think you are, deciding whether he lives or dies?" Miss Farthingale demanded. "This man is sick and we brought him here because we were told you're the only chance he had. You don't have a choice, you've got to try."

"Who's you?" Nitti asked, realizing for the first time there was a woman with Doxdater, "comin' up here in your fancy shoes to tell me what I can do?"

"I'm Andalusia Farthingale, and Mr. Doxdater and I promised we'd get this man the best help we knew about."

"You gotta pretty sharp tongue, ain'tcha?"

"These are my Sunday-to-go-meeting manners. You don't want to make me mad."

"What are you doing here? You don't sound like anyone from these parts."

"I came to celebrate Susan B. Anthony's lifetime work in behalf of women's rights. She taught school here some years ago so she has friends still living in Canajoharie who support her cause."

"Oh yeah, I remember hearing about her, she's a meddler. Should have stayed a teacher. Never had much use for those women's rights groups. Don't ask permission for what's yours, I always say, just take it."

"I'd think you'd be one of their charter members, you're the most asin-," Miss Farthingale caught herself, "most assertive woman I've ever met."

"Your high and mighty talk don't make no difference to me. All of you better get off my property."

"I don't know about Mr. Doxdater, but I'm not leaving until you promise to take care of this man."

Nitti silently considered her predicament before thinking out loud. "My dog wolf is so old I can't sic him on ya and I can't bury both of ya if I shoot ya, so okay."

"Good," Miss Farthingale said. "I'll pay you a dollar a day for your trouble and we'll buy you whatever is needed for his recovery. Here's five dollars to start with."

"Now you listen to me 'cause from now on you ain't running this show. When you leave here today never come back or tell anybody about our bargain. Nobody ever. Monday before daylight I'll leave a list of my needs under the rock by the big spruce on the road. Mix up the days you buy my supplies and don't go to the same stores for the same things. Don't make a pattern. Wait till sundown to put the supplies behind the big rock and be sure you ain't followed."

"He's a Jew, you know," Miss Farthingale added as though some Hebrew rituals should be accommodated in his recuperation.

"I don't care what he is. I don't do no prayin', I just do the fixin'. Now let's get him in to my place."

Nitti led the way through the heavy woods to a small clearing barely holding back the forest from engulfing her log cabin. Doxdater pushed the cart to her door and lifted Moses' limp body, which would have been difficult to carry for a man twice as strong as the blacksmith.

"Leave him on the doorstep. I'll take care of the cart later," she commanded. "If he lives, I'll send him on his way so he doesn't go through the village. Now go and never speak about today." Nitti, surprisingly strong for her reputed age, grabbed Moses by the collar, dragged him into the cabin and slammed the door.

Chapter 10

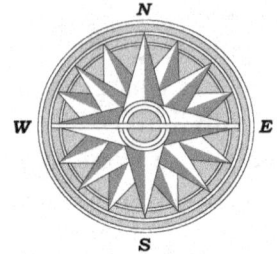

His withdrawal from the coma into the chaos of primordial disorder was not unlike the passage from the womb into an environment of threats. The animation of his hearing was the first faculty he discovered, and the bewilderments it brought blocked his retreat into nothingness. Committed to the inescapable now, a reflex opened his eyes to reveal what his ears had detected. He surveyed unfamiliar space, its proportions and features nearly obscured by the dim light or out of sight from the position in which he lay. Again the raucous, startling noise erupted behind his pallet goading him to roll on his belly to detect the source. A parrot, big as a crow, challenged him with blinkless staring, while a second voice, scratchy and in a higher register, rose above the din to order the man in bed to go outside to relieve himself lest she have to wash the bedding yet again.

"Piss your pants, piss your pants," the parrot squawked annoyingly.

"Shut up, Shakespeare, or I'll chop you up and feed you to the pigs," the old woman cackled.

Then in one continuous motion, she pulled the man to a sitting position, threw his arm over her shoulder and helped him out into foliage-sprinkled sunlight and relief. Even this slight exertion left him chilled and trembling. Seeking the warmth and protection of his bed, he climbed under the blankets and fell asleep.

Unaware he'd slept another six hours, he woke to the ache of an empty belly. "I'm starved," he called out to whoever would hear him, then added, "Where am I?"

"You're at Mohawk Nitti's, and I'll tell you when to eat and how much. You're a lotta bother to me gettin' you back into this world, an' I ain't gonna see my healing ruined by a hog."

"How long have I been here?"

"Longer than you and me wanta recollect. Stop yammering and eat your vittles, not fast or you'll puke it up," Nitti said.

Still in bed, he propped himself against the wall of the cabin and spooned the watery stuff into his mouth with less pleasure than he'd anticipated.

"This stuff is too salty," he complained.

"Never you mind about salty, you been pissin' away all your naturals. You need salt, and if you hold that gruel down you get potatoes to ease your leg cramps. Boy, you been hibernatin' longer than a bear, and you better wake up and do some livin' cause you ain't got that much time left." He wondered if that pronouncement was as ominous as it sounded or just the woman's way of speaking.

"Why are you doing this? Do you even know who I am?" he asked, thinking about his identity for the first time.

"I thought ya might be a Jew 'cause a your privates, but all your questions now make me sure of it. You're here because I promised Hiram Doxdater and that hard-assed woman I'd try to heal ya. And I don't care who ya are if you need fixin', Moses Morgenstern."

"Eat your gruel, eat your gruel, eat your potatoes, eat your potatoes," the parrot chattered.

"Shut up, Shakespeare," Nitti commanded, "I'm doin' the talking."

The potato restoring the salt in his mouth tasted better than the gruel, and he asked for more.

"That's enough for now," Nitti told him. "Tell me, young fella, whada you doin' in this part of the world?"

"I sell knickknacks and notions, small things mostly for women they'd have to go to the city to buy."

"I knowed that, I already looked in your cart."

"Did you see anything you'd like for dressing up? If you did, take it."

"I got nobody to dress up for," Nitti said. "No, I mean why was you on the barge in the first place?"

"I was going some place, Chicago maybe, but some place west and I have to earn a living, so I brought merchandise to sell. I, I feel so tired. I want to - - -." Suddenly overcome by the fatigue of an invalid in recovery, Moses' head tilted forward and he succumbed to sleep.

Nitti unfolded a tattered patchwork quilt and tucked it high around his shoulders rather than risking awaking him by dragging him onto the bed.

When he awoke he found his surroundings less threatening, but sensed he was being closely watched. A shaggy wolf-like animal, fierce-looking but non-threatening, stood beside his chair methodically sniffing Moses' entire body. Too surprised to be frightened, Moses thought he must be dreaming until he heard Nitti call, "C'mere Wolf, you know he's goin' ta live so leave him alone."

"Thanks, I thought I was having a vision."

"I bet you had your share 'lucinations the way you talked crazy from the time they brought you in."

"Is that a tame wolf?" Moses asked trying to divert their conversation away from his nightmares.

"Not sure, but he sure look like one, don't he?" Nitti cackled. "Wandered in here one day when he was a pup about the time a farmer I know shot a full grown female he caught raiding his sheep."

"Why was he looking and sniffing me all over?"

"Wolf is kinda my second opinion, the way doctors have. He done that all the time you was sick, checking my diagnosis the same as big-time saw-bones have friends do. Wolf could tell long before me you was getting better. If you was dying he'd leave you alone."

"How can you tell for sure he knows?"

"'Cause I seed him do that many times over the years. Just two years ago a farmer run over by his team never made it and last year a girl, milking her cow, was kicked in the head. She lingered a good two weeks but Wolf knowed both was going to die and they did."

"Dead or alive, dead or alive," the parrot horned in.

"I'm hungry," Moses announced.

"More gruel and potato and you need to stand up for a spell."

While there was little one could do to relieve that monotony of gruel, Nitti proved creative with her variety of potato recipes and Moses welcomed the increased portions she allowed. He felt no inclination to doze after the meal this time, but the vertical posture of standing took more adjustment than expected. A couple of times dizziness tempted him to return to bed, but he resisted and the urge abated, which he regarded as a minor triumph, encouraging him each time to push even harder.

At first he viewed the rapid rate of his recovery as miraculous, each day bringing more endurance and strength, enabling him to relieve Nitti from the routine chores necessary for her existence. Graduating from washing their clothes, to working the garden, to cutting fire kindling - which provoked Nitti to warn if he cut his leg off she wouldn't mend him all over again - Moses joyously regarded increasing vigor as proof he was well on his way to recovery and the resumption of his journey.

Then unpredictably he relapsed before reaching a plateau from which it took weeks to resume his recovery in smaller increments. When he grumbled about his progress, Nitti replied, "Go out there and try pushin' that cart. See how far you can go. Nature's tusslin' with you and she's gonna win, so stop getting' so riled up. You'll know when it's time to leave. B'sides, I'm gittin' to enjoy your company. Never knowed a man willin' to work his share an' then some."

At a creeping pace that frustrates the young and confirms the wisdom of some elderly, Moses and Nitti in the passing weeks wove an intricate tapestry of harmony, trust and affection. Conversations enhanced by spontaneity and mutual respect lasted for hours, Moses learning from all she said as well as her silences. Occasionally they were interrupted by Shakespeare croaking, "Speak up I can't hear you. Speak up I can't hear you," in diction better than Nitti's.

"I've wondered how the parrot ended up here," Moses said.

"You can't fool me, young fella," Nitti replied, catching him in his subterfuge. "You really wonderin' bout me. Well, I'll tell you, when I was a lot younger a patent medicine salesman come to town. He always put on a show with his talkin' parrot before he gave his sales spiel. Got more customers that way, he claimed, but I figured more would buy if he gave them a taste of Shakespeare first, then did his sellin' before givin' the real bird show."

"Well I'm sittin' on a wall a little way off, eatin' blueberries when all of a sudden his parrot flies over to me and starts eatin' berries right outa my hand. Well, the bird won't go back to the tonic salesman, no matter what, so I walks over to the owner with the bird eatin' my berries and hands him over, but before the man can get Shakespeare in the cage he takes off and perches on the church steeple, which I think is kinda funny 'cause I heered better talk come outa that bird than the preacher. I guess some folks might think I was irreverent, but I give up that worry an' just try to do the best I know how."

"That's quite a story, but how did the bird get here?"

"He don't come down the rest of the day, an' thinkin' I'm to blame and should help out, I come the next day with more berries to sit side the owner. He kinda takes a likin' to me and tells me the parrot's breed is an Amagona, the best talkin' kind, which he named Shakespeare. Well we're waitin' and waitin' an' he says parrots can live up to eighty years an' he's already owned him ten. And he talks to me a lot about the curin' business, tells me which remedies is fake and how some have dope in them to make ya forget you is sick, but don't cure nothin'. Then he tells me how to make potions outa everyday stuff in the woods, 'cause he once worked in a morgue and seed firsthand what can help or hurt sick people. I learned a lot from him."

"Well after the third day and the bird don't move he gets around to sayin' he likes me a lot an' I should go with him 'cause he can't wait anymore. But I know he only wants the bird back and to get me alone in his house wagon outa town. When I told him I ain't goin' he told me to stuff my ears real good and he cusses out the parrot, and maybe me. Then he hitches up his horse and leaves town an' he ain't gone ten minutes when the bird flies down to my shoulder an' been with me ever since."

"Have you taught Shakespeare to recite anything?"

"Oh yeah. Right after the Civil War, the miller across the river handed out copies of the Gettysburg Address to anyone who bought fifteen pounds of corn meal. So I learned Shakespeare that, but mostly things like 'a stitch in time saves nine,' 'gone but not forgotten' and 'all's well that ends well.'"

"That last saying was written by William Shakespeare."

"Who's he?"

"He's a great English playwright who the parrot was named after."

"So that's where that come from."

"How old do you think Shakespeare is?"

"You a cooney one, ain't you, but I see right through you. I always heered Jews was smart but never knowed one till you come along. You wanna know how old I is, but don't wana ask straight out. Some say ninety-eight, others a hundred and one. Three years one way or other don't make no difference to me."

"You're a marvel, Nitti. I'll never forget you."

"Well show me how much you 'preciate me by fetchin' water from the crick so's we can have supper."

After supper when Moses had washed the pewter dishes in the creek and Nitti's cooking area was as orderly as it was ever going to be, they talked until the burning logs stopped hissing to give way to miniature fireworks and dying embers were ready to be banked for the next morning. Then Wolf was let out for the last time till morning and an Indian blanket was draped over a rope passing from the cabin's center upright to the back wall, creating two separate sleeping spaces.

In the morning the procedure was reversed, ending the nocturnal estrangement of two yards. Breakfast, chatting and timely chores began the day. Lunch allowed an assessment of progress before Moses took a nap and Nitti disappeared to return with a trout or rabbit for supper.

The restorative combination of increasing exercise, hearty food, rest and time returned Moses to a vigor surpassing any in his life. Hours spent repairing the roof, mortaring chimney stones and caulking the log walls restored the cabin's resistance to the uncommonly cold nights predicting a vicious winter.

"Ain't you ever goin' stop?" Nitti asked Moses. "You already cut enough firewood for two years."

"I think winter is coming early and I want you to be all set before I leave. I tried pushing the cart and I can handle it. It's nearly time to be on my way."

"Don't be in such a hurry, you'll live longer," Nitti joked.

"It's good we got the honey out and shut down the hive," Moses said, changing the subject as the approach of his departure was saddening. "The potatoes are all dug along with the turnips and in a couple more days all the apples will be picked and the pumpkins, too. You've got a pretty full cold cellar."

In the days when trees dress in lavish colors to outdo each other and the first frost comes as a surprise even to the keenest naturalist, Nitti became increasingly less active and words spoken were not as tart as those she'd used with Moses in ill-disguised affection. Deciding the change could no longer be ignored, Moses questioned Nitti.

"I don't feel good," was all she volunteered, disturbing Moses enough to insist on a fuller explanation. "I got a fierce belly ache and I'm passin' blood, Mr. Nosey," she yelled.

"I'll get you to a doctor. You need attention right now."

"They never been able to cure people not as sick as me. Fact is they gave up on people I cured."

"But we've got to do something. I'll take you to New York, there are lots of doctors there with new treatments.

"I wouldn't last the trip."

"Oh, Nitti, don't make me give up on you," Moses said in a voice weakened by distress. "Where are your family and relatives? They should know about you, maybe they can help."

"I ain't got no family or relatives, least no one would claim kin to me."

"What are you talking about? How about friends?"

"I got no one but you, Moses, and you'll be leaving soon."

"Not as long as you need me, so let's go over your cures and mine and see if any will help you."

One morning when Nitti felt too sick to get up and he'd cleared away the uneaten breakfast, she asked Moses to sit with her.

"You been more like a son to me than I can tell you, better than any friend could be."

"I love you, Nitti. You gave my life back to me."

"I'm an old lady who'd die pretty soon anyway and you come along just in time to give me what I was missin', so's I need ta tell you a few things. I come down from the Mohawk Indian Nation, the first and biggest in the Iroquois confederation. Kantengehaga, they was known as, 'people of the place of the flint,' which I reckon was around here 'cause their camps was along the Mohawk Valley. Our early medicine tells of them bein' originally set free from underground by Tareyawagon, who guided them here by the river. They was the fiercest warriors and I heered they was cannibals way back, but I never seed proof."

"Are there many Indians living around here now, Nitti?"

"Not Mohawks, they was all drove out ta Canada after the Revolutionary War. I guess 'cause they sided with the British."

"But you never said you went to Canada."

"That's the story about me I want you to know. My grand daddy was a chief of one of the most powerful tribes in the Mohawks. He was forced ta leave home ta go to Canada with his wife and daughter, an only child. One of the white soldiers guarding our tribe raped her, my mother. All her life she tried to keep it secret that I was a breed, but it get out somehow no matter where I go and Whites an' Indians drive me away as soon as they find out an' I don't belong no place."

Not a word was missed nor a nuance lost to Moses' concentration. The anguish recalled by those scarring abuses slowed Nitti's narrative to simple, sparse words absent of revenge, generous in forgiveness, but more horrid for her than the pain she now suffered.

Every day he sat at her bed attending her with his presence, the only comfort he could offer. Every day he watched her wince and shake, leaving only to let out Wolf and cook gruel and potato, the legendary restoratives, the sole nourishment she tolerated. Early on it became evident to both toilet necessities were beyond her capacity alone, and she accepted Moses' assistance without embarrassment to either. Her periods of consciousness became shorter and less frequent. She would wake for a few minutes to speak of trivia, falling back to sleep and returning to pick up on the conversation where it had stopped. Her body became more frail, bones seemed to surface where none had been before, and lusterless eyes fell farther back in her skull to make her ghostlike.

The first snow of the season fell to bring more silence to the cabin. In some mysterious vigil Shakespeare went silent and Wolf lay less close to Nitti's bed than was his custom. In the shortening days of December, Nitti awoke less frequently, but always with startling clarity to ask the time and place where Moses and she waited. Helpless to provide any relief, he nevertheless always asked what he could do for her, to which she'd reply, "You doin' it."

As her agony increased, she'd call out for a swig of applejack, which initially burned going down and made her choke before it took effect. In the times when she slept, Moses routinely prayed for her out loud in Hebrew and once, awakening without his notice, she heard him and joked the strange lingo hurt her ears more than it healed her guts. Just before the periods of delirium set upon her, she urged Moses to leave while he could still push his cart through the snow, and when he replied he'd go with her all the way, her answer was surprisingly coherent and detailed.

"You give me friendship I never had before I used up all my livin'. I want you to have the cabin an everythin' in it. All the land, too, as long as you stay here. If you leave, burn down the cabin. Look out for Shakespeare and Wolf, they's used ta me an' they's good company. If you leave, let Wolf loose, he needs ta be free an' go where he wants. Take Shakespeare, he cain't make it on his own any better than you an' me. He needs a hood over his head when he ain't inside with you. I don't care where you put me down long as I's facin' the risin' sun. If you leave, be sure everything in the cabin is burned."

December twenty-first, winter solstice, the passing of the year's longest night making way for the sun's ascent, found Moses cramped from sleeping in a wooden chair next to Nitti's bed. He bent to feel a faint pulse and hear shallow breathing. The parrot, mute but vigilant, monitored each of the man's movements, a sentry for the protection of his mistress; Wolf stretched out at Nitti's side, farther away but ever faithful. Moses rubbed the stiffness from his legs, rose to peek through a slot in the shutters and discovered no new snow had fallen. More awake, he felt the chill in the cabin and realized the fire had burned out. Nitti's organized chaos, which she called a cupboard, yielded a single match, perhaps her last, with which he coaxed twigs and logs into a fire.

Satisfied the blaze was well fed, Moses went to Nitti as Wolf got up and went to the far side of the cabin as though waiting to be let out, but refused to leave when the door was opened. For a few moments, the dog fussed, lying down and getting up, restless in either position. Again Moses commanded the dog to follow, but Wolf never moved from his circling, lying down and getting up. Moses, remembering Nitti's words about Wolf's power to detect death's approach, held the dog by his long winter coat and led him to the bed.

"Lie down, Wolf! Lie down!"
When he released the dog, it returned to the far side of the cabin.
Nitti was dead.

In a final day at the cabin, Moses examined Nitti's belongings of a lifetime, a pitiful eulogy to her worthiness. Honoring the instructions of her oral will, he would return all signs of her to nature's regeneration. Only the tumbled-down chimney stones, impervious to fire, would mark her enduring spirit.

At dawn the next morning he arose and wheeled out the push cart from the protection of the shed to move it to the big spruce by the main road before another snow trapped him. When he returned, he called Wolf to let him out to return to the habitat from which he'd come.

"Come on, Wolf," he urged then scanned the dark cabin, but there was no response. The dog lay dead beside Nitti.

"Well Shakespeare, it's time for us to go. Let's say goodbye to Wolf and face Nitti east."

The parrot remained motionless on the chair back while Moses slipped one of his socks over the bird as a makeshift hood to shield against its departure into the winter's cold. Shouldering his knapsack, Moses placed the bird in a large side pocket of his coat, smashed out the shutters to create a draft, and with a deft sweep of the fire poker, hooked blazing logs from the hearth, scattering them throughout the room. The fire crept across the marsh-grass floor mats, eating slowly up the chair legs, jumping to catch bed clothing and set the cabin ablaze. The stifling heat drove him out the door to stand for two hours at the edge of the clearing to witness the creation of a purifying memorial. First the roof fell in with a great display of pyrotechnics. One by one the upright supports gave way, causing the walls to collapse inwardly upon the cabin floor in a fiery sandwich, a funeral pyre even Nitti would have approved.

In his last act of respect Moses swept off his hat and bowed low to Nitti, accidentally dislodging Shakespeare from his coat. Before he could recapture the parrot, it flew swiftly into the fire to preserve the trinity.

Halfway across the dormant daisy meadow to the big spruce, Moses paused and turned to see a plume of smoke rising from the virgin forest, healing one of its own. One loud explosion violated the silence – a salute from the blunder-buss set off by the fire.

"Don't worry, Nitti. I won't trespass on your property anymore," Moses said.

Chapter 11

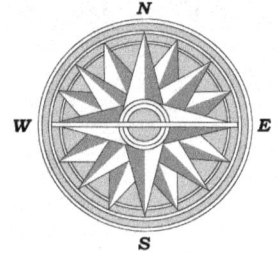

W hen Moses neared the big spruce by the road, he saw a
donkey standing near his pushcart. The animal showed no
uneasiness at his approach and allowed being inspected for
an owner's mark. Finding no brand or tag, Moses tethered the donkey
to the back of his cart with a length of tape from his merchandise and
started down the road, little traveled in winter. Smoke plumes of
distant chimneys in the clear, cold air gave assurance of nearby
habitation to the traveler. Moses reasoned it was probable the hamlet
would have a livery stable or blacksmith who'd know the animal's
owner. Thankfully the route was all downhill with only a light snow
cover, easing the travel. He passed several farms scattered along the
road for the next two miles and then entered an unfamiliar village.
Most of those he passed looked on in puzzled amusement and one
fellow replied when asked what the community was named.

"Mister don't you beat all. You come to a town and you don't
know where you are and you're pushing the cart with the jackass
loafing behind when it should be pulling you and the cart." Then,
without answering Moses, the man hustled away shaking his head and
chuckling to himself.

Mindful his errand was to locate a livery stable or blacksmith and
not delay for wiseacres, Moses moved along till his inquiries brought

helpful directions to Canal Street, which lead to the river and the establishment of Hiram Doxdater, blacksmith.

"And what can I do for you?" the sinewy bare-armed man in a leather apron said without unbending as he cradled a horse's foreleg to pull off a worn shoe.

"Excuse my interruption, sir, I found a donkey up the hill a few miles south of here with no mark of ownership. I wondered if you might know anyone whose donkey has strayed so I can return it."

"Ain't been no donkeys around here since way back to when the canal barges was towed by mules," Doxdater said, lowering the horse's leg and turning to his visitor whose voice he could not associate with any of his acquaintances. He stood mute before Moses whom he guessed had long since gone to his grave. Doxdater, a God-fearing man, was certain some revenant had come to punish him for his sins.

"Are you not well?" Moses asked, sensing the blacksmith's distress.

"Dizzy spells come upon me when I stand up too fast," Doxdater lied, and then unable to concentrate added, "and what might you need of me?"

"As I said, I found a donkey up country with no owner's marks so I thought you would know where it belongs."

"Let's go outside and take a look at the beast," Doxdater said, relying on the crisp winter to clear his head and order his thoughts. Doxdater avoided looking directly at Moses because it had unnerved him, but the pretext of examining the donkey might allow him to carefully observe Moses without being detected.

The blacksmith inspected the animal in needless detail from different angles, all the while peeking at Moses. He remembered the nearly lifeless body taken to Nitti as younger, less sturdy than the man standing before him; this one bearded, the other clean shaven, but neither had any permanent physical characteristics to differentiate them. Then for the first time he noticed the pushcart. Surely they were one and the same. Elated he'd solved the puzzle, he dismissed the hobgoblins of guilt and was about to reveal his earlier connection with Moses when he remembered his oath of secrecy to Nitti.

"Looks like this is a breed I never seed or heard of. It's definitely not from around here. I think you got a nice donkey, Mister. By the way, what did you say your name wuz?"

"Moses Morganstern and I guess from the sign on the building you're Hiram Doxdater."

"At your service." Unsure if Moses ever knew the identity of who carried him to Nitti, Doxdater was careful to keep his secret pledge, but how could he be certain the sick man on the barge and this fellow were the same? This new fellow could have stolen the cart and grown a beard to change his appearance. How he wished Miss Farthingale was around, she'd know how to find out. Too many unknowns accompanied the arrival of this Moses. Anything was possible, even ghosts.

He'd take charge of things, shake the hand of this fellow to see if he gripped warm flesh and bones.

Doxdater's huge paw wrapped around Moses' with enough force to crush a handful of walnuts, but the stranger never whined; all the more reason to suspect a ghost, as they never felt pain.

"Are you sure you're not ill?" Moses asked, having watched Doxdater's growing agitation.

Forgetting his earlier excuse for the distraction caused by Moses' presence, he said the first thing that came into his head.

"I've been having a little trouble with my eyes lately, though I can see good enough to know you're not a run-of-the-mill gent. Where ya heading?"

"Chicago."

"I don't think ya'll get far in the weather up here, 'specially pushing that cart in the snow."

"A few miles at a time will suit me. There's no hurry."

"There are some stretches with no houses for miles. Ya don't wanna get caught out there in a storm. Why don't ya take the train, one comes through here twice a week."

"I'm tempted except I'd have to leave my new donkey-friend behind and you've confirmed my opinion it's a special animal."

It restored Doxdater's composure to talk to Moses, and as the conversation lengthened, the blacksmith found his earlier mistrust of the stranger baseless. To Doxdater's disappointment, Moses related nothing of himself prior to his arrival at the forge, preventing any backtracking to Moses' presence at Nitti's or the barge.

"And what might be takin' ya to Chicago?"

"I've never been there."

"Is that the reason ya come to Canajoharie?" Doxdater asked, hoping Moses would unconsciously reveal something of his past, disappointed when Moses' response was simply "No."

"Ya talk in riddles, Mister Moses, if ya don't mind my saying so," the blacksmith observed, now feeling comfortable enough to press his inquiry.

"It's simple. Searching for something is the most important part of my life, but I must do something first to discover what that is."

"Ya think you'll find it in Chicago?" the blacksmith asked, baffled by the explanation.

"Probably not, yet I pledged to go there. I'm on a kind of treasure hunt, going from one clue to the next, never knowing if I'll reach the final prize."

Moses saw he was confusing Doxdater and changed the conversation. "Do you think my donkey should be shod?"

"If ya goin' on that trip, yes."

"Could you do that while I look around town for a meal?"

"No need to do that. I'll shoe the beast, then fix somethin' for us ta eat. Make yourself comfy while I bring in the animal." The smith, gone longer than necessary to untie the tether and get the donkey into the forge, returned clearly exasperated.

"I cain't get tha critter to move an inch, just lies down when I pull the lead line."

"That's strange, followed me without a bit of trouble."

When the donkey saw Moses come out from the forge it rose and went with no resistance to being shod. Doxdater took off his cap, scratched his head in disbelief and mindlessly fired a shoe till it was white hot and too fiery to fit. With surprising agility he swept up the fire tong, whisked the shoe from the coals, quenched it in the water tub and held it on the anvil to be hammered into shape.

On Doxdater's third failed attempt to raise the donkey's hoof for a fitting, the smith, chagrined that the animal had prevailed complained, "this dang jackass won't gimme his foreleg, it's liak tryin' to move a taproot."

"Let me see if I can help," Moses said, first rubbing the animal's muzzle and speaking calmly in its ear, then cradling the legs while the smith attached the shoes.

"I ain't never see nothin' like that, there's magic between you two. Have you named him?"

"He's a special animal and deserves a special name," Moses declared, cupping the donkey's jawbones in his hands to look straight into its eyes. "Henceforth you will be called Numbers."

"What's that?" Doxdater asked.

"It's a book in the Old Testament about a donkey that led the way."

"I guess I'm never gonna understand ya, so we might as well eat rather than jaw. Feed the donkey and the horse while I fix somethin' for us. Always feed livestock ahead of ya self then ya knowed they'd eat."

"You reminded me, Numbers will need to be fed along the way to Chicago and I don't know where to get feed for him."

"Any farm along the way can supply ya. If you talk ta the old lady while her husband's busy workin', she'll swap ya feed for a few of them trinkets outa ya wagon. If ya deal with the old man he'll want cash."

In keeping with hospitable, hard-laboring, country folks, Doxdater prepared a hearty, generous midday meal. Two kinds of meat, sweet potatoes, turnips, corn, breads, cheese and condiments were washed down with hard-cider and coffee. When the plates were empty and the warmth of the forge enhanced the feeling of well-being, Doxdater loosened his belt, tilted back his chair, took a burning twig from the open fire and lit a pipe of aromatic tobacco.

"Ya know meetin' ya has set me ta thinkin' about a lotta things."

"Such as?" Moses asked.

"Well for one, an' I hope ya take no offense about me askin', but what's it like bein' a Jew?"

"How'd you know I am?"

Doxdater, trying to recover from a misstep, grasped the first reason that came to mind. "I guess from your last name."

"But Morganstern is German."

The smith, running out of diversions, made a final attempt to extract himself from his muddled inquiry. "'Cause ya knowed the Bible so good. I guess my question was outta line."

"No, no, I'll answer this way. If you're a Jew, you must always remember you're a person, same as everyone else is a person. A Jew is different only in the eyes of those who think he's different."

"Ya know, Mister Moses," the smith said, rocking forward to tap out his pipe in the fire, flooding the forge with the smell of Kentucky burley, "I'd be mighty pleased if ya stayed over the winter and helped me cut ice outta the river ta ship to New York City. Then when spring comes ya can be on ya way in the best of weather an money in ya pocket."

"That's more than neighborly of you. I'd like that; still, I can't ignore the search I'm on. As soon as I settle up for the shoeing, I'll be on my way."

"It's too late for ya ta start out taday. The light will be gone in a couple of hours," Doxdater noted, trying to delay his new friend's departure. "Why don't ya stay the night and get an early start? Besides, ya need sled runners on that cart for the weather ya'll run inta."

"You're too persuasive, Doxdater. Make the runners and tell me your price," Moses replied, trusting the smith to be fair.

"Well, ta tell ya the truth, I kinda had my eye on the straight razor with the ivory handle. I'm thinkin' of shavin' off my beard."

The morning came stone cold and hard edged, setting the pines to whistling and contracting the water trapped in the hardwoods to ice, cracking their bones with sharp, snapping noises. The snow, unusually light for this time of winter, lay packed, giving no indication travelers had passed through this desolation. All evidence of Canajoharie grew faint, then vanished. No sounds but the crunch of Moses' boots on the snow and the donkey's occasional snort disturbed the season's hibernation. Even the raucous crows were quiet.

Doxdater's good advice to attach runners on the push cart equaled his counsel to travel west along the river's less hilly north side to maximize exposure to the sun in winter's low declination, if it ever reappeared. Physics' law that a body of water tends to moderate adjacent temperatures was no comfort to this traveler, for the Mohawk was frozen over. The bent strip of gunmetal gray riveted to a stricken land was no enticement for a passerby to pause and marvel at the valley river.

The bottom land where Moses entered the route west soon gave way to a series of gentle, snow-covered inclines and though the donkey gave no indication of tiring Moses put his shoulder to the back of the cart-converted-to-sleigh to share Number's haul. On one sheltered plateau they passed a grove of wild apple trees, all denuded of their foliage except the nearest two, which still retained two parchment-brittle leaves, refusing to yield. They waived in the wind like semaphores, signaling they still survived in this wasteland.

Over the crest of a rise beyond the apple trees, Moses looked down on a shrub-choked compound of ramshackle farm buildings enclosed by tumbled stone walls. Its open windows contrasted with those shuttered, reminded Moses of the mythical Greek god with one hundred eyes; fifty for guarding, fifty for sleeping. As he remembered the legend, Argus at his death was turned into a peacock. Little chance here.

A few miles past the derelict farm a teamster, on a flat-bed sleigh carrying long pine timbers dressed for building, stopped to chat. "Howdy stranger. That's quite a contraption ya got there."

"Works better than wheels in the snow."

"Where ya from?"

"Canajoharie."

"I never heard proper-talk like that in Canajoharie. I mean before that."

"Poland, and you?"

"Oppenheim."

"Germany?"

"No, up the road a piece. Where ya headin'?"

"Just west."

"Ya don't look like a drifter and not with that jackass. It sure is different. Never run across a breed like that. Hear there's some dirty weather comin' our way tonight. Ya don't wanna get caught out on the road after dark. Bleeker's is about eight miles ahead. It's a good place to stop. Grub's pretty good, mostly teamsters stay there, and I reckon they'll take in your jackass in the horse barn if he don't keep the other livestock awake with his brayin'," he chuckled.

"Thanks," Moses said.

"Real nice talkin' to ya. I'll be on my way," the teamster called over his shoulder as he slapped the horses' rumps with the reins and yelled, "Giddy-up!"

In the next hour Moses estimated he'd traveled four miles, passing only three farms, each insulated against the punishing winter with heavy mattings of corn stalks packed around their foundations and rising a few feet above the sill. Except for paths from the house to the barn, there were no signs of occupancy as country folk burned well-seasoned wood with no tell-tale smoke rising from the chimneys.

At one farm's hillside a free-flowing spring piped to a livestock trough offered man and beast refreshment too good to pass. Having first unhitched Numbers to bend and drink from the tub, Moses bowed and caught the water in his mouth as it spilled from the pipe. For several seconds they drank the clear, fresh liquid side by side before Numbers moved to forage the grass washed free of the snow by the spring's overflow. Moses reminded by the donkey's example that it was time to eat, pulled out a chunk of bread and cheese, amused that man and beast were enjoying a bucolic buffet - observing Doxdater's rule that livestock were always fed first.

Surveying the countryside before him, as unfamiliar as all he'd traversed, Moses realized he was never lonely traveling alone. He never failed to revisit his family and friends in prayer, but he suffered none of the nostalgia of separation. In every new public forum he'd entered, he'd met many good people and a few scoundrels whom he refused to judge, but commended their favorable qualities and rejoiced in their redemption. He always looked for the frequently concealed but ever-present positive attributes of people, which when awakened were enriching and benefitted others. In the generosity of his humanity, he sought the companionship of animals to understand his effect on their behavior, benefitting both the vulnerable creatures and himself.

He carried like a disfigurement the outrageous behavior of the rabbinical scholars in New York City who ignored ever-present social injustices to ponder yet another interpretation of archaic texts. Wasn't the Pentateuch, the focus of their concentration, a library about the calamity of such behavior?

It was dusk when he reached Bleeker's hospice, a long fieldstone building originally housing a rope walk to supply towlines to the horse-drawn barges, now converted to ease the weary travelers of both water and road. To the rear of the roadhouse, a large barn and several small service buildings enclosed a lot fast filling up with rigs and wagons from the west, substantiating the Oppenheim teamster's forecast. With the pushcart covered and parked in a sheltered area, Moses fed and stabled Numbers in one of the few remaining stalls before entering the hostel to find the innkeeper.

The proprietor, a man of undetermined age and accent, more accurately his lack of accent, offered no clue to his origin, education, compatriots or any other influence. Heavily pomaded black hair parted in the middle of his head and combed straight to either side, eyebrows diabolically turned up at the temples, ice-blue eyes, an aquiline nose, and a pencil-thin mustache over a chiseled chin made him a dominant figure. Nature's comic attempt to disguise a man of uncertain purpose was dispelled by the authority of his decisions and the strength he leveraged from his agility. Hospitality was offered with an excellence of manners and precise elocution. At introduction, his uncommon courtesy to those he sheltered established the behavior he required of all.

These unwritten house rules were rarely broken, but never without sweet, swift justice. A drunken, brawling teamster, half again the innkeeper's size, learned to his chagrin the code of conduct was inviolable as he was ejected in a debilitating half-Nelson armlock. Without one pomaded hair of the head of the master of Japanese jujitsu being put out of place, the offender was ejected and banished in perpetuity.

The fare of the table was wholesome and generous. The common room, rustic yet comfortable, provided a display board for messages and served as a forum for the exchange of the region's news, meetings, reunions and dining hall. There was no other place along the valley like Bleeker's, and for all the accommodations the price was right. Perhaps the most unorthodox of the proprietor's innovations was the house rule that all rooms must be cleaned by guests upon departure equal to preoccupancy, thereby reducing the hostel's labor costs and qualifying the individual for future admission. This was the widely known Lyman K. Bleeker House serving central New York State since 1865.

"Good evening, sir," the host of Bleeker's said to Moses with genuine cordiality. "With what name may I address you?"

"Moses, Moses Morganstern, and I presume you are Lyman K. Bleeker, owner of this hostel."

"You are correct. Many have traveled our way, but I do not recall a Moses in our twenty-two years of service. And how has the journey been that brought you to our door?" Bleeker asked, ever respectful to solicit no intrusive information.

"Unlike any before," Moses replied, indicating an adventure without revealing his mission. He immediately liked Bleeker, who'd offered his friendship and shown interest in his guest's welfare.

"How long will you be with us, Mr. Morganstern?"

"Certainly until the weather clears and the roads are packed down to a level my donkey can pass over."

"You say you arrived by donkey? I've seen many teamsters stop here with mules, but never a donkey."

"Yes, sir, this is an unusual beast. I've never seen such a donkey, and others can't identify its breed."

"I'd be curious to see it. When I was a young boy, my father was a missionary and we lived in several eastern countries where donkeys are the main beast of burden, so I became familiar with those plucky little creatures."

"Why don't we go to the stable and have a look before the weather gets worse?" Moses said.

They opened the door against a gale that almost snuffed out their kerosene lantern and walked in heavy snow that blotted out their tracks before they reached the barn. As the lamplight ran across the stable floor to the farthermost stall, Numbers looked up for a moment before returning to his feed.

"Numbers, Mr. Bleeker wants to look at you, so behave," Moses said in a tone too serious to be taken seriously.

"May I?" Bleeker asked, taking the lamp from Moses to inspect the donkey.

Like an acolyte incensing the devout, he passed the lantern several times over the donkey's back, noting its distinctive colorations, before kneeling in the animal's bedding to inspect Numbers' belly, cannons, shanks, fetlocks, pasterns and hooves, all the time uttering "remarkable" or "extraordinary." When he'd completed his meticulous examination, Bleeker rose, returned to his military bearing, fastidiously rearranged his attire and said, "I never will be able to understand what I've seen. There is no explanation for the donkey being in this country, absolutely no precedent for breeding this species. Wherever did you find this animal?"

"I didn't. It found me."

"Oh Mr. Morganstern, I sense you jest with a humor more sophisticated than usually encountered in these parts, but please tell me where the donkey came from."

"In truth, I found the donkey standing under a tree outside Canajoharie and when no one claimed, it, took it to be my own."

"Preposterous," Bleeker replied, unsure if Moses was continuing to make light of him, but politely giving notice he was not a gullible rube. "May I tell you something about the beast?"

"Please."

"Your donkey is about four years old and has probably reached its full growth. This species is identified by its conformation and coloring, always a solid light brown whereas others carry a dark stripe from the neck backwards. It is of the Equus Hemionos derivation that migrated from Siberia into Western Manchuria, to Turkistan, Persia and Syria. It is probably the type associated with the Old Testament stock."

"That's very interesting. I'm grateful for your expert opinion because no one else could explain why he was special."

"Is there anything unusual in his behavior?"

"Well, he seems protective of me, and if anyone tries to move him he makes it impossible by lying down. He also responds as though he knows what I'm saying."

"They're very keen, you know. I'll never understand why people associate stupidity with a jackass. By the way, you should know how fleet they are. Without a lead, they can run up to forty miles per hour. It's getting cold; shall we go in and dine?"

"I'd like that and again my thanks."

Meals were taken in the common room at a long refectory table accommodating sixteen at a time. Two and occasionally three seatings, taxing the resources of the kitchen, were served when foul weather, such as this night's, drove the teamsters off the road. None of the help ate until all guests were served, limiting the wasting of food through carelessness in preparation. Grace was said by Bleeker at each seating before the meal was served, as he believed it kept men more civilized when they were away from home and increased their appreciation of the food when it arrived. Chewing tobacco and smoking were forbidden inside the hotel or barns, relegating the indulgers to the outside porch, where aesthetics, health and safety were not jeopardized by missed-spittoon nor hostel and barns at risk from fire.

Bleeker's rules seemed restrictive at first to the newly inducted, but patrons rarely failed to return to this modestly-priced haven for lonely men who spent their lives on the road. It soon became apparent even to the slow-witted and boisterous that all benefitted from Bleeker's commandments, a term he used to dignify his house rules.

Little was known of his generosity to those in need, for beneficiaries of his largesse were sworn to secrecy and never obligated to repay him; his only request was that they help others as they'd been helped.

An astute listener, Bleeker acquired a considerable amount of weather, news and biographical intelligence, filtering all for accuracy. It was a rule of thumb that biographies and anecdotes were usually delivered in subjective extremes and the truth lay somewhere in the middle, but weather was reported with surprising accuracy. Residents and travelers alike along the Mohawk Valley had learned to respect its weather changes, and woe to those who ignored the warnings of this conduit east from Lakes Erie and Ontario, incubators of meteorological mischief. Most tavern owners along the Valley's East/West Road simply accepted weather's occasional treacherous caprices and made no use of teamsters' reports of climatic conditions that could affect travelers' patronage. Such variations resulted in a continuous imbalance in the supply and demand of food. If provisions ran out, sales and good will suffered, and excess inventories earned no profit on the investment. Bleeker's sensitive monitoring of these factors let him succeed where others failed.

Chapter 12

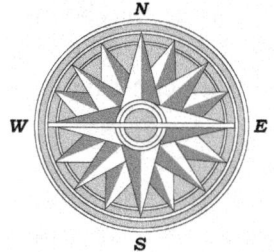

Moses sat close to feel the fire-inducing tranquility, his mind floating in free association, captive only to the flames' ever-changing abstractions. In two absorbing hours of Bleeker's casual comments, penetrating perceptions emerged to support Moses' earlier impression of the innkeeper's extraordinary intellectual capacity. Certainly the reach of this learned and curious mind extended beyond this crossroads inn or the county bounds of the community. It was unlikely his competence had escaped consideration for public office and equally improbable he'd commit to that orthodoxy. What anchored him to this simple rural retreat?

Moses, so caught up in his thoughts, rudely blurted out, "What are you doing here?"

Bleeker quietly replied, "Are you questioning me or yourself?"

"I'm," he stumbled, "seeking truth?"

"How do you define truth?" Bleeker countered.

"I don't know. I'm searching for the wisdom to describe truth, then I'll know how to find it."

"You don't find truth, it finds you," Bleeker replied.

"All right. Truth is fact."

"Many assertions of fact are demonstrably questionable. For example, beauty is in the eye of the beholder, which allows both fact and fiction. Truth is a fact, but a fact may not be truth. That's why you must let truth come to you; you cannot manipulate truth by trying to hasten its arrival or pretending you've found it."

"Now I appreciate Doxdater's confusion when he asked me a question and said I answered with a riddle."

"The Canajoharie blacksmith?"

"Yes."

"He found a riddle in you, maybe his first, and attempting to solve it changed his world forever. The riddles you solve will bring you wisdom, with wisdom truth can't be far behind."

One by one the teamsters reluctantly left the warmth of the common room for their cold beds, looking first through the frosted windows to check the size of the storm. The snow fell in diagonal sheets, winds gusted backdrafts down the chimney to whirl ashes on the hearth and quicken the blaze. Moses and Bleeker, indifferent to the hour and comfortable with each other, turned the conversation in a biographical direction. Before continuing the conversation, Moses considered how much he'd reveal, expecting the innkeeper's good manners to respect his privacy and dismissing Bleeker's compelling silences as a manipulative device to seek more information.

"I'm a Jew," Moses began and went on to describe how his family had resigned themselves to the grip of poverty in Poland. As the youngest of eight, Moses unlike his siblings was unwilling to submit to a continuous, hopeless life. But inexperienced, he could not imagine the hardships of an immigrant could be as severe as those at home. As he described the privation of his solitary trip to Hamburg, often existing on cabbages left in the fields, it now surprised him he'd had the endurance to go on.

"When I regained consciousness in the convent infirmary, I felt transported to another world, a feeling I'd never had. I suppose the nuns' peculiar style of clothing had something to do with it. Their large wing-like head coverings made them appear to sail through the air."

"Did you have any professional diagnosis of your injury?" Bleeker asked.

"One might call it that, but the nuns seemed to trust the doctor's five minute examination, and I was in such a hurry to get to America I didn't question his opinion."

"How old were you at that time?"

"In my seventeenth year. I remember the thing I most worried about was keeping the money in the waistband of my pants a secret."

Moses described his introduction to Alfredo and Ludwig who, despite their contrary temperaments, became fast friends, surprising Moses and themselves. In considerable detail he told of witnessing New York's indifference to people's poverty and the prejudicial extremism practiced even within the differing sects of Judaism. His voice lifted, reflecting the happy memories of welcoming newly-arrived immigrants and the productive people who'd changed from rascals to useful push-cart vendors.

He understated how the success of his business in New York had given him confidence to expand into Boston and Philadelphia and the notion to explore opportunities in Chicago. It pleased him to recount his meetings with Osgood, Jasper, the Happy Harpy and others on the west-bound Erie Canal barge. The omission of the Red-Tailed Hawk's avionics, Nitti's healing and Lightning Lance was purposeful, lest they sound like the hallucinations of a fool. Finished, he sat in silence watching the fire, wondering if he'd been too candid.

Throughout his life, Moses had preserved his privacy, rarely discussing experiences or feelings. As the baby in the family, he was treated kindly, but his seven brothers and sisters seemed satisfied not to explore thoughts and behavior and his father, preoccupied with grieving over his wife's death, was incapable of ministering to the emotional needs of a son whose mother had died.

Bleeker reclined quietly in a chair across the hearth from Moses, his composure beginning to annoy the younger man, who felt he'd been left dangling by the other's failure to jump in and tell his story. After engaging in a long, drawn-out theatrical silence, Bleeker sat erect and spoke.

"I am the progeny of an English missionary's and Bedouin maiden's catalytic assignation - straight out of Arabian Nights. My mother died when I was quite young," he said, his voice faltering, "but we stayed on at the oasis village just north of the Atlas Mountains where my maternal ancestors had lived for years. At home and in the mission school we spoke both English and the Afro-Asian dialect of the Berbers, which nudged me toward becoming multilingual. Alternating weekly attendance at church and mosque also made me bidoctrinal or agnostic, depending on the day of worship.

"A voluminous library, eclectic by design and not without vexation in desert transport, was the indulgence of my father and my passport to the world outside the little village. Schooling came easily, and I was soon tutoring the teacher, not without some embarrassment to the mission's elders. Father, who preferred exporting problems rather than working them through to the benefit of all, packed me off to a supposedly academically challenging institution in England. To my disappointment, a student's intellectual nonconformity was not encouraged, and in fact subordinated to maintain faculty infallibility and incompetence. My persistence in questioning a master's assumptions and the demonstrably proven faulty conclusions he reached, which I was quick to point out, earned me the rod and ultimately expulsion."

Bleeker paused, a smile showing from the memory of a father's atypical reaction to the punishment of an unruly son. "With his usual equanimity Father noted his satisfaction that his son had the courage of his convictions and dismissed their academia as third class ignoramuses, which were regarded as low as one could sink. Having dispatched academia, Father devoted the rest of a long letter to reassignment in the Holy Land and his intention to make the entire twenty-five hundred mile journey to Jerusalem by caravan, a strenuous effort for a man in his sixties.

"His letter expressed great joy and exhilaration at the prospects of a long nomadic trek immersed in desert culture and the spiritual regeneration of solitude. The suppressed sadness over his wife's death, now many years behind him, returned as he prepared to leave her resting place forever, but he said she surely would have wanted him to move on and even more so now that I was living in England. He congratulated me on my twenty-first birthday, a maturity milestone entitling me to a distribution of benefits from my grandfather's estate, and enclosed a detailed map of his route with estimated arrival dates at points along the way. His letter closed with an uncustomary note of affection to the effect 'it would be gratifying to see his beloved son at some oasis on my path.'"

Bleeker became more animated with each recollection, reliving years past, chortling with no embarrassment presumably over some incident he declined to disclose.

"Through some outrageous reasoning, it became critical at the time to beat Father at his own game, which I later admitted was delayed, childish rebellion. In any event, having no obsession with sand or camels, I set out to walk through Europe and the Middle East to welcome Father when he arrived in Cairo. From there I would accompany him on the last leg to the Holy Land. My journey to southern France and east along the Mediterranean Sea, except for a few minor threats from thugs, was a rewarding adventure offering wondrous sights, agreeable people, tolerable weather and a wide variance in palatable cuisines. Intrigued by the prospects of exploring what was just around the next corner, my curiosity was in constant conflict with an unyielding timetable, and irritably I stayed close to schedule, swearing to revisit certain locales, which of course no one ever does.

"I arrived in Cairo five days before Father, self-congratulating my punctuality but cursing my alter ego for rushing me past places of interest. For four days I toured archeological landmarks around Cairo until on the fifth day Father arrived behind a bushy, gray beard, clothed in a turban and caftan, leaving only his eyes and tan brow exposed."

"It must have been a deeply emotional reunion after twelve years," Moses said.

"Indeed," Bleeker replied, "but all that time apart vanished when I hugged him and smelled that familiar odor of light sweat he gave off when he exercised. I no longer worried if he was safe, I was safe now. Perhaps it was the beard, but he seemed to have aged beyond his sixty-odd years. Of course, the mind is very clever in supporting one's own opinion, assuring reality is as we discussed earlier."

"How long were you in Cairo before leaving for Jerusalem?"

"Nearly two weeks. Father insisted on visiting all the sights on the Upper Nile Valley, including those I'd just seen. However, in all fairness his scholarly expertise increased my appreciation of the ancient world. He even convinced me to wear a burnoose, which I found quite comfortable but inadequate for the task of making me look as majestic as the desert people. I'm sure I'd be an embarrassment to Mother's family."

"Next you'll be telling me the Red Sea parted and you were off to Jerusalem," Moses joked.

"Not so. On part of the journey we followed much of the route in Exodus and contrary to my expectation our journey to Jerusalem passed a succession of immensely interesting Biblical sites. As we walked the lands of Hebrew exile, my father's scholarly reach made the ancient text come alive - every well or mountain guarding a legend."

As though some outer force, of which Bleeker was unaware, controlled the story, it was delivered in a series of interrupted phrases, hinting his narrative might run down before its end.

"I stayed with Father in Jerusalem for nearly four months -- until he had settled into his work at the mission."

Then presumably, Bleeker was deeply moved by what was to come, for he rushed to end this painful episode.

"I thought it prophetic Father never intended to move again when he donated his library to the mission. He became increasingly contemplative, spending much of his free time walking in the desert, politely refusing company, absent for longer periods. One day he never returned. I often wonder what he was looking for."

Bleeker, though visibly fatigued, gave no hint of ending the saga, but he arranged his sentences more deliberately, ordering words with care before offering them to his midnight companion. With minimum description of city or province, country or continent, land or sea, he told of circumnavigating the world always facing the rising sun. His infrequent references to archeology, geography, weather and exchange rates employed only if they advanced his analysis of the natives' cultures. His unconventional methodology, particularly in comparing the classes, often earned him the reputation of troublemaker and a quick exit from the country.

Crossing the International Date Line as a deckhand on a sailing ship, he learned a sailor's life was not for him. Panning for gold on an exhausted site earned little but humility and the incentive to get paid for his labor steered him to San Francisco, where he subsisted on the paltry wages of washing dishes and waiting on tables in a hotel by the Bay. Amid the hub-bub of California, a territory trying to find its identity, he searched for his. Once again, he set his course east toward the rising sun, but being a child of the Sahara and unable to pass up an exploration, he detoured to the Mojave Desert.

Springtime's floral extravaganza of blues, reds, purples, yellows and greens, an apology for Winter's fierce deluges, was not to be ignored, nor were the exotic rock sculptures eroded by winds that chased tumbleweeds in unordered direction. Recently discovered deposits of a mineral, commercialized under the name of Borax, drew a large number of laborers to the area to mine and mill the raw material, and Bleeker joined them long enough to refill his depleted treasury.

He went looking for the indigenous natives, but the Mojave Indians, once a fierce tribe now consigned to raising corn and making pots, evaded him by melting into the shadows of the rocks or blowing away in dust devils. Common sense prevailed over impulse, and he stopped pursuing them until their curiosity emboldened them to parley. They showed a simple nature, patient and non-committal, commenting on non-controversial subjects. Bleeker described to the Indians the enormity of his motherland Sahara and the peoples' complete dependence on the oases. When he and they had satisfied the restrained curiosity of polite strangers, Bleeker bid the Mojave tribe farewell and reset his compass in a north-northeast direction to intersect a transcontinental railroad under construction. Arriving at the easternmost point reached by the construction crews, Bleeker joined the roughnecks laying track and driving spikes for labors' wages to reline his pockets. One day the gang-boss announced each shift would work longer hours to meet the company's goal of thirty more miles of track before winter set in. To clarify the assignment, he showed the men a crude map that ran the rail line through the heart of an Indian hunting ground, a direct violation of a U. S. treaty granting the land to the tribe forever.

Bleeker quit. After drawing down his wages, he walked off the job to warn the tribe three days distant. He was greeted by skeptic and young braves boasting they could protect the tribe's domain with no help, especially from an untrustworthy white. At considerable risk, Bleeker bypassed the naysayers and appealed to the council. Once again, many suspected Bleeker was trying to trick them and argued for his expulsion. At last a wrinkled elder called for silence and reason.

"My brothers, think of what this stranger is doing. He comes to us and asks for nothing, risking his safety if the story is true and the railroad finds out he has warned us. If it is only a story with no truth, we have lost nothing but will be more vigilant. If it is true, we will be prepared. He knew before he came he'd be punished if he lied to us and helped the railroad take our land. Remember, he asks for nothing. Let us keep him among us for two months, treating him with respect as long as he walks upright. In that time we should learn the truth and if he has acted in honor, repay him for his kindness and release him to go where the winds blow him."

All in the council put their differences to rest except one named Shadow Dancer who continued to grumble over the decision.

"Did you stay?" Moses asked before realizing how stupid the question was.

"I had no choice," Bleeker replied, shifting his weight in the chair and crossing his outstretched legs, more relaxed than in earlier phases of his narration. "Throw another log on the fire, good fellow. The finish of my story is about one log's worth away." Bleeker was now clearly enjoying the recounting of derring-do, and Moses was swept along with his enthusiasm.

"For three weeks the tribe on alert with lookouts at their boundaries, waited for a trespasser, but noted only Shadow Dancer who rode out each morning to check the fish weirs but never returned with a catch. The chief asked Shadow Dancer why the fishing was so poor and was told the weirs had been broken by bears, but now repaired, should soon yield good catches. Dissatisfied with the answer, the chief ordered a brave to carefully check the weirs for any new repairs and estimate the fish trapped. All the weirs seemed to be of original construction and were full of fish, raising the question of Shadow Dancer's regular absences from the camp. Still unwilling to make accusations of any mischief, the chief directed a scout to track Shadow Dancer whenever he left the camp.

"By the end of the first day's tracking, the chief learned Shadow Dancer had been seen leaving the railroad laborers' shed arm-in-arm with the big boss. Swigging from a whiskey bottle and laughing uproariously, he staggered to his pony. Unable to mount his horse until boosted by a laborer, he rode out of the camp stuffing a wad of money into his leggings and shouting from his precarious perch. Several miles from the tribe's encampment, he left the trail to bushwhack through a thick undergrowth on his way to the fish weirs. By the light of the moon, he counted and recounted the money the big boss had given him. Apparently satisfied the agreed amount was all there, he scooped out a hole under a cottonwood tree and buried the cash. Still drunkenly clumsy, he clubbed some fish in the weir, wrapped them in ferns and returned to the tethering-meadow near his wigwam. Just within the encampment, two braves stepped out of the shadows and delivered him to the waiting council.

"I see you fish at night, Shadow Dancer," the chief began.

"It is best to take the fish from the weirs in poor light when they can't see you," Shadow Dancer replied.

"But, here you are just home from fishing and the moonlight is bright as day. Do you always hide some of your catch under the cottonwood tree by the river?"

"I cannot follow your meaning" Shadow Dancer answered, trying not to slur his words.

"I mean, do you always hide your fish and any other catch under the cottonwood tree by the river instead of bringing such things back to your wickiup to make a feast for your people?"

"I give them to the tree to lift to the Great Spirit in the sky as a sacrifice for bountiful harvests and good fishing," he replied, hoping to end the chief's questions.

"Are these the fish you catch?" The chief asked, holding up the wad of money, "and what do you use for bait?"

"No," Shadow Dancer cried out feeling trapped. "No, I took some of the fish to the railroad men who paid me with the money I hid to surprise the tribe."

"So much money for so few fish?" the chief persisted.

"I've been selling fish to them all week."

"And have you sold anything else belonging to the tribe? You must sell many things to get this much money," the chief charged, throwing the wad of bills on the blanket before him. "Tonight you must tell us everything you've said to the railroad men and don't leave anything out, your life depends on it."

Bleeker paused, sipped some water to relieve a drying throat and returned to his tale.

"By morning, Shadow Dancer confessed to the council he'd divulged all the features of the terrain in the tribe's hunting grounds, river crossings, hideouts, trails, location of the encampment, number of braves, children, elders, ponies, type and number of weapons. When all had been established by repetitive questions, the chief, council and an escort of braves rode to the railroad to stop some distance but in clear view from the laborers' shed. The chief, unarmed, rode closer toward the laborers just finishing their noonday meal.

"Railroad boss," the chief called, "We should speak, railroad boss."

A tall, bony, bespectacled, balding man ambled out from behind a chuck wagon. "Start talking."

"We come in peace. You are at the border of our hunting grounds. We did not ask you to build your railroad in our direction. You never told us you were coming here. Our treaty with Washington gives us our land forever. No one will take this land from us. No railroad will cut our hunting ground in two. We leave you in peace, but know this, railroad boss, if anyone breaks treaty, if anyone enters our land he will be cut down like grass."

The chief raised his hand in friendship, returned to his council and escort and left the clearing to disappear in the border scrub.

"Did the tribe release you after that?" Moses asked.

"I was free to leave, but the chief's fairness and temperance throughout the entire incident persuaded me to ally myself to the tribe's cause and help them appeal to Washington to enforce the treaty. As I expected, there were several ambiguous conditions in the treaty that could be interpreted to favor either side, and I felt the Indians would have a better chance if they were first to force the issue. As it turned out, they won seven of the ten issues in contention, but within eight years the new administration in Washington reversed the earlier findings and a rail line was driven through with much blood lost before the tribe was exiled to a reservation."

"And Shadow Dancer?" Moses asked.

"His tongue was cut out so he'd never again lie, and he was banished from the tribe."

"But none of this explains why you came here," Moses said.

"Oh, but it describes part of my odyssey - you as much as anyone should understand the irrational drive that forces one ever onward. I was certainly not an obsessive sightseer nor a dreamy romanticist, more like an explorer with no objectives or expectations. For three years I traveled east from the tribe, timbering, farming, herding along the way to Chicago, a brawling collection of roughnecks, harlots and robber barons trying to shoulder their way to competing with the northeast metropolises. I sailed east along the Great Lakes to the western terminal of the Erie Canal celebrating its twenty-fifth anniversary and boarded a barge for New York City.

"For two years I worked in the city's largest library, advancing faster than my peers, before catching the attention of one of its wealthiest patrons who hired me to build a collection for his athenaeum. It was there that I reached the goal of my journey -- a lovely English lady of mythic perfection who was the governess to my employer's children. We professed our love in marriage and I experienced bliss beyond all imagining. Then one day she fell ill and we were told she had tuberculosis and must recuperate outside the city in the restful atmosphere and clean air of a rural locale.

"I remembered this beautiful valley from my earlier trip on the canal. We moved here at the beginning of Spring's metamorphosis and watched tender greens of infinite variety predict the exaggerated palette of wildflowers, counted and catalogued the plumage and songs of returning birds, raised and ate vegetables five minutes from harvest in our garden. Ours was a unity of body, mind and spirit with the promise of each morning and the peace at day's end. Neither of us realized how full a life we were living in the rapidly passing eighteen months of our marriage, never rushing from one thing to another to crowd it all into whatever time was left, but everything important got done at our pace. One of our pleasures was a walk to the river to watch its continual changes almost minute by minute. We'd challenge each other to describe what we'd see next time, and of course both of us always failed.

"One fall day at dinner when the crimson sumacs slashed the banks of the river giving credence to the name, Bloody Mohawk, she looked at me for a long time before saying, 'I don't want to go to the river anymore, it's dying.' Then she kissed my forehead, went to the bedroom to lie down and never woke up."

Regaining his composure to finish the story, Bleeker said, "You asked me why I am here. I'm here because I discovered everything I ever wanted is here."

Chapter 13

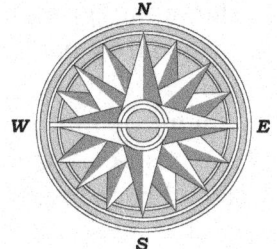

Moses was awakened by the glaring rays of a rising winter's sun that contradicted a notion of the previous day's blizzard. He squinted against the blinding light for orientation and stretched out the stiffness of a night's sleep in a large wooden armchair under the weight of a great bearskin. He peered over his furry horizon discovering the fire was almost out, Bleeker no longer sat next to him, and he was alone in the chilly common room. He straightened his legs to their full length to test if they would hold him then slowly rose. His visible breath commanded attention to the fire, which he fed with kindling and logs. Impatient with the wood's delayed ignition, Moses bent to blow the coals just as the fuel burst into flame to singe his beard.

"You've enjoyed a much needed trim courtesy of our hospitality." Bleeker chuckled as he entered the room in a black burnoose covering all but his face and hand. "I understand from barbers singeing closes the ends and strengthens the hair shafts."

"I prefer scissors," Moses replied.

"You're an early riser and build good fires without being asked. Perhaps I can persuade you to work for me until the weather warms for traveling."

"I thank you for the offer, but if I delay my journey just once, I may never learn who I'm meant to be."

"Nobody could know this better than I, my friend. Let us prepare a breakfast to ease your journey."

Alongside the cooks now fixing the day's first meal for the rising wagoners, Bleeker and Moses prepared food of a near-eastern, ceremonial significance, celebrating gratefulness for their meeting and prayers for their welfare when they parted.

By eight a.m. Moses had fed and watered Numbers, completed every teamster's obligatory chore of mucking out his animal's stall, hitched up the skid-modified push-cart and descended the last hill from which Bleeker's hotel could been seen.

At first the ice-coated branches of the leafless hardwoods covering the land to the horizon entranced Moses with their beautiful abstractions, but as each new place looked like the last, the repetitious vistas tricked him into questioning his progress. No one had preceded him to mark a passage in the snow, and the shadowless white wasteland distorted the route he traveled and deceived his vision.

Near noon, judging from the sun's elevation, he sighted a farm surrounded by conspicuously green, coniferous trees in the hollow of a hill, a welcome relief to nature's dazzling crystal display. Despite a lack of evidence the house was occupied, Moses halted Numbers by the front entrance and rapped on the door. After several attempts that brought forth only reverberations in the hollow interior, he concluded the farm was abandoned and was preparing to leave when the door was opened a few inches. A young woman, obviously cautious about talking to strangers, was detectable through the narrow slot.

Moses, quick to sense her nervousness, backed away from the door to stroke Numbers' muzzle. "I wonder if I could draw some water from your well for my donkey?"

"It ain't likely. The well's froze solid."

"Perhaps there's a brook nearby that hasn't frozen over?"

"Everythin's froze 'cept my kitchen well-pump. If'n that goes, I'll hav ta melt snow for the livestock."

"Would you fill my pail for me?" Moses asked, holding it toward her at arm's length.

"I guess I can do that," she replied, snatching the bucket and slamming the door behind her. In a few minutes she reappeared wearing a long, black, boiled-wool coat, easily handling the full pail. Moses, trying to make no gesture to alarm her, set the water down Numbers' side opposite the woman and watched the donkey drink his fill.

"Where ya headin'?"

"West."

"Where'd ya come from?"

"Last night I stayed at Bleeker's."

"Ya come a good piece already today. Ya must be in a hurry," she said, watching Moses as he attached Numbers' feed bag. She drew here coat tighter against the wind that whistled through the evergreens. "Would ya like to come in by the fire?"

"That's very kind. I won't stay long. Would you mind if I ate my meal while I thaw out?"

"Ya need to tie up the donkey?"

"No, he'll stay put until I leave."

The woman slammed and bolted the door before leading Moses through an empty hall and a sparsely furnished room to a kitchen with one window shuttered against the winter. Most of the room's light was provided by blazing logs in a massive fieldstone fireplace, its chimney occupying much of the wall near the blind window under which a soapstone sink caught the drip of the recently activated hand pump. Logs for the fire jammed more than half the darkened side of the room. Beyond the firewood stack there were three unmatched chairs tucked tight against a small table and a rope-bed, leaving little space to navigate the room. When Moses' eyes adjusted to the semi-darkness, he realized that a little boy lay in the bed quietly watching every move of the newcomer.

"This here is my boy Horatio. He'll be five this spring. Right now he ain't feelin' too good with the croup, but he's a lively one when he's up to snuff. Gets around real good for a deaf kid."

"How long has he been deaf?"

"Ever since he had the epidemic and almost died from the high fever. Shortly after he got better he couldn't hear. Doc said he never would get all better. Around me and his daddy he done real good, but now there's only me to depend on since his daddy got killed last spring in a log float down river to the mill."

"I'm sorry," Moses said. "Have you ever taken him to doctors who specialize in this problem, big city doctors in New York?"

"We don't have no money to do that. I mean I don't have no money. Price, that was my mister, Price and me was just beginning to make the farm pay off when he was killed."

"Well, let's try to think of something," Moses said to reassure the woman there might still be hope. Then after a thoughtful pause, "Would you like to share my food?"

"Me and Horatio ate just before you come." The woman looked at her son for a long time before asking Moses, "What did you mean let's try to think of something?"

"I was thinking the boy could learn sign language or reading lips so he could communicate with others."

"Are there such things?"

"Oh yes, many deaf people get along about as well as you and I once they learn these skills."

The woman sat silently staring at Horatio, showing her suffering for the boy.

"Where would he learn this? How much would it cost?" she asked, impatient to pursue a treatment for her son.

"I don't know for sure, you'd have to investigate," Moses said, not knowing how to advise the woman.

"How come you know so much about readin' lips and sign language?"

"A friend showed me how they work."

"Show Horatio how they work."

"It's not that easy, especially with a child."

"Then show me how it works."

"It takes time and a lot of practice."

"I should have know'd it," the woman said, discouraged.

Moses ate his meal, sorry he'd given the woman false hope.

"Maybe you could stay over a few days and teach me," she persisted, not yet ready to give up. "I'm a quick learner; you could write down the easy words like 'yes, good, thank you, sick, help, eat,' things like that. Can't you stay a couple of days? The weather's no good for travelin'."

"I really must be on my way, but I'll try to find a book on signing and send it to you. I don't know your name, who should I send it to?"

"I'm Molly. Just send it to me at the general store in Capin Corners. I'll pick it up when I go for provisions in the spring."

"Thanks for the comfort of your kitchen," Moses said, rising and putting on his great coat. "You take good care of Horatio and yourself."

"What's your name, stranger?"

"Moses," he said as she let him out the front door to see him off.

She stood stoically, pulling her shawl tight against the chill.

"Goodbye," Moses called, unhitching the feedbag from Numbers and turning him in the direction of the road a hundred yards away. When they reached the entrance in the stone wall enclosing the farm yard, Numbers stopped.

"Come on now, Numbers, we've got a good distance to cover before dark," Moses urged, but the usually responsive donkey only dug his hooves deeper into the snow with each of Moses' increasingly impatient commands. After unsuccessfully demanding the animal move, Moses walked to the outside entrance in the wall and offered Numbers a treat to follow him, only to receive a mocking bray.

Although a biting wind chilled Molly, she could not leave the comical testing of man versus beast before its conclusion. After half an hour of trying everything short of whipping Numbers, an option too repugnant for Moses, he stroked the donkey's muzzle while speaking softly, but an attempt to hold the donkey's bridle was met with head tugging until the animal understood Moses was not leaving the house.

"Put him in the barn and out of the wind," Molly suggested.

"If there's plenty of hay, I'll sleep out there."

"You come inside. I ain't worried about no man sleepin' in the house 'cause I keep a loaded shotgun next to my bed. I'm only offering a night's lodgin' and a couple of meals and you can be on your way."

"I'll pay you for your trouble," Moses replied.

"Just get your beast settled and bring in whatever eggs been hatched."

When Moses was alone in the barn, he held Numbers' head a few inches from his to look straight into the animal's eyes.

"Why are you doing this to me, Numbers? Haven't I always treated you kindly? All of a sudden you've become obstinate for no reason. I don't care if Bleeker says you're not a hybrid, you're as stubborn as an old mule."

The donkey blinked large liquid eyes and hung his head, as though pleading innocent to the charge.

"I could stop giving you treats and helping you push the cart up the steep hills, you know."

The donkey shook his head up and down several times, appearing to foolishly pantomime that Moses was the master and the donkey his obedient servant. Then, as though recanting this arrangement, he snorted several times, brayed loudly and set the woman's horse to whinny, the cow to moo and the chickens to crowing in rural discord.

"Now see what you've done," Moses barked. "You've probably soured the cow's milk. This lady is kind enough to let us stay the night and you repay her by upsetting the livestock."

Molly, having come to the barn to learn what was delaying the traveler, was greeted with the extraordinary spectacle of an animal again arguing with a human and winning. She couldn't remember how long before this day she'd laughed. Withdrawing before he saw her, she returned to the kitchen and was soon joined by an exasperated Moses muttering to himself. His good nature returned with the warmth of the fire, and in a few minutes of introspection, he was able to laugh at the incident.

For the first time, he became aware of the woman as an individual, her high cheekbones, and how the set of her jaw and unflinching, dark eyes reinforced the determination of her voice. Long hair, black and shiny as crow's feathers, was pulled back tightly from her forehead and caught in a ponytail that fell just below broad shoulders. Her movements, quick, quiet and sure, were perfectly suited for a lonely existence.

As she sat by the fire, head bowed momentarily paying homage to the turnips she peeled, the light turned the contours of her black hair to a silvered sheen. Unaware she was being watched, she unexpectedly turned to move a cooking pot before Moses could divert his eyes. Moses, unsure if she thought she or the fire was the object of his staring, reached for his coat as a pretext for something just remembered and extracted a tortoise shell comb.

"Numbers and I would like you to have this," he said, including the donkey as a donor to depersonalize the gift. "Seems that's the only thing he and I have agreed to today," he added, giving her the comb.

For a moment, it lay in her open palm as she studied the variety of its subtle, transient amber hues in the flickering firelight.

"What's this for?" she asked, indicating one might construe it as a bribe for her favors.

"It's for you."

"What would I do with this? It's for a fancy lady. I'm a farmer." She spoke in flat tones with no hint of self-pity, only acceptance of her reality.

"Why, I've seen many women just like you wearing these when they go to see their friends or a party or - " Moses immediately attempted to correct his choice of examples, "or church or the general store."

"Mister, what are you tryin' to do with that fancy comb? Get on my good side?"

"I don't know what you're talking about. Good side, bad side? I don't know anything about your special sides. It was only a present to thank you. If it offends you, I'll take it back."

Molly broke off the conversation to respond to a request from her son, unintelligible to all but a loving mother.

"Nah, I think I'll keep it till I find some pretty young woman who deserves it," she said as both turned their attention to the pump that belched water into the soapstone sink with each of Molly's strokes.

Ill at ease from their misunderstanding of how the gift might be given or received, they occupied themselves with the drama in the fireplace. Alternating winds sucked the flames high up the chimney or blasted air downward to scatter ashes and threaten to extinguish the fire.

"We're gettin' a storm. I kin always tell when the wind is from that direction. Good thing you and your beast ain't on the road," she said.

There's not much to do when marooned in a blizzard with a little sick boy whose mother rations her speech to short sentences, no more often than every fifteen minutes, Moses thought as he listened to the wind rattle the clapboards. He was grateful to the woman for offering Numbers and him shelter, but remained puzzled that she would trust a man to spend the night in the room where she slept. Such overconfidence seemed reckless. He quickly dismissed the notion she was adopting some artifice to seem more desirable before submitting to Moses. It would be interesting to know if she was speculating on his reaction to her bold independence.

"When do we start?" she asked, nudging him from fanciful musings.

"When do we start what?" he added.

"Start to learn me to sign."

"We can't get much done tonight," he said.

"We'll do more than if we don't start at all," Molly persisted. "I seed you watchin' Horatio at supper. What was you thinkin'?"

"I'd say he's a very bright child, the way he handled his food and anticipated many of your moves. Where do you suppose he gets that from?" Moses joked, bringing a faint smile to Molly's lips with the flattery.

"Let's get goin', we're wastin' time."

Horatio watched them, curious about their expressions and gestures, mimicking the two before he fell asleep. Molly's pursuit of a promising communication breakthrough with her son was tireless, practicing signing late into the night.

When at last she lay back in her chair, her face white with fatigue contrasting with dark circled eyes to make a mask, she said, "My head won't hold no more. I gotta sleep."

"You did very well," Moses replied, standing to stretch. "I haven't signed for some time and I was afraid I'd forget, but it all came back. If you have an extra blanket, I'll sleep by the fire."

"No, you come to bed and sleep on the other side of Horatio. I let the fire run low for the night to save logs. In bed us three can all keep warm."

The crackling of rapidly igniting logs woke Moses to find Molly had stoked the embers to bring the fire ablaze while Horatio, proof of children's quick recuperative powers, sat in bed cooing to himself and twisting his fingers in signing imitations. In the windowless kitchen it was difficult to guess the time, but Molly was dressed and fully awake. "We need to keep the path to the barn open. It's already filled back up," Molly said.

"Let me do that," Moses said, sitting on the bed's edge to lace up his boots.

"You work on that. I'll call you when breakfast's ready."

"Where's the shovel?" Moses asked, glad for an outdoor chore and the chance to relieve himself.

"Outside by the door where any rightminded person would put it. And don't pee in the path," she cautioned as he left the kitchen.

The night had dumped a foot of snow to cover halfway up the cornstalk-insulation around the foundation of the house. The slight depression in the snow still traced yesterday's path to the barn, but drifting would soon erase the way if he let the storm get ahead of him. Moses had reopened about half the hundred yards to the barn when Molly's welcoming voice called him to breakfast.

"You're a good worker," she said, "Ya move faster than most farm hands I know."

"That's probably because unlike me they don't have to go anywhere."

"Where ya goin,' Mister?"

"That's a very short story that takes a long time to tell."

"Are ya running from a woman or the law?"

"Neither. How's Horatio doing this morning?" Moses asked, already aware of the boy's improvement but anxious to shake off her questions.

"He's better, a couple more days and he kin go outside if he don't get lost in the snow, which puts me to mind, the rest of the path to the barn needs clearin' so's we can feed the livestock. Don't look like this is ever goin' to stop."

Finished with breakfast, Moses put on his coat, hat, and boots and headed towards the door.

"Oh yeah," she said, "You might also clear the way to the privy. We oughta use it as long as the storm don't block us. It's cold out there, but a helluva lot easier than emptyin' the chamber pots. And every time ya come in bring an armful of wood, we're goin' to need it."

Moses completed clearing the remainder of the path to the barn in less than an hour but realized the intensity of the storm would again fill up the path by dark. In the stable, Numbers' heehaw seemed a donkey derision for doubting the animal's good judgment to take shelter at the farm.

"I know, you were right to dig in your hooves and not go back on the road yesterday," Moses said, snuggling Number's head in an act of atonement.

"Do ya always talk to animals?" Molly said, surprising Moses.

"This is not your run-of-the-mill animal. Numbers is wiser than a lot of people and besides, we're good friends."

"Ya beat all," she replied. "What ya got in this cart?"
"Notions, grooming items, sewing necessities, mostly small items for women."

"Whatcha gonna do with 'em?"

"I'm a push-cart salesman. I serve people in small towns or big cities' poor neighborhoods that can't get to stores."

"And that's what you're in such a hell-bent-for-breakfast rush to do?"

"No, but I must earn a living."

Molly decided she'd never understand him and wouldn't spend any more time trying. Having fed the livestock, they gathered the eggs and Molly milked the cow while Moses mucked out the stalls.

Their fresh footprints in the new snow marking their return to the house made clear the path to the barn would need shoveling once more before going to bed. By chance he looked at the roof of the house and was concerned with the load of snow it was carrying. An additional snowfall during the night could cave it in, but despite his aches and fatigues, he returned to the barn to find some implements for the task.

After several attempts with a long bean pole, he settled for a ladder and rake. Two hours later he'd removed the threat, piling snow banks around the house half way up the windows. Tired and cold, but satisfied with his remedy, he went into the kitchen and fell asleep in a chair by the hearth, still wearing his coat and boots.

When he awakened from his nap, Molly looked up from her sewing and in a rare admission of dependency said, "I don't know what I'd done if ya didn't come along to help."

"You would have thought of something," Moses replied, immediately regretting he sounded mean. "As far as I can see, you handle things very well. Think of how you've run this farm since you've been a widow; the planting, the harvesting. That takes a lot of gumption and good common sense."

"But I ain't never had a blizzard to get through alone afore."

"It's just different, not any harder than what you've done."
"I think ya weak in the head from all that work. Ya need some grub to get ya vitals to working."

"I'll help you get through the storm. It won't be bad, you'll see."

Warmed from the fire, Moses peeled off his greatcoat and placed his boots on the hearth to dry. It was good to be sheltered from the storm - a storm more violent than any in his lifetime, but one unable to vanquish his feeling of peace, secure inside, well-fed and cheered by the companionship of Molly and Horatio.

"Ya don't look so peaked since ya got some food in ya," she observed.

"That's what I needed."

"Looks like ya stuck here for a while 'cause ya ain't goin' nowhere in this weather. Now we got plenty of time for signin'," she said, excited by the prospect. "Let me show ya the signs we made last night to see if I remember them right."

"You don't quit, do you?" Moses said.

"Who was it said that's why I get along so good," she replied, pleased she'd caught him with his own words.

"Let's include Horatio. He's interested, seems to think this is a game we're playing, and if he feels that way, he'll learn quickly. It's the same as making it fun to read; children learn faster."

Molly made the sign for eating. "Is that right?"

Moses nodded in approval, inspiring her to pick up an apple, pretend to eat it, make the sign and encourage Horatio to imitate her. She repeated the process over and over before handing the apple to Horatio. The child studied the fruit for a moment, took a big bite and made a perfect sign, drawing applause from Moses and Molly.

For five days while Moses and his two pupils lurched through the practice of signing, the storm almost entombed the farmhouse with snow halfway up to the second floor. Keeping the way open to the barn required three or four clearings a day by Moses and Molly. Once Horatio came out to watch them and, as his mother predicted, he was temporarily lost when a blanket of snow slid off the roof and covered him. The ever rising banks towering over the way to the barn became increasingly difficult to top with new snow shoveled from the path. Familiar landmarks became distorted into disorienting, alien sizes and shapes. More than once Moses wondered how Molly and Horatio would have survived alone. A claustrophobic person might find this unbearable.

When supper was finished and Horatio put to bed for the night, Molly would occasionally break their fascination with the fire to make an irrelevant comment about the storm, their only common experience, which she hoped would open a conversation to reveal more of Moses.

Once Molly looked up from the dancing firelight and said, "I reckon ya never had snow like this where ya come from."

"They have heavy snow in parts of Russia, but I never saw it because my family moved to Poland before I was born."

"I didn't know ya wuz a Polock," she said, using the common slang with no intent of derision.

"I'm not. I'm a Jew."

"How long do ya figger this will go on?" she said, quickly retreating to the noncontroversial storm.

"I have no idea, but when it's over, the roads will still be blocked for a long time."

"So ya'll be stuck here?"

"Yes, if you can put up with me, but I'll be on my way as soon as I can."

"Ya no bother to me, ya been a big help," she replied, deciding not to include 'and comfort' as it was too telltale. "How's my signin' comin' along?"

"You learn very quickly," Moses answered and added to keep his comments impersonal, "and so does Horatio."

"If ya went tomorrow, da ya reckon Horatio and me could git along good enough?"

"It depends on what you mean by good enough. Could you understand each other better than before you started? Yes. Could you be as fluent as possible? No."

"What's that mean?" she asked, guessing before he answered that Horatio would still be handicapped. "How long would it take ta make us fluent?" she persisted, liking the sound of smoothness in the word 'fluent.'

"Maybe four months, maybe longer. No one can tell when to stop learning signing until they know all the words they need - some keep at it until they can sign all the words in the dictionary."

"What's that?"

"It's a book that tells you the meaning of most of the words in any language."

"Where da ya get this dic-, dicshun - whatever it is?" she asked, fired up by the prospects of such knowledge.

"At a library. Some city stores have them. A few people own them."

"Do ya have one?"

"Yes. I bought one when I came to this country to help me read and write English."

"Can I see it?"

"Next time I go to the barn I'll get it out of the push cart," Moses said, cautious about his growing involvement with the woman but intrigued with her awakening intellect.

Molly, for the time being, controlled her impatience to explore the wonders of a dictionary, but being disciplined, redirected her energies to signing with Moses. As the fire burned down to coals and chill reclaimed the kitchen signaling their day was ending, Moses tested her on the signings he'd previously taught. He tried to trick her, but in the range of her growing vocabulary, she always caught him. With the review of their past lessons complete, Moses was ready for bed, but she added a log to the fire and insisted on learning more, keeping him at it late into the night.

"You're a born student," he told her when she finished her first attempt at linking the words in an understandable sentence.

The density and vastness of the blizzard seemed immeasurable. A twenty-four hour fall now took Moses the better part of the day to keep the passage to the barn open, and reaching above his head to deposit the shoveled snow on top of the ever heightening piles was exhausting. Molly's day was equally tiring from carrying the neatly stacked logs alongside the front door to the kitchen's dwindling supply. Further from the front of the house and now buried in the snow was a jumbled pile of split wood that never reached the front door to be stacked for the kitchen, for who could have ever predicted such a record-breaking blizzard.

One day Moses returned from the barn and handed the use-worn dictionary to Molly, who took it as carefully as a conservator holds a masterpiece. She stood rooted to the floor, her eyes moving from the book to Moses and back again, connecting the three in the gift of learning.

In idle moments she'd huddle by the fire, her minimal ability to read straining to decipher the meaning and pronunciation of the words. Too proud to ask for help or hesitant to bother Moses, she'd locate a word she knew and use it to sound out words with the same letters. She quickly understood that alphabetizing the contents was the only reasonable approach, but was unable to decode the letters in brackets after each word signifying pronunciation and grammar.

Late in the second week the storm's fury was spent, having distorted familiar landmarks into continuous, shadowless, formless whiteness. None of nature's creatures emerged from snow tunnels or the protective thickness of marshes; the open skies could not tempt the birds beyond their cover.

In some places, the snow had climbed up to reach second floor windowsills, helping to insulate the house from the polar blasts. When Moses could no longer deposit snow on top of the banks to the barn, he led Numbers and Molly's horse back and forth over the path to pack down the accumulation. He estimated food supplies, carefully managed, should be adequate till spring. Moses, now relieved of shoveling, exercised the horse and donkey and hauled in a large supply of logs from the sprawling pile.

Each day, time was reserved for studying the dictionary with Molly. Signing increasingly replaced the spoken word to involve Horatio and especially at meals when mouths were filled. Once after Molly failed to correctly form a sign with her hands even after Moses repeated demonstrations, she became frustrated until he placed her before a mirror and, standing close behind, stretched his arms around her to guide her hands.

"See, it's easy," he said, then suddenly caught the reflection of his embrace and backed away.

With no hint of annoyance, Molly returned to more simple signing with Horatio.

Spared nature's destruction, the three returned to normalcy's hum-drum - bathing - an arduous winter's ceremonial. A large, boat-shaped, copper tub was drawn close to the fire and water heated in a variety of kettles, pots and pans. It was no small undertaking to pump and heat the eight receptacles of water, dump it into the tub, soap, scrub and rinse, then empty the tub and repeat the process twice.

What was an ordinary bath for Horatio became the introduction to a ritual of manners for two dissimilar strangers who would bathe in each other's presence. Waiting for Horatio to fall asleep, Molly tried to dismiss her ambivalence about the intimacy ahead with chores, while Moses sat by the fire wondering if cleanliness was more important than modesty. Without speaking, Molly filled the kettle and pots with water then set them on the fire for the next person to bathe.

Moses, not wanting her to feel he was abandoning her in the venture, said, "I guess it's as good a time as any for a bath."

"S'pect so," Molly replied, poking at the logs to get more draft under the blaze.

"How long does it take the water to heat?" Moses asked, knowing the answer. "Do you have any more pots for heating?"

"That's the lot," she answered. "I heered city folks have hot and cold running water, never have to heat like us."

"That's true, but pipes break in freezing weather, making a mess in the house," Moses offered as a consolation.

"Did ya live in a house with runnin' water?"

"In New York City we had a bathroom and a furnace and gas street lights at night, but all that didn't make our life any better than what you have. There are so many people you never get to know anyone. It never gets quiet enough to really think or appreciate the world, but you can shut the bathroom door and take a bath in privacy," Moses said, bringing his anecdote full circle.

She rose to check the temperature of the water. "Guess it's true about a watched pot never boils. Why do ya think that is?"

"I suppose you're so busy watching the pot you don't do anything to distract yourself and time passes slowly."

"Ya know that kettle come down in our family a hundred years."

"I imagine it would have interesting stories to tell if it could talk."

"I learned me one my granny used ta tell. One summer when they was livin' in a lean-to while this house was bein' built, a bear wandered down ta steal some food outda cold cellar. When Granny tried to shoo him away, he chased her up ta the lean-to. She barred the door, then he tried ta climb through the open window. With no gun or club, she thought she was a goner till she spied the boilin' kettle. She had ta empty the whole kettle on his head before he took off. Ain't that somethin'?"

"Now I see where you get your courage."

"Let's see how the water's doin'," Molly said, knowing the time to fill the tub was approaching.

"When you empty all the pots in the tub, how deep is the water?" Moses asked.

"With or without me in it?"

"With you in it."

"'Bout six inches. Be deeper with you."

"Hmm," was all Moses said.

"Now we gotta agree on somethin'. When one of us is in the tub, the other's gotta lie on the bed facin' the other way. Agree?"

"Agree," said Moses, relieved she'd so simply solved a possible problem.

"And another thing, as soon as the hot water's emptied in the tub, the one goin' next should refill the pots and stoke up the fire under them."

"How do we decide who goes first?" he asked.

"Hold ya fingers behind ya back and the one who guesses closest to the total of ya fingers and mine chooses who goes first. Ready," she said.

"I say eight," Moses guessed.

"And I say eleven. Show them," she called, showing three fingers to his four.

"I win," Moses laughed.

"Okay. Who goes first?"

"I yield my right to decide to you."

Chapter 14

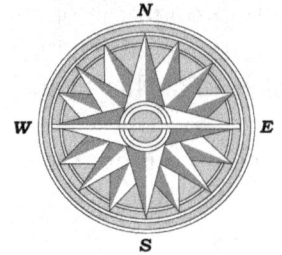

Early one morning when the reach of the sun neared the vernal equinox, Moses awakened to find Horatio standing at his bedside signing, "I love you." He pulled the little boy under the bedcovers beside him and they cuddled until his beard tickled giggles from the child. Moses pointed to the boy's mother, presumably asleep, then brought his forefinger to his lips for 'quiet' and settled down, hoping to return to sleep. For a few minutes Horatio lay motionless, but rested he began to fidget. Moses' beard, the object of Horatio's attention, was curled around the little boy's fingers then parted and brushed into wing-like projections. Completing his tonsorial creation, Horatio pulled Moses' beard up, covering all the man's face but the nose. No longer able to suppress the giggles, the little boy buried his face in the covers.

Molly, ever aware of her son's waking moments, was roused but pretended to be asleep while peeking at the man and child at horseplay and was rewarded by their joy. In the weeks since the stranger, now her best friend, her only friend, came seeking water she'd discovered absolute trust, the excitement of knowledge and the warmth of quiet affection. He was a generous soul who practiced the belief that a gift had no strings attached. She often thought of his comforting calm through the storm and his help in its aftermath. Thanks to him the livestock survived, the roof escaped collapse and they kept busy improving their signing, discovering the wonders of the dictionary and learning from games Moses made up. Her most vivid memory was of Moses putting aside his chimney repairs to embolden Horatio to hold his hand and jump from the roof with him into a huge snowpile, disappearing then emerging like two snowmen.

As the winter melted away to bare the earth and warm days and cold nights gorged sugar maples with sap, the man and boy set taps in the wrinkled trunks and hung buckets to catch the golden liquid for boiling. One day Moses, unaware of Molly's presence, signed Horatio if they wanted honey next winter it might be time to make a box-housing for a beehive and start a colony near the hollyhocks. Moses had never said how long he'd stay, but now it seemed he wouldn't leave before the flowers bloomed.

Like all creation's deliveries, the long-awaited birth of spring was not without winter's labor pains. Trickles of water, which began slipping between the frozen earth and rapidly melting snowpack, now turned to liquid sheets sliding downward to swampy low areas, diverted only by the erosions they cut. Fortunately the barn and lesser outbuildings were set on a slight rise, providing a natural drain away from them, but the house resting below a concave hillside was exposed to serious undermining unless the run-off was turned aside. Trenching would take too long even for a farm crew, impossible for Molly and him.

"The horse, why not the horse?" Moses suddenly exclaimed at their breakfast.

"What about the horse?" Molly asked.

"I'll hitch up the horse and plow a deep furrowed arc up the hillside to carry the water around either side of the house."

"Did ya ever plow?"

"No," Moses said, temporarily puzzled by the potential obstacle to his resourcefulness. "Have you?"

"Ya forgit I'm a farmer. I'll teach ya."

When spring's inundation receded to open land and established vegetation grew rapidly as bamboo, the thought of leaving tugged at Moses. But the prospect of Molly struggling alone to keep ahead of Nature postponed his departure. They sowed grain in patches, avoiding the seed-rotting, soaked spots, hoping the early growing season would not pass them by.

"This here's gonna look like the moths got it," Molly said good humouredly as she surveyed the uneven growth of their planting.

"When your neighbors see it, tell them you had a greenhorn farmhand, but you fired him," Moses replied.

Returning from the barn one day, Molly reported, "My mare's gonna foal."

"How can that be?" Moses asked.

"Musta been the time ya donkey broke tether and ya found him in the mare's stall eatin' her oats."

"Looks as though he went in for more than oats. Guess you're going to have a mule to help you work the property."

"Another mouth ta feed. We'll be lucky ta work the horse through harvest."

"Well, since Numbers was responsible he can fill in for the mare."

"Never thought a donkey could mount a mare, being at different levels and all," Molly said.

"You'd be surprised what a male can do when he sets his mind to it," Moses replied.

It was a summer of bountiful prospects. The maple sap had been collected, boiled down to golden syrup one-twentieth the volume of the tree's gift, decanted into large glass jars capped with paraffin wax and a glass lid and sealed with a wire loop under tension. Bees made their daily appointed rounds between flower and hive. Blossoms on the apple and cherry trees gave notice of the fruit to follow. Green grain grew as though each stalk was in a race with its neighbor.

Nature's industry encouraged Moses and Molly, with Horatio's supervision, to repair all the winter damage to house and barn. Even the privy seemed less of an outcast. Moses dammed up the brook where it ran through a swale to make a pond and taught Horatio to swim. Its more practical uses, he told Molly, were water storage for the cattle and ice for the cold cellar, now rescued from neglect. Molly matched his industry, repairing and making his clothes, planting a kitchen garden and quilting. Horatio progressed with his signing and ventured further into the dictionary. Though not as skilled as his mother, he surpassed Moses at milking the cow.

Their frequent chores in different places in the barn reinforced their mutual dependence with no threat to individuality, but this was more evident as they separated to different parts of the farm on more distant errands. Sharing work and pleasures with Molly and Horatio had become so natural Moses was unprepared for the tension that finally surfaced between staying and his goaless journey.

At last the persistent goading of his conscience drove him to get an idea of the effect his learning would have and he hitched Numbers to the cart for a test. The donkey accepted the harness and pulled the loaded cart with ease until he reached the opening in the stone wall where he stopped, snorted, dug in his hooves and brayed twice. No treats or threats could persuade the animal to pass through the wall's opening and when Moses walked out of the farmyard down the lane towards the main road pretending to leave, Numbers brayed twice, turned and started back toward the barn.

Several times over the following weeks Moses tried to coax Numbers to haul the push-cart out of the farmyard but was frustrated by the animal's disobedience. With harvest season now underway, Moses decided to direct all Number's energy to bringing in the crops and postpone working on the animal's stubbornness. Horatio, observing the test of the man and beast, decided the problem could be resolved if Numbers could speak and was often found in the barn trying to teach the donkey to sign. While the donkey's uncloven hooves made this impossible, the project was not totally unsuccessful because Numbers and Horatio became friends.

With the ripening of August and September, harvesting became a race to gather the yields before the arrival of damaging rains. When the picking, digging and reaping had been completed, the three spent a few lazy days sitting on the porch looking at the spirit-regenerating wonders of the world -- buzzing insects, diaphanous butterflies, acrobatic birds, ever-changing cloud murals, squirrels busy collecting winter stores, a woodchuck nervously popping its head from a hole and deer gathering at dusk at the pond made a tapestry of tranquility. Now the world seemed at rest for days to be lived.

With the afternoon's heat retreating, twilight signaled each to the last chores till morning. Molly, the first to rise from her place on the porch, took a look at the sunset, breathed the cool of the evening and went into the kitchen. Hand-in-hand Moses and Horatio strolled to the barn to feed the livestock, gather eggs and milk the cow. A quick dousing of arms, hands and faces in cool wellwater from the outside pump gained entry to the kitchen with its enticing aromas.

At supper that evening, Horatio complained that his bedtime was getting earlier and earlier even though he was growing older and older. Moses explained that this very day was the autumnal equinox, when night and day were equal and days would begin to get shorter than nights till just before next Christmas. Then nights would grow shorter than days. However, the celestial lesson was no consolation for Horatio's disappointment that his bedtime would remain the same.

"Can I sleep in the barn tonight?" Horatio suddenly signed.

"Why?" Molly inquired.

"Because Numbers is acting lonely and we're friends."

"What do you think?" Molly asked Moses.

"I don't see any reason why he shouldn't, but he can't take a candle in there," Moses replied, continuing the signing so Horatio could follow the exchange.

Anxious, Molly walked Horatio to the barn, laid blankets on a hay mound near Numbers, kissed him goodnight then hurried back to the house, aware his communication was severed not only by their physical separation but also by his silenced ears.

"He'll be fine," Moses assured her. "If the animals get disturbed by anything, they'll wake us up. Ever think of his getting a dog?"

"I sure hope he's going to be fine like you say," Molly answered, too distracted to answer his question. Her thoughts drifted off to other times and other places before returning with a melancholy ditty.

> When Ah was born Ah was the runt of eleven
> Four was boys and the girls numbered seven
> Mind ya pappy or ya won't git ta heaven
>
> Boys beat girls all the grown folks said
> They cin plow and git the livestock fed
> Girls cin only plant an asparagus bed
>
> By five Ah was wearin' hand-me-downs
> While my older sisters were practicin' frowns
> Or passin' the time makin' dandelion crowns
>
> At ten Ah was milkin' and swillin' pigs
> Or cleanin' dung off rich men's gigs
> Or cleanin' dung off poor men's rigs
>
> By twelve my body began to redo
> My lookin' and thinkin' seemed brand new
> And boys got grabby when they's close to you
>
> At sixteen Pappy said Ah was growed like the rest
> It's almost past time to be leavin' the nest
> Take what you can, don't wait for the best
>
> At seventeen Ah tied the knot with a fella
> In my hand-me-down dress and a fancy umbrella
> Like the storybook prince and poor Cinderella
>
> He drove his wagon to a place by a hill
> With a surroundin' stone wall and a waterin' rill
> And rundown house from his pappy's will

> We started to work on the day we arrived
> With the land gone fallow we barely survived
> In spite of toilin' we barely survived
>
> 'For long he beat me to make me work more
> And yellin' and cussin' me out like a whore
> Wouldn't believe his was the child that Ah bore
>
> When my sweet boy Horatio was only four
> His Daddy without warnin' walked out the door
> Killed by a tree he returns no more

Molly, as if waking from a dream, stopped her song and returned to Moses' presence.

"I'm goin' ta bed," she said.

"I'll look in on Horatio and then sleep on the porch," Moses told her. "It's still warm enough outside."

"No, Ah want ya with me."

Consummated, they fell away from each other, consumed by the ferocity of their coupling, spent for an indeterminate time, stripped of their separate identities.

Neither slept the slumber of lovers, nor tried to revisit their extravagance not yet a memory. The man and woman now lay in separation.

He said, "I will leave tomorrow."

"I know. Ya made the land give me and Horatio a big harvest. Ya helped make Horatio and me whole. It's time for ya to go."

"The weather is right for traveling. With any luck, I should reach Buffalo before it turns bad."

"What will ya do if the donkey won't budge?"

"I'll push the cart myself as I did before Numbers appeared and leave him with the boy. But don't say anything until we know."

Before the sun rose to wake the farm animals and while the resident birds sang their last pre-dawn encore, Molly rose to wash and dress, taking care not to disturb Moses. Waiting for the fire to come up, she prepared the batter for bread and biscuits she'd bake for his trip. A quick trip to the cold cellar for a side of ham and a slab of cheese completed her pack of provisions.

The aroma of the baking dough coaxed Moses to consciousness. Fighting the temptation to return to the warm bed, he wrapped himself in a towel, walked to the pond and dove in. His instant awakening was not much faster than his departure from the pond for the warmth of the fireplace.

"Good morning," he said, still shivering from the cold bath.

"Good mornin,' Moses. I guess ya lost ya mind, swimming in that cold pond, so it's probably time for ya ta leave," Molly replied, trying to laugh away the sadness of his departure. "When ya finished dressin', will you get Horatio?"

"Of course. It will be hard saying goodbye to him."

"Maybe ya better tell him when I'm not around. He thinks it upsets me if I see him cry."

Moses entered the barn undetected to find Horatio signing to Numbers that the two of them would always be best friends and every night would sleep together to keep the donkey from getting lonely. To Horatio's delight, the animal dipped his muzzle into the feed, appearing to nod in agreement. *How wonderful,* Moses thought, *to have a child's innocent make-believe.* Seeking not to violate the boy's privacy by spying, he backed out of sight and slammed the barn door to announce his presence.

"Will you sit down here with me for a moment, Horatio? There's something I want to tell you while your mother's cooking breakfast," Moses signed.

"I hope it won't take too long. I'm getting hungry."

"I've been here almost a year and your mom and you have made me as happy as I've ever been. Some things I couldn't have done without you two, some things you couldn't have done without me. In a way we've been a family."

"We lived through a harsh time and learned how to pull together and survive even if we have another bad winter."

"You and your mom learned quickly how to sign so you can understand each other, which makes everything easier. You're a very smart boy and I know you'll be a very smart man. Each day you're more of a help to your mom, so I don't worry about how things will turn out for you two. I think I've done all I can and now it's time to continue the trip I was on when I stopped here for water."

"Will you come back, Moses?" the boy asked, standing up feeling it gave him more courage than sitting.

"I can't lie to you, Horatio. I don't know. I'm looking for something I can't describe. It's like you before you learned to sign. Is there anything you want to ask me?"

"Will Numbers go with you?"

"I don't know, but if he does, remember the mare is going to foal before long and you'll have to train a baby mule so you'll be busy. Anything else?"

"Can we go in for breakfast now? I'm hungry. And will you tell Ma I didn't cry?"

"And will you help me move the push cart out of the barn? It's easier for two men to handle," Moses said.

All through breakfast, Moses caught Horatio stealing glimpses at him and Molly. Each time the boy looked up from his food to ask for another blueberry pancake or the maple syrup, he'd glance quickly at the adults to try to read their feelings, then return to eating. Attempting to avoid confronting his departure, Molly and Moses discussed the condition of the farm -- the preparedness of a full silo, the weatherproofing improvements in the house -- subjects both knew were intended to make her feel secure and assure him he'd done everything possible for her welfare.

At last when there was no more breakfast or conversation to keep them, Molly said, "I've packed enough to feed ya for four days."

"Thank you for looking out for me."

"Ya probably should think about goin'. Remember the days are gittin' shorter."

"I'll help you clean up the breakfast things," he said.

"No, there will always be dishes to wash."

Upset by their imminent separation, Moses and Molly had thoughtlessly stopped and substituted speech for its faster exchange.

Hurt then feeling left out, Horatio jumped up from the table and began signing, "I though I was part of the family. Why can't you tell me everything that's going on? I can see neither of you want to say goodbye and I don't want Moses to go, but he says he has to, and he's always told the truth."

"Horatio's right, I have to go and now."

Moses left the house headed straight to the barn, fetched Numbers and harnessed him to the push cart. Loading the sack of food Molly had prepared, he stopped and cradled Horatio against him, stood and held Molly at arm's length in a long silence. Neither spoke as they captured a memory.

Then Moses lowered her arms and turned to the Numbers. "Giddy-up."

The donkey disregarded the command.

"Giddy-up, Numbers."

Only statuesque immobility.

"You heard me, now come on we've got to go," Moses said. Losing his patience, he added a pointless appeal. "We mustn't keep these people standing here."

Each verbal command to Numbers, not understood by Horatio until Molly signed him, became more ludicrous than the last as the donkey planted himself more securely, setting mother and son into howling laughter.

Moses, unable to pretend to be angry any longer, appealed to the donkey's good nature. Holding his muzzle with both hands, Moses looked directly into the face of the animal and spoke sadly.

"Well, I guess I'll have to leave you and go on by myself. It will be very lonely without you. Won't you reconsider your decision?"

Numbers remained unwilling to capitulate, staring back with unblinking, warm, brown, liquid eyes at Moses as though saying to him, "Don't be a silly ass."

The absurdity of the situation won out and Moses joined the two to laugh at himself. He unharnessed Numbers, saluted Molly and Horatio and pushed his cart through the opening in the stone wall enclosing the farmyard onto the undulating country road.

Molly and Horatio stood watching Moses on his way, disappearing over a rise in the road to reappear moments later on another hill. When he no longer returned to their view, the boy and the woman realized Numbers had remained untethered where he'd been unharnessed. The boy signed to his mother and she responded, telling him his idea was a good one. Horatio stood facing the donkey, stroking his muzzle for a long time, and then signed Numbers not once but twice and a third time. The animal gave a snort and trotted through the opening in the stone wall enclosing the farmyard and down the road towards Moses.

Chapter 15

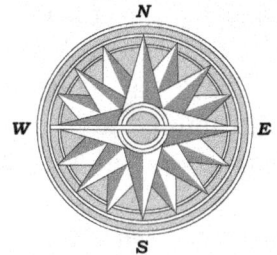

Three miles along the road west of the farm, Numbers caught up with Moses puffing and huffing up a hill, laboring under the illusion the cart was heavier than the last time he'd pushed it. The donkey, frolicking in reunion, brayed with such force goats in a nearby meadow choked on their cuds and the somniferous drones of mating male cicadas were stilled, to the puzzlement of the species' females.

Moses, proclaiming his pleasure with the donkey's arrival, attempted to return the salutation but only managed to sound like a goose honking.

Without any persuasion, Numbers backed up to be harnessed to the cart, ready to share Moses' journey.

Never fully appreciative of his dependence on Numbers until the third mile of solitary travel, Moses reproached himself for taking life's blessings for granted. He'd always assumed his humane treatment and the donkey's obedience -- a good master and dutiful beast of burden -- fulfilled the relationship, but the animal's refusal to leave the farm when they stopped for water displayed an uncanny awareness of Molly's and Horatio's needs. Then as conclusive affirmation of the donkey's prescience, Numbers remained bound to serve Molly and Horatio until they released him to join Moses on his journey.

Back on the road, Chicago was no longer the magnet of his destination but merely a stop along the route to somewhere. His obligation to family and employees to evaluate opportunities in the muscular city by the lake remained and he'd meet it, but building a retail business of specialty items was no longer his interest.

He put aside his musing for the more immediate concerns of coming to a town soon that would generate enough sales for barge fare to Buffalo or perhaps even Toledo before starting the last leg of the journey to Chicago. Canal travel, he rationalized, would offer plenty of time to write to his family more frequently, and caught up in self-redemption, he committed to mail a letter at the next town with a post office.

There was still considerable harvesting to be done in the fields. Farmers trying to stay ahead of rainy delays worked long past dark to save their crops from the rot of the season's typical storms. Those fortunate enough to have gathered their perishables were speeding their produce to market from byways to his road, their increasing numbers predicting the proximity of a town. With summer's nurturing, the stone-cold loneliness of wagoners crossing empty winter miles never seemed to have existed. Exuberant camaraderie was common currency as most teamsters had come to know each other. In fact, the absence of a highway veteran became known in both directions of his route within days. Newcomers, though treated civilly by most, were not accepted as regulars for several years. However, Moses, no exception to this rule, received unusual attention if not acceptance because of the odd cart piled high with uncommon merchandise and numerous questions to be asked about the "hand-painted jackass" pulling the contraption.

"Howdy stranger! Did you forget the two back wheels to your wagon this morning?" one good-natured driver inquired.

Another observed, "I see your nag got shrunk in the wash," while a third wondered, "What's that goin' to be when it's growed up?"

There was nothing malicious in their teasing, and the banter made Moses feel no less at ease in this land than any his journey had led him to.

As the day warmed to bake away the dew, any disturbance to the dirt road raised clouds of hazy dust. An approaching sheep drover and his flock surrounding him were made legless by the agitated particles, giving them the appearance of walking to heaven through unwashed cumulae. Moses' quick glance at his own pants confirmed this morning's change to clean clothes was a wasted effort.

"Hail!" the drover called after whistling instructions to his dog to keep the sheep from straying.

"Hail, sir drover!" Moses replied, keeping alive the pretense of the man with the sixteenth century garb and manners.

"I beg you sir, please address me as shepherd, drover has such a callous sound to it. I was once a drover of goats, but one cannot establish and affinity for those creatures, they are so wayward and perverse. Sheep are more in keeping with my spiritual persuasions and contemplative way of life -- congenial, obedient and appreciative, a soothing relief from people's prattle."

"Is your farm nearby?" Moses inquired, guessing the man lived in a secluded section and missed an occasional encounter with others despite his derision.

"Oh, no! I'm a hermit...protector of the rights of individualism, a font of solitude by God's will, by choice and by myself." He chuckled, pleased with his joke. "And what, may I ask, brings you this way with so strange a contraption and indeterminate hybrid?"

"I'm a push cart peddler with goods to sell women."

"But you're not pushing the cart, the beast is pulling it, and you'll find no women on this country road."

"True, but my friend Numbers likes to help," Moses said, gesturing at the donkey. "And I was hoping to sell your young ladies something," he added, pointing to the sheep, indicating they were prospective customers in this ridiculous exchange.

"For sure you jest. My females are as finely dressed as needs be until they meet their maker," the shepherd said, wiping away a tear with such an exaggerated gesture it would not go unnoticed by Moses.

"What is your destination?" Moses asked.

"The Brothers of Mercy Abattoir."

"Is that a monastery?"

"No, a slaughterhouse."

"Seems an odd name for a slaughterhouse," Moses commented.

"I named it that to ease my conscience. Becoming so attached to the creatures, I feel better thinking they're going to a religious retreat. After all, I'm a shepherd with an obligation to precedent."

The solemnity of the shepherd's mission seemed to demand a moment of silence, and the road's dust was so drying to the throats of both men, words were rationed not wasted.

"Pigs. Have you ever thought about pigs?" Moses asked. "You might not feel as close to them. I mean, you might not identify with them so much."

The hermit recoiled from the suggestion of pigs, pantomiming his revulsion to their odiferous unpleasantness by holding his nose. Moses, attempting recovery from his faux pas, quickly returned to the primary subject of sheep.

"Maybe you'd be happier keeping the sheep and carding their wool for the carpet companies or the textile manufacturers."

"Yes, yes. There are so many choices when one stops to think about what life offers. Perhaps I should return to my pasture and contemplate the significance of our encounter. You've given me a whole new perspective. Thank you for the confusion," the shepherd said before whistling his dog to turn the flock around, all disappearing in a cloud of dust.

At an uncalculated distance farther along his way, Moses came to a crossroads with a watering trough on the east corner, church on the south, a general store on the west and a school on the north. At the trough he caught the cool, clear water from the pipe to the spring in cupped hands while Numbers glupped his fill from the large, round, wooden tub.

As he leaned back against the cart to enjoy the quiet, he was startled by shrieks of childish delight coming from the schoolyard across the way. Investigating, he found a dozen little boys and girls crowding close to a tall, skinny, middle-aged man wearing a black stove-pipe hat and an ill-fitting, plaid suit short in the sleeves and trousers. His general appearance and jerky movements resembled a string marionette in action as he hopped from one foot to the other, his stove-pipe hat remaining secure, defying the law of gravity. His hands were constantly in motion, pulling a flag-decorated line fifteen feet long from his coat sleeve or rubbing his vest before leaning down to extract an apple from a little girl's long hair, then throwing the apple into the air to land on his shoulder, run down his arm and disappear while he doffed his hat and bowed to his overjoyed audience.

Moses joined the youngsters to get a better look at the performer and performance. Startled by the intrusion of a stranger, the children pulled away from Moses until he asked and received permission to stay, the consenting nods outnumbering reluctant murmurs. To avoid towering over the children, Moses sat cross-legged, enraptured by the juggler's skill. It took but one slight-of-hand trick to lure the youngsters back from their attention to Moses to the land of disbelief.

The juggler completed his routine with six apples circling in the air until each in turn as it came down was split in two while the others floated skyward. When the last apple was halved, he handed each child a portion.

"More! More!" they begged, hoping to substitute a blackboard for black magic, but the juggler with perfect showmanship had timed his entertainment to conclude as the school bell ended the recess. The children slowly returned to class, chanting how much they loved the juggler as the school room door closed behind them.

"You certainly made those children happy," Moses told the juggler. "I'm glad I came along when I did or I'd have missed a great performance."

"Kids are so responsive. I've never had a bad performance when they're in the audience. Now I only perform for them."

"From what regular line of work do you earn a living?"

"Stimulatin' young minds is my only business."

"But they can't pay you. How do you survive?"

"It's a long story, but I see I'm goin' your direction so if you want company we could talk on our way."

"I'd like that. Just a moment while I get my cart."

"What you got in the cart?"

"Small household needs, mostly women's things -- hairpins, needles, thread."

"Where you takin' 'em?" the juggler asked.

"I'm going to sell all along my way to Chicago."

"Chicago, eh. Tough city. I used to play there on the vaudeville circuit. Tough but not near as mean as Erie and Kankakee. If they didn't like your act, they'd throw rotten eggs, fruit, even bottles at you. Say, that's a peculiar lookin' donkey. Can't say I ever see his likes before."

"He's from a breed common in the Holy Land. My name's Moses, by the way."

"Mine's Herbert T. Ruggles. Some got to callin' me Ruggles Juggles after seein' my act, but then just shorted it to Juggles. Did you bring the donkey from the Holy Land?" Juggles asked, always interested in pursuing a fanciful tale.

"No," Moses replied rather abruptly, not wishing to relate his discovery of Numbers to another doubter. "You were telling me about your career in vaudeville before we were sidetracked by my push cart. Have you given that up? You're very good, you know."

"I keep my act by entertaining kids. I had to give up vaudeville 'cause somethin' came up."

"It must have been discouraging to give up a talent that made people happy."

"Haven't you ever had to quit somethin' you really liked?" the juggler asked.

"Not yet. I'm not sure what I'm meant to do."

"That's real peculiar," Juggles said, becoming silent for a moment to consider such a quandary before abandoning the subject. "You seem like a smart feller, decent too, and I suppose we'll never meet again. Might as well tell you my story. I'm an orphan, grew up in a Philadelphia asylum with seventy other kids. Some of the kids came to the home after their parents died, the rest ended up there when their parents just left them at the door. Most like me never knew their mother or father. When I got a little older and smarter I began to realize each time a new kid came in the orphanage got more money from the state so I figured I was worth something. But I felt like a piece of goods to be labeled with a dollar sign.

"The only person who didn't treat us this way was an old man with a mustache who came every Christmas and handed out presents to the kids. He tried to be fair all around, but he always seemed to favor me. One of the kids said he looked like me. I didn't pay any attention to that 'cause he had grey hair and a mustache."

"Did you ever find out who he was?" Moses asked.

"Don't get ahead of me. When I was fifteen, the orphanage moved to another buildin' and records were left around in open cartons in the cellar. I found them and read every damn one before they were recovered and locked up. I learned my mother's first name was Harriet, but only an X for her last name. She was listed as a school teacher who had been disowned by her family. There was no record of my father."

"What about your Santa Claus?"

"He comes later in my story. As soon as I found out about my mother, I ran away from the orphanage to look for her. 'Course I'd never been in the outside world before so I never thought about how I'd live. It didn't take long to learn I had to eat and have a place to stay and to get along I had to work. I was lucky 'cause a circus was passing through town and they gave me a job hauling water for the animals, pounding tent stakes, cleaning up the mess before the show left town."

"That's a hard life for a fifteen-year-old boy," Moses said.

"I figured by travelin' with the circus it would take me to lots of towns and I could look for my mother. Wrong! The only time I had off was when we were on the road. Along the way I became a good friend with one of the clowns who taught me how to juggle. He was so good he used eggs and they weren't hardboiled. The first time I tried it, my breakfast was spattered all over the floor. Occasionally if my friend was sick, 'cause he drank a lot, I'd substitute for him. After I'd been with the circus about two years, my friend said he was quittin' to go with the vaudeville and offered me a job in his act and I took it."

"Was that better than the circus?"

"Much, 'cause the layovers in each city was two or three times longer than the circus stops, so I could look for my mother."

"Nevertheless, you were still always traveling with no home of your own," Moses replied, reminded of his own life.

"I got used to it. Matter of fact, I became so restless bein' in one town a week was about all I could take. For twenty-five years I played circus side shows, carnivals, vaudeville -- I even tried plays but they said I was fidgety and spoke the lines the way I wanted. About this time in my life I was doin' a show in Philly and got the urge to visit the orphanage. I wasn't too sure why, but I had to do it. They was nice as pie and told me they'd been tryin' to locate me for some time. The old man who brought us presents every Christmas had died and his will specified a lot of money be donated to the orphanage and even more if they located me. Well, the old man's lawyers called in the orphanage people and me and after a lot of questions and even an eye test they was satisfied it was me. It turned out he was my mother's father but not until he was dyin' could he take back the daughter he banished for havin' a child out of wedlock and by so doing he was able to accept me as his grandson. The old man hoped I'd find her and tell her how sorry he was, and he left me a legacy to live off while I searched."

"Ah! So you verified your name Ruggles came from him and your mother," Moses said, relieved a part of the mystery was solved.

"No, his name was Bankhardt. My mother must have given me a false name to hide me from my father."

"What a story."

"For five years I've visited every school I could, using my juggling to entertain teachers as well as the kids, hoping I will find her or someone who has information on her."

"You know so little about her. How will you find her?" Moses asked.

"I won't. She'll find me."

"I don't see how," Moses said.

"Look in my eyes," Juggles told Moses. "What do you see?"

"One iris is green, the other is blue."

"That's how she'll find me."

Moses and Juggles walked westward, discussing a range of unrelated hypotheses in no particular order as newly-met often do, and having no previous association but being reasonable people, they felt no constraints in the conversation.

Moses quickly learned Juggles' continual use of schools' and municipal libraries' sources to search for his mother had stimulated an appetite for knowledge not encountered in most people. Juggles prioritized each leg of each search based on facts rather than unsubstantiated opinion, but perhaps most remarkable of all was the great distance he'd covered. Moses wondered if Juggles' quest would ever be rewarded. And would his own?

Not far from where the Mohawk River bends ever so slightly south from the eastern course of its flow to the sea, the two parted, Juggles to visit schools, Moses to sell his goods and write a letter to his family. At this place three hamlets, once separated, had swollen to breach their boundaries and spill all over each other, leaving a stranger ignorant of what town he entered or left. The only vestige of these communities' identities were the Greek, German or Indian names chosen by the founders suggesting scholarly pretension, and the architectural preferences for brick on the north side of the river while those on the south showed off their modesty with wood.

By day's end Moses had sold a surprising amount of merchandise to the north side matrons in their dormered mansards. It seemed reasonable that a few more sales of this volume would pay barge fare at least to Rochester, a real landmark of progress to Chicago. That night by candlelight in the stuffy room above a local tavern's bar, Moses wrote a ten-page letter to his family, employees and friends recounting his experiences to date. Putting pen to paper emphasized what a long time it had taken to go such a short distance. He knew his delays at Nitti's and Molly's could not be reasonably explained in a letter, so he simply mentioned them as temporary stops necessary for his and others' wellbeing.

A hearty breakfast and a trip to the post office satisfied his stomach and conscience sufficiently to resume his sales coverage on the northside of the river. He crossed to the south and entered neighborhoods of small wooden houses occupied by laborers' families. Purchases were more deliberate and for smaller dollar amounts, reflecting the policy of two nearby, large manufacturing plants that dominated the market's work force and kept pay scales and family incomes low. One factory produced national brand firearms and the other typewriters, a relatively new device with which a competent operator could print a full-page letter in less than ten minutes, a marvel by anyone's standards.

When Moses' sales continued to be disappointing, he returned to his original strategy of calling on prospects too busy to visit stores only a few miles away. Heading towards the town's outskirts, he stopped at homes where his service was welcomed and purchases invariably were accompanied by the customer's eagerness to chat.

Moses' instinct was correct for by midafternoon he'd sold the day's quota and stopped to eat while Numbers grazed. Resting his back against a massive oak and warmed by the autumn sun, he listened to the giant shed its acorns and watched squirrels scurry to gather the scaly cups for the winter ahead. The idyllic course of the river weaving its way to the horizon transported Moses to that place between sleep and wakefulness of carefree surrender.

As quickly as he'd yielded some instinct roused him to confront an object silhouetted against the sky where there had been none before. Unable to identify this intruder with the sun in his eyes Moses changed position.

Standing before him was a man dressed in a mountain of leather.

"Who are you?" Moses asked directly without first offering the courtesy of a greeting. The stranger lumbered closer to blot out the sun.

"What are you doing here?"

The only response from the stranger to Moses' question was to squat and sit cross-legged face-to-face with the peddler.

The man's overpowering physical presence was made more formidable by his silence. A strong odor of herbs escaped his mouth with each breath he exhaled; deep-set, unflinching, dark eyes peered out from beneath a broad brow accentuating his high cheekbones. A roughly chiseled nose and jaw confirmed he was an Indian even before Moses saw the jet-black hair tied in a ponytail.

"What do you want?" Moses demanded.

After an unnecessarily long visual inspection, the Indian answered in English deformed by an undetermined accent. "You late."

"What do you mean, I'm late?"

"You late," the Indian repeated, becoming irritable. "You brother wait, four harvests pass, you don't come. I walk Mohawk from great falls in west to Hudson and back two times look for you. You not anywhere. You come late. Lightning Lance not wait much longer."

"Lightning Lance! You said Lightning Lance? Where is he?" Moses demanded.

"He wait for you there," the Indian said, pointing west.

"I have to go to Chicago, that's west. Is he there? I promised a lot of people I'd go to Chicago."

"You do what must be done."

The Indian's ambiguous reply annoyed Moses who surprisingly didn't object when told, "We go now," but complied by hitching Numbers to the push cart and following the leather man.

Trailing his gruff guide allowed plenty of time to study the Indian's peculiar attire without being observed. Clad in a great head-to-toe coat of leather patches, he looked like a giant vertical armadillo and despite the weight he carried moved with remarkable agility. The only deviation from the scaly mammal's appearance were calf-high leather boots with crow feathers dangling from the laces and his long, ash staff, grooved its whole length by a vine that had encircled the sapling.

For the entire afternoon the Indian set the pace, always keeping Moses at his fastest stride, and even when the sun cast long shadows warning stragglers to reach their night's lodging, the Indian showed no concern for seeking such comfort. At last Moses, who'd not spoken since they started out, called ahead to him.

"Numbers and I need to stop for the night and get some food and rest. Is there a town nearby? We probably should have stopped at the last one."

"No town. Two more miles we stay my cave."

"What do you mean, your cave?"

"Many caves where I walk, I stay."

"What do you do for food?" Moses asked, feeling guilty he'd not offered the Indian any of his bread and cheese.

"People feed me, I do jobs for them, slaughter pigs, sheep, cows; dig outhouses, fix kettles, short jobs no one wants. No more talk. We hungry, beat dark."

The Indian pointed to a thicket not unlike dozens of others on a ridge three hundred yards ahead. In the age of glaciers a huge sheet of stone had sheared from the summit and slid down to rest against the base of the hill, snugly sealing a cave except for a narrow gap on its leeward side behind the heavy underbrush. Nearby a spring bubbled up to fill a hollow gravel deposited by that same geological landslide. The men and beast together bent to satisfy their thirst from the long hike before the Indian nudged Moses and pointed at Numbers then at a stretch of lush pasture for grazing. Another poke in the ribs and more gestures energized Moses to tether the donkey and follow the Indian into the cave to prepare for the night.

The cave's entrance was shaped like a large vertical pea pod, only the opening at the middle large enough for a man to squeeze through sideways. Several small fissures in the stone ceiling ran diagonally upward to the exterior surface of the hill encasing them to serve the dual purpose of admitting light and venting fire smoke. The temperature in the main chamber, while cooler than outside, was well above that of the fissures where the Indian stored food.

With a survivor's efficiency the Indian started a fire, retrieved smoked venison and dried corn from a cold cache and, using a hunting knife carried inside his leather coat, chopped the food into stew-sized pieces. The corn and meat ingredients were dumped into a kettle and mixed with a minty aromatic liquid, cooked until steaming, then equally divided into two surprisingly delicious portions.

When both finished eating, the Indian removed the crude utensils, scrubbed them clean with sand, indicated that one of the two piles of balsam branches was Moses' bed, then lay down on the other and fell asleep, all without a word. Wearied from the day's long trek, Moses was quickly overtaken by a series of short but vivid vignettes --

surrealism co-existing with reason as though that were the natural order of slumber.

"Good morning," the man at the crossroads said as Moses guided his cart towards the fallen tree where the stranger sat.

"Good morning," Moses replied. "It's a fine day to be about."

"Don't let appearances fool you. Who knows what lies ahead? I see you're still peddling knick-knacks, gim-cracks and rick-racks. Do you ever sell any? Your cart looks fuller than ever."

Moses, who'd been trying to recall where he'd seen the stranger, suddenly remembered the fellow, but he'd been quite indecisive in their earlier meeting.

"Now I remember. You're the shepherd who was so protective of your sheep. Aren't you concerned about their welfare now you're not watching over them?"

"Not at all. Do you recall my dog Shep? Really my righthand man, to coin a phrase. He turned into a very smart, responsible young fellow and looks after them as well as I ever could."

"But you must miss no longer guarding your flock? What do you do now?"

"I guard people, some very special, some like you who aren't special yet," the ex-shepherd said.

"You're certainly not very flattering," Moses replied, amused by the other's candor. "How far are you going on this road?"

"As far as need be," the ex-shepherd answered, telling Moses nothing.

They walked and talked for several miles till the road crossed a stream on an arched stone bridge where they rested and ate the remainder of Moses' bread and cheese. It was not long before the combination of exercise, food, warm fresh air and the murmur of flowing water caused them to stretch out and be hidden in the full, green grass at the stream's edge.

Raucous laughs and obscene exchanges by two men woke the ex-shepherd and Moses from what both thought were exits from a retreating dream to enter another. Realizing the uproar was no fantasy, they raced up the bank to the road where the voices had come from and saw two drunken ruffians looting the push cart.

"Leave my merchandise alone," Moses demanded. "Put back every last one of my goods."

"Make me," the burly ruffian challenged, continuing to shovel handfuls of goods out of the cart into his burlap sack.

His partner, a simpleton, echoed the dare in a tentative whine. "Make him."

Moses snatched the bag from the burley one, causing the goods to spill on the road. As he bent to retrieve the items, the simpleton pinned his arms against his back. The burly one, at first caught off guard, now moved in to punch his vulnerable victim, but was suddenly jerked back in the choking crook of the ex-shepherd's staff and pulled helplessly over the edge of the bridge into the stream below. The simpleton, hearing his partner's yell of terror, stood rooted in confusion at the bridge's edge for a moment before jumping to join his pal.

With the sound of splashing water Moses awoke, realizing it had all been a dream.

"Get up. Eat. We go," the leather-covered Indian said, shaking Moses from his pallet.

Shaking off the remnants of fast dissolving fantasies, Moses groped his way through the cave's entrance to relieve himself and check Numbers before splashing cold-water wakefulness on his face from the nearby spring. Back in the cave, the Indian hurried Moses through a piece of roasted rabbit and stewed apples before departing but fifteen minutes from the time he'd been roused.

By the second day's sunset, they'd left the steep ravines of the Mohawk River for its gentle, rich bottom lands where farmers raised bumper crops. The obvious absence of craggy hills or bluffs seemed at first to disprove the possibility that the Indian was housed only in caves.

Then their last mile led to a large untillable field surrounded with trees and jammed with a jumble of rock slabs of all sizes and shapes –

a glacial monument to Nature's capricious disorder in the midst of a gentle rolling land - ominous at first sight.

From the edge of the ruins, Moses watched the Indian pick his way to a collision of rocks forming a mound, take two steps down and disappear. In a moment he rose above the rubble and returned to Moses saying, "Go to me," while pointing at the mound.

"I can't take my cart in there and I don't want to leave it. What do I do?"

"No one touch. Think evil spirit's graveyard. Safe."

Moses, reluctant to leave his cart and Numbers at the grassy perimeter, nevertheless followed the Indian back through the rubble and descended to enter a vault, weathertight except for chest-high chinks easily plugged with well-used corncobs lying ready. In the center of the chamber a spring bubbled up through the ground. This cave was stocked with firewood, a kerosene lamp, a bearskin and some smoked and canned provisions, indicating a frequently used site.

"You light fire. Boil water. Me get chicken," the Indian said and left the chamber before Moses had the presence of mind to ask where he'd get a chicken.

The big iron kettle of water had been boiling but a few minutes when the Indian returned with a plucked hen. In a few deft movements with his hunting knife he gutted the bird, singed its skin and tossed it into the pot.

"Where did you get the chicken?" Moses asked.

"Farm over hill."

"You can't go around stealing chickens any time you feel like it," Moses protested.

"They tell me I geld colt last spring, get three chickens. Get two duck. Don't like duck. Take chickens up to three before do more jobs for them," the Indian explained, making clear his action had been just and needed no additional discussion.

The second evening's simple meal was prepared and eaten as swiftly and silently as the previous day's. For two days the Indian had spoken but a few sentences, so it seemed significant when just before settling down for the night he broke his silence.

"Alert all signs come your way. Set course with Manito protector, red tailed hawk."

It was clear to Moses that the Indian's few words, though crude and scrambled, were an unmistakable warning to be vigilant. For a while he lay awake trying to recall the events of the days when he'd seen a hawk circling overhead, but succumbed to the day's exertion and fell asleep.

As he traveled, countless road signposts indicating distance and direction to the next settlement welcomed him by wiggling their upright supports provocatively and waving their cross bars. Occasionally Moses found himself at a crossroad where some prankster had turned the sign ninety degrees, but always his good sense of direction was confirmed by the sign bending its cross bars arm-like to point the correct way.

In a small hamlet he saw a lone man despondently sitting with his head between his knees.

"What's your trouble, good fellow?" Moses asked and instantly recognized the juggler.

"It's Sunday and the children won't be back in school till tomorrow."

"Why don't you go to the church and perform for them there?" Moses asked.

"I tried, but the pastor suspects me of witchcraft because I do magic tricks," the juggler said, "and not only that, but the library's closed and I don't remember if I've been this way before."

"Things can't be that bad," Moses suggested. "Starting tomorrow juggle for the children, and when you're finished before you leave town collect all the seeds from their apples and plant them along the roads you travel. When they become trees, you'll know you've been this way before."

"Oh, that's a marvelous idea," the juggler said. "Just for that, I'm going to show you a new trick." And with that he made Moses' donkey disappear.

"Get him back, will you? I must be on my way."

"I'm afraid I've forgotten how," the juggler said.

He came wide awake from his dream. The Indian was gone. No sign of his presence suggested he'd ever been there. Moses rushed up to the opening to the cave, fearing his donkey would also have disappeared, but the panic vanished when he saw Numbers grazing peacefully by the perimeter of the scattered rocks. Then as Moses turned to retrieve his clothes from the cave, he saw a red-tailed hawk lazily circling as it moved west.

Chapter 16

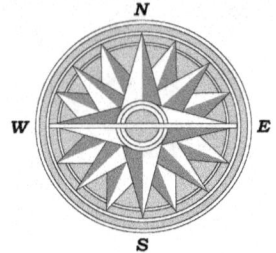

To My Beloved Family and Friends:

Greetings and hopeful expectations this letter will arrive to find you in robust health and cheerful spirits. I'm sure you'll share my disappointment that the time spent to reach Chicago has far exceeded my most pessimistic estimate and hope you'll understand the only previous letter written in my year's absence reflects there was so little progress made in my assignment I had nothing to communicate. God forbid my lapse into silence should ever alienate us because of any misinterpretation that my affection and responsibility in your behalf has wavered for one instant.

It may be worth noting since the letter referred to above, I have traveled two-thirds of the miles crossed in only one-quarter of the trip's time, which unfortunately does nothing to rectify the earlier delay, but I am at last in Chicago and offer the following observations.

You may recall when expansion into Boston and Philadelphia was considered, I questioned the assumption that selling approaches which had worked in New York would apply in other markets. Perhaps my initial success made me unduly cautious, but it seemed more knowledge about our prospects in both cities would be a distinct advantage. I'd *hoped to find information on populations -- numbers, genders, incomes, races, places of domiciles and retailers patronized. Finding limited data on these social statistics, I had to rely on my New York experience. That and a flexibility to quickly adapt to customer preferences helped us penetrate the Boston market.*

When we moved to enter Philadelphia, I mistakenly believed their people, made gentle by the Quakers among them, would resemble the conservative Bostonians. That was a mistake that set us back about six months. Once again, without adequate Chicago market facts I am forced to study on sight prospective customers and build an information record to aid us in making appropriate product offerings, always remembering our customers are a special segment of the total population described in general as follows.

Chicago is or soon will be the fifth largest city in America. Successive immigrations of French, English, Irish, Germans, Italians, Poles, Jews and others from Middle and Eastern Europe are the origins of rapid growth which supply a large labor pool for the steel mills, railroads, water transport and meat packers.

As many immigrants recently arrived from agrarian communities, they are novices even in the semi-skilled trades. It is my impression the rapid growth of the foreign-born and the location of manufacturing and transportation companies makes it a noisy, restless city of undetermined identity -- a boisterous teenager trying to act grown up and not knowing how. Newcomers understandingly gravitate to settle among their own for the comfort of a familiar culture, slowing their assimilation into the greater community. Our selling practice of taking the product to the customer gains from this ethnic clustering, but we must always remember we are guests in their homes.

In summary, Chicago probably offers a profitable niche for push cart business; however, the person you choose to locate here will need to develop different merchandise offerings to serve the special ethnic and economic groups.

I am hopeful that in maintaining the principles on which the company started, you will enjoy a rewarding future. You are much better prepared than I was on my first day of peddling, so use all we've learned to satisfy customers and guard against trying to sell them what you think they should have, rather than what they want and need. Finally, remember the business belongs to you. Keep unceasing counsel among yourselves because all of you will share in the failures and successes.

Since I left your fondly remembered companionship a dozen months ago, the same inner voice that led me out of Poland has been reawakened and I cannot deny its call. Now it is unmistakably insistent that I leave the business and search for my real identity. It deeply concerns me that I am unable to be more specific as such a nebulous separation could risk estrangement. I must confess this force, whatever it is that propels me from one day to the next without any hint of destination or purpose, deeply affects my peace of mind, but I hasten to add that along the way I've been treated kindly. Only one or two days of fasting have deprived me of an adequate diet and there has never been a night, not of my choosing, when I slept without shelter. It is my good fortune to have a donkey help move the push cart across the countryside, and to free me from being immobilized in winter, a blacksmith generously fashioned skids to replace the cart's wheels, useless in snow.

Although a few sewing items and notions were sold to pay for my living expenses en route, the majority of inventory was retained until I reached Chicago and is accounted for in the enclosed report on purchases made here in the city -- proceeds are being sent to you via U. S. Postal money order. I have been advised by a lawyer my following instructions for disposing of my company ownership constitutes a valid legal document, therefore my request follows -- I, Moses Morganstern, twenty-one years of age and being of sound mind, authorize my portion of ownership in Morganstern and Company be distributed as follows: ten percent of the shares equally divided among current non-family employees and the remaining ninety percent of shares equally divided among living family members.

Tomorrow I will take the donkey and cart in whatever direction the day dictates. Not knowing where I'll be, you'll be unable to write me, but I will strive to keep you better informed with more frequent letters than those written to date, and I will always keep you in my prayers.

> *Honor bound to you always.*
> *With deepest affection,*
> *Moses*

Moses, pen in one hand, letter in the other, studied the text, sobered by the estrangement so easy to read in his message. He remained motionless longer than he realized, as though doing otherwise would permanently sever connections to his family. At one point in the letter he'd attempted to describe his experience as a young boy alone, leaving Poland for the New World, symbolically represented by America and New York, naively thought of by him and others as interchangeable synonyms. He ultimately abandoned any attempts to describe his amorphous call, convinced that if he was unable to satisfactorily explain it to himself, he'd never make it understandable for others.

The finality of his withdrawal from family and friends, routines and responsibilities left Moses in estrangement. He thought of Numbers pulling an empty cart into he-knew-not-where for which no one could store up the right inventory.

Unaware he'd descended into apathy, he left his bed more infrequently and for a short time neither day nor night registered in his nothingness. Then hallucinations occupied the void with third-person strangers.

In his world of indistinguishable days and nights, some bird-like harbinger pecked at his window till he was fully aware of the arrival of another intruder.

No less puzzling, the second meddler took command of the visitation. Looking more gaunt than need be because he dressed in black and carried a black satchel, the man repeatedly asked unanswerable questions before stripping Moses of his covers and underwear to poke the shivering patient with long bony fingers then retracing his earlier route of exploration with a listening device. Presumably Moses' signs and sounds justified no more of the black-suited man's time, and he held out his hand palm up for his fifty cent fee and departed.

Moses concluded he must be unique to deserve such professional attention and began a recital of his lineage by trying to name his parents and siblings in ascending or descending order, but invariably substituted Adam and Eve and the seven generational issues that followed.

Once Moses dreamed he was pushed out of his mother's birth canal into a world of foreign complexities, and he scolded her for dying before preparing him to solve puzzles, but relented and told her he hadn't meant to be ungrateful for making him and wished her well. Then he wet his bed and like a defenseless infant cried out for nurturing.

On a sunny day when all the doors of the building had been stored for the summer, Moses' curiosity, exceeding caution, sparked enough energy to rouse him from bed and crawl about the floor. Unsatisfied with the monotony within the range of his vision, he moved on hands and knees outside the building to cross a small yard with a marsh. The water, warmed by an uncommonly hot spring day, softened the mud to a child's squishy delight. Tiring of luxuriating in his newly-discovered spa, Moses attempted to move on but found he was stuck in the mire. Helpless, he called to be rescued, not with the wordless cry of an infant, but with a distinct 'God help me.'

Spellbound, he scrutinized his metamorphosis from a baby to a man lying in muddy grass aside his cart two empty lots away from a road house. He struggled to remember what had happened after he stopped for a meal in the ramshackle building, but he could not control his mind.

He had been mistaken about the weather; it was raining. He had crawled under the cart for shelter to a new line of sight and discovered Numbers was missing.

An attempt to rise awakened fury in the extremities of his body, and he fell back, tasting the salty sweat of painful effort, even in the rain.

Again Moses struggled to roll into a sitting position then lost consciousness.

Later, how much later evaded him, Moses awakened to cautiously test his body's tolerance to a range of motion, registering pain with each effort. Uncertain he wanted to risk revealing he was conscious to anyone present, he peered through half-closed lids. The view was fuzzy and so limited his sense of touch became dominant, revealing he was lying on a warm, dry, feather bed pleasantly scented to stimulate his faculties to full wakefulness. The room was quiet and overly ornate; plush red furnishings choked the space and noises of the outside world -- femininity carried to the extreme by a woman who took her gender seriously. The word "boudoir" came to mind, a place of unimaginable intrigue with a grande dame or prostitute presiding over pleasure or perfidy and at times each trying to act like the other.

His stirring prompted a woman's soft drawl from the darkest corner, teasing him with the possibility he'd fallen back into another episode of hallucinations not physically uncomfortable but no less disturbing.

"Ah most give ya up for daid."

"I feel like I could be," Moses said, unsure who was speaking. "Who are you?"

"Ahm Angel, but ya sure ain't in heaven, not yet, though ya come close to it. For right now, Ahm ya guardian angel."

"Where am I?"

"In ma place, about seven blocks from where Ah found ya in the rain last night."

"I don't understand any of this. Could you come here in the light so I know who I'm speaking to?"

All at once with no sound of her approach she appeared at his bedside, dressed in a long, flowing, ghost-like gown.

He saw a woman, perhaps not yet twenty, heavily rouged but unsuccessful at masking a care-worn face. Her thick, pale, bleached hair was piled high atop her head to add several inches to her stature. Black brows arched over large, dark inquiring eyes in jarring contrast to her alabaster complexion. By conventional standards she could have been considered beautiful except for a wall-eye, independent of the other, that drifted slightly away from her directed vision.

"What happened to me?"

"Ole Rush, he give ya ah Mickey strong enough to kill a bull."

"Rush, Mickey? Where did this happen?"

She calmly recounted the attack on him, and he wondered how a young person could become so unmoved by violence.

"I still don't know what you're talking about."

"Ahm talkin' 'bout last night when ya come in to the Butcher Block for a meal and lodgin' and Rush wanted to buy ya donkey real bad but ya wouldn't sell it."

"Who's Rush?"

"He owns the tavern, the Butcher's Block; the Block everybody calls it. He offered ya twenty-five dollars for that donkey, and when ya told him there wasn't enough money in the world ta buy it, he started yellin' and cussin'. Then he cooled down right quick, got friendly to show there was no hard feelings and bought ya an apple jack. That's when he slipped ya the Mickey."

"A Mickey is a knockout potion?" Moses verified.

"Yeah, ya was gone before ya put the glass down."

"How do you know all this? I never saw you before."

"Ah was on the upstairs landin'. Ah seen it all. Then Rush went out to lead ya donkey and wagon into the stable, and when the donkey don't budge, took a whip to him and the donkey reared up and knocked out three of Rush's teeth and broke his nose before he ran away."

"That doesn't explain why I hurt all over."

"When Rush got banged up and lost the donkey to boot, he comes back inside in a killin' rage and the first he sees is ya, so he picks ya up and beats the hell outa ya before dumpin' ya and the cart down the road from his place so they ain't no connection. Ahm the only one who knows all this 'cause the help's gone home and the night customers didn't come in yet."

"What happened to my donkey?"

"He's long gone, and he better not come back 'cause Rush'll shoot him."

Disregarding the possible penalty of pain for movement, he sat upright in bed, preparing to go out and search for Numbers, discovering only a momentary ache and his nakedness.

"Where are my clothes?" he asked.

"Ya was one God-awful mess when Ah got ya here so Ah washed them. They's almost dry."

"I still don't understand why you were at the tavern, why you cared what happened to me and brought me here."

"Ah thought Ah told ya, Ah entertain at the Block. Ah'm a singa."

"But how did you get me here?"

"Business was slow last night and with Rush hurt bad and all, we closed up early. When Ah come by and see ya still breathin', Ah figger nobody else will take ya in and ya don't deserve nothin' like that. 'Sides, Ah kinda favor stray dogs, being one myself if the truth be knowed, so Ah get a drunk ta help haul ya up here."

"Aren't you going to get in trouble with Rush?"

"He don't know Ah watched him beat ya up and nobody but the drunk seed ya with me."

"I must get dressed and out of here before you get in trouble. May I have my clothes, please?"

Angel, as illusional in name as in appearance, vanished into the shadow but broke the spell by returning with his clothes a moment later. She laid them on the counterpane neatly folded and warmed, their freshness as fragrant as the bed linens, then sank into an overstuffed chair to watch him return to the land of the living as he dressed.

He pulled on his pants, noting his money still seemed secured in the waistband and rejected the impulse to make certain it had not been replaced with worthless paper. Surely anyone who'd risked her safety to help him could not be a pickpocket. Then wavering, he considered it might be acceptable to check the cash, particularly if he were to give her a suitable gift. Uncomfortable with that rationale, he concluded the only real sign of gratitude would be a heartfelt thank you and immediate departure to protect her from Rush learning she'd aided him.

"I will never be able to repay you for your kindness. You are a fine woman and may God reward you." Moses held out is his hand to take hers before parting. It was too small, soft, an insufficient defense against the likes of Rush. "Thank you," he said, pulling her close for a hug and leaving her befuddled.

On the first floor of her building, Moses located a rear door to a service alley from which he exited to the street, reducing the chances anyone would suspect he'd come from Angel. The previous night's soaking rain had given in to a grey, moist, dimming overcast that hung low to crowd the soggy tenements into an indefinable mass. He made his way along almost deserted streets to the city center, identified by a soot-soiled, stone church bearing a cross of such proportions as to seemingly jeopardize the building's stability. Opposite it stood a monotonous, bulky sandstone police station for the eleventh precinct, more commonly known as the tenderloin district because it offered the best cut of vice and graft in the city.

The cold-eyed precinct captain sat behind a massive ebony desk so highly polished a nightstick, the only object on its surface, seemed suspended in air.

"You are?" the chief demanded, neither introducing himself nor offering Moses a chair.

"Moses Morganstern."

"State your occupation," the captain demanded.

"I'm a peddler of notions and sewing supplies."

"Vagrant! Meggs, did you get that?" the captain yelled to an underling in the back room. "Residence and license number," he continued, yelling for the benefit of the invisible scribe.

"I'm just passing through and not selling any goods."

"Just passing through, is it? Is that how you describe entering an orderly business establishment and seriously injuring the proprietor, not to mention trying to cheat him on the sale of your donkey?"

"I didn't do that. I told the owner the donkey was not for sale. Now that you've brought that up, where is my donkey?"

"You tell me, Mr. Morganstern, where you hid the beast. I don't suppose you had it licensed, either."

"I wouldn't sell the donkey to the owner, so he drugged me, and I was unconscious when he took the donkey somewhere. And that's why I came to the police in the first place. I want to file a complaint against him for assaulting me and stealing the animal."

"Are you getting all this, Meggs?"

"Yes sir, chief."

"Well, Mr. Moses Morganstern, if you were drugged and unconscious all this time, how did you know what happened? We do detective work, Mr. Morganstern, we deal in facts. So tell me how did you know these things you just told me happened? Were there witnesses?"

"How else could it have happened?" Moses asked innocently as though unaware the captain might be trying to trick him into identifying a witness or discredit his complaint. In any case Angel could be in danger, and he needed to help her find protection from Rush by throwing the captain off the trail that led to her.

"Think about it, captain. Why would a poor man like me in a strange city want to cause trouble in a tavern where he only wanted supper and a night's sleep? And why would he sell his donkey, which is all he owns and needs for his work?"

"You tell me, 'cause that's not the way I heard it from Rush."

"But you just indicated there were no witnesses, so it comes down to his word against mine."

"I never saw you before today. Why should I believe you when I've known Rush for thirty years and he says you came into the

Butcher's Block and began to drink heavily? When it was time to settle up, you couldn't pay the bill so you sold him the donkey. Then when he went outside to take possession of the animal, you wanted more money, and while you and Rush were arguing the donkey ran away. That made you crazy drunk and you beat up Rush before passing out."

"That's not the way it happened. I'm a peaceful man. I want to go before a judge with the tavern owner present."

"With no witnesses, as you seem to think, it doesn't appear you've got any complaint. I'll tell you what you really want, you want to get out of town before Rush recuperates. Our force is limited, and there are just so many people we can look after. Rush might just get to you before we can. And Rush is going to be really riled up if he knows you've been laying Angel. There's no mistaking her perfume, you smell like you took a bath in it. Now get out of here, Mr. Moses Morganstern, before I remember I haven't locked up my quota of vagrants for the day."

Moses' petition had failed, and even worse, it linked him with Angel who'd be unaware she was in danger. With little time to rescue her and escape to a safe haven, a place yet to be determined, Moses moved evasively to confuse anyone following him. At the door of the police station, he asked the guard for detailed directions to the railroad station and spoke of going back east to his family. Once out of sight, he walked an indirect route to Angel's, arriving in that narrow protective interval of dusk and darkness, when she usually left for work at the Block.

Feeling sure no one had traced him, he cautiously entered Angel's building from the rear alley, worrying she might have left by the front door as he entered from the back. No one was in the first floor hall nor the stairs. In his hurry, he almost rapped on her door before listening for voices. All clear. Three short raps. Was she still there? Then the door opened.

"Well ain't ya--", she said, before Moses touched her lips with his finger, motioning her to a whisper, "--the sight. What brings ya back here?"

Moses entered and shut the door to a slit to survey the hall for witnesses of his arrival. Assured no one had seen him, he turned to Angel.

"I went to the police to file a complaint against Rush, and they're as unlawful as he is. What's worse, they think you and I were together. The captain smelled your perfume on my clothes. You've got to leave before he gets to Rush. Have you friends or family who can hide you until you find a permanent place away from here?"

"Ah seed him have bad spells before, but he'll get over it in a few days. Ah'll just wait him out like before. Besides, my family won't take me back and all my friends live right here."

"You don't understand. I can't leave you here, Rush will take out all his rage against me on you and the police will cover it up. If he was the only one, I'd stay to see you weren't harmed, but I can't take on the police force."

"Where would we go?" Angel asked, beginning to yield to Moses' reasoning.

"I don't know yet, but away from here as fast as we can," Moses answered, adding his most persuasive appeal, "because Rush is not going to believe nothing happened when he hears your perfume was on my clothes. Come on, we don't have any more time to lose."

"Awl right," she conceded. "Ah won't be long in packin' ma clothes. Ah'll only take ma favorites."

"No, Angel. We must leave right now."

"Can Ah leave a note with Mabel on what ta do with ma things?"

"Now," Moses commanded, grabbing her long black cloak as he pulled her into the hall. "Lock the door so it appears you haven't left in a hurry. Leaving your clothes undisturbed should also help. When we get on the street, start walking towards West Main Street and go as fast as you can without calling attention to yourself. If you meet anyone you know, say hello and keep walking. Turn onto the next side street as though you're going to the Block, then make turns at the next two streets to get you back on course. Remember I'll always be behind you in case there's a problem. Ready? All right, let's go."

When Angel had walked two hundred yards ahead, Moses started to follow with the push cart. As it was not uncommon to see vendors about after dark making their way home from a day's work, he attracted no attention. Within ten minutes, Angel came to a major intersection with its cluster of small stores and evening shoppers. A young man recognizing Angel stopped her to talk.

"If Ah don't hurry ya gonna make me late for work," she flirted, never breaking her pace. "See ya later at the Block and don't bring ya wife," she purred over her shoulder then turned at the next corner.

Another mile and they'd leave the Tenderloin District and the captain's jurisdiction to enter the residential section, a gradual transition from poor to wealthy in fewer than ten blocks. Close to the homes of the affluent, Moses watched a middle-aged couple look disapprovingly as Angel passed them, and as they came towards him, heard the woman say, "It's a disgrace to see common prostitutes walking our streets. Where's Officer McCarthy at a time when he's needed?"

Still agitated, the woman stopped the next pedestrian coming her way to air her complaint and gesture menacingly in Angel's direction.

Moses quickened his stride to draw within easy speaking distance of her. "Angel, we might have a problem. The couple you passed a block back think you're a street walker and will call the police. The next stretch where you see nobody on the street, stop. I'll catch up to you quickly and help you into the cart. Cover up so only your face shows...not your shoes, not your dress, not your hair, only your face. I'll pull the tarp over you, and if anyone approaches I'll rap the side of the cart. Remember, lie absolutely still if I rap on the cart."

Moses had only just relayed his instruction when she stopped, signaling him to catch up with her. His effort to sprint while pushing a full cart to Angel winded him, but despite the delay of finding a comb that held her hair in place, freeing a shoe caught in the wheel and unsnagging her dress from a bolt, Angel disappeared within three minutes. He hastily drew the tarpaulin over her and continued their exodus none too soon as they encountered pedestrians along their way.

Reaching the section with the most opulent mansions, a man

dressed in black suddenly ran out a driveway pursued by another some distance behind yelling, "Stop thief! Stop thief!" Immediately behind the pursuer a pack of yelping, ill-assorted dogs joined the chase. At first the man Moses presumed was the thief appeared headed for dense undergrowth across the street, but he swerved to come directly at Moses brandishing what appeared to be a revolver.

"Uncover the cart," he ordered. "I'm getting in."

"But--" Moses objected.

"You heard me," he said and snatched the tarpaulin off the cart. "Holy Mary," he gasped. "She's dead."

"I know," Moses answered, lowering his voice respectfully, "she's my sister," at which point the pursuer arrived fortified by a gardener armed with a hoe.

The burglar, but a youth, still immobilized by the sight of a dead woman, quickly surrendered a toy pistol and the stolen articles.

"I'm eternally grateful to you, sir," the owner told Moses as the servant, unprepared for taking custody of a prisoner, tried binding the thief's wrists with the captive's belt but abandoned that when the boy's pants fell down.

"You must come to my home and let me find a suitable reward for apprehending the scoundrel and recovering these heirlooms," the homeowner said, inventorying the stolen articles.

"That's very kind of you, but I'm rewarded knowing your valuables are intact and no one is hurt. However, I would like you to think about letting this youth go if he promises not to steal again. He only had a toy pistol."

"Well, I could consider that. After all, no harm was done and he is very young."

"Will you promise not to steal again, young man? Do you realize next time you could be shot or killed? Do you understand and promise? This could be your last chance," Moses said, adding, "Do it for all the dear departed youths whose lives have been snuffed out. You have the second chance they haven't had."

"I promise, Mister. I'll starve before I steal again."

"Well, I guess that about does it then," the homeowner said, telling his gardener to release the youth.

"And I'll be on my way," Moses said.

"Surely you could wait till I get some money from the house for you."

"Thank you. That's not necessary."

"If you insist," the homeowner replied, moving swiftly alongside the cart. "I can't for the life of me imagine what was in the cart that stopped the thief in his tracks," he added as he whipped back the tarpaulin to expose Angel lying as though in the early stages of rigor mortis.

"My God, it's Angel," he gasped, recoiling from the presence of death.

"I know," Moses said reverently, "one of heaven's own. She's my sister and I'm taking her to a more peaceful place. If you're the God-fearing man I think you are, pray she'll rise again," and he hurried the cart away.

Chapter 17

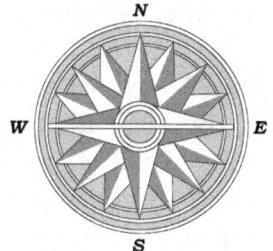

They had fled almost fifteen miles into the country when the sun rose to warm their backs. No longer concealed, Angel hobbled along in impractical, dress-up shoes while he pushed the cart at a fast pace, anxious to get far beyond the grasp of Rush and the police. From the beginning she'd grumbled about being cooped up under a smelly tarpaulin in the small cart and, with each jolt on the road leading her away from danger, cursed it would 'jar the piss out of her.' Apparently the episode of the robber and the robbed had failed to convince her of the value of subterfuge, while the uncertainty of a future in an unfamiliar but safer place seemed to threaten Angel more than standing her ground and facing Rush's violence. Moses told her there was a difference between courageous and foolhardy and just because she'd survived Rush's previous beatings, there was no guarantee he wouldn't kill her this time.

Finally when Moses agreed it seemed not overly risky to let her out of the cart, the release from cramping confinement and the invigoration of walking lightened her spirits. An interminable recital of the fancy dresses she'd been forced to leave then dominated their conversation, or perhaps more accurately her monologue, during their first morning on the road. When the dirge for her wardrobe's abandonment lessened, Moses remarked that walking the distance she'd covered out of the cart must have been uncomfortable, and longer stretches lay ahead.

"It's a shame to spoil such beautiful shoes," Moses said, appealing to her vanity. "We'll buy a pair of well-fitting work shoes at the next town. But for now, put on these women's moccasins given to me by an Indian." Her sore feet were all the persuasion needed, but the suggestion of replacing the evening gown was postponed for another time.

"Where are we headin?" she asked offhandedly as children inquire with little interest in the destination so long as it had a name.

Moses knew the question would eventually arise as surely as it could not be answered, and so as not to add his uncertainty to hers, said they'd stop at the first place they came to that served food. That seemed to satisfy her, and they went on in silence for a while before she acknowledged her change to moccasins had been a good idea.

"Ya really think he'd hurt me bad?" she asked as though she had been considering returning to Rush.

"I think he might kill you, or worse, maim you so badly you'd be completely dependent upon him till he decided to throw you out."

Her brow wrinkled in thought before she committed to raise a question whose answer might disappoint her. "Would ya've helped me if Ah done nothin' for ya?"

"Of course," Moses answered, "just as you helped me – a stranger."

"Ah just knowed it was the right thing ta do. Ah didn't think 'bout what might come after. Who are ya, anyway?"

"You know my name is Moses. Who am I beyond that? How many of us know who we are?" he said, tempted to answer her question only with a question. Then, reminded she deserved a considerate reply, he gave her an account of himself.

"I'm five feet ten and weigh one-hundred sixty-five pounds, have dark hair and hazel eyes," he began, never having talked about himself before. "I can tell you I'm a Jew by birth – however that doesn't mean I adhere to all Hebrew practices. I was a New York City peddler who expanded the business to Boston and Philadelphia, but if you asked one hundred of my customers about me, you'd get one hundred different descriptions.

"Most people live by following rules and repeating customs over and over, then passing them on to the next generation. People are too often satisfied by this formula and never discover who they were meant to be. They end up recognizing only the rules and customs in others and never know the individual. It's unlikely I'll ever learn who I am until I remove myself from me -- to get out of the conventional existence and find the real Moses."

"Ya sure don't talk like any man Ah evah knowed," she said.

"Who are you?" Moses asked, presuming she'd never thought of it and amazed by the candid self-appraisal she gave without a second thought.

"Ah'm worthless 'count a ma skewed eye."

"Does it interfere with your vision?"

"Ah see good, but people think ah ain't right."

"That's what I meant, you're letting others decide who you are."

"They sees me in ma pretty dresses singing at the Block and says Ah'm nothin' but a two-bit whore, that's all any man would want of a woman with a wanderin' eye, but Rush took me in and Ah only been his woman until now."

"Angel, I think of you as a good, kind person. See how there can be two entirely different opinions and that's all they are, just opinions."

"Just when Ah think Ah'm followin' ya, ya lose me."

"Don't let that upset you, I confuse myself all the time. I go just so far and then I can't go any further."

"Ain't that the truth?" she asked, surprised to hear a man admit his shortcomings.

"The only truth I know right now is we're both tired and hungry and need to have a meal at the town up ahead."

The town up ahead announced its existence by belching clouds of black smoke before the irregular shapes of its buildings marred the symmetry of the horizon. It proved to be a place of big people, big voices, big prejudices, animated by boisterous laborers as they were funneled into factory warrens of twelve more hours of mind-dulling repetition.

Before they'd passed the first mill, Angel became the object of hurtful insults from employees waiting for the gates to be opened for the start of the noon shift. Moses watched her recoil from the first slur before stiffening to shrug off the obscene talk not new to her. When it was apparent their hazing was not working on Angel, their vulgarities were directed at Moses, speculating on his relationship to the woman. Moses stopped in front of the biggest heckler, smiled and began to sign. The workers seemed dazed by the confrontation, but the more the worker was puzzled, the faster Moses signed. Finally regaining his bullying bravado, he yelled, "There's no point in trying to talk to them, they're deaf," and the mob deflated into twos and threes.

When they were out of hearing of the workers, Moses insisted the ready-made clothing store should be their first stop, hungry or not, arguing continued travel in the way she was dressed would wreck her finery. There was no need to mention a change of clothes might reduce the scornful vulgarity. She did not object to buying her clothes before eating though she was faint with hunger.

"Ah guess Ah'm ya woman now, so's Ah better do as ya say."

Both content and tone of her quiet submission suggested to Moses that she entrusted her future welfare to him and would yield to his judgment. If he showed no interest in having sex with her, would she believe her disfigurement repelled him? Or if he made unwelcomed advances, would it degrade her self-image to an object, returning her to feeling trapped as she had with Rush? After several tries, but arriving at no successful answer, Moses concluded resolution should not be attempted on an empty stomach.

In minutes denim and flannel transformed Angel into what he hoped was an unrecognizable country girl, a regression before a mirror she might reject. Sturdy shoes and floppy felt hat completed the attempted head-to-toe disguise. Her dark eyebrows, pale complexion and ashen hair so mismatched with the drab clothing as to remind him of itinerant artists who attached all their subjects' portraits to the same previously painted images of a man's or woman's torso in order to simplify the rendering.

It was evident the perils of their flight had not effected their appetite. By his count Angel gobbled a slice of ham, thick as the skillet it was cooked on, flapjacks, fried eggs and two mugs of coffee before sampling a half-dozen biscuits with honey and a pint of milk. She burped then excused herself, shielding her mouth with the back of her manicured hand.

"Ah only eat two meals a day," she said as though justifying that such an extraordinary consumption was not unusual.

"I would hope so," Moses chuckled, then realizing his gaffe added, "how else could you wear those dresses so well?" Then attempting to remedy the bungle of reminding Angel of her abandoned wardrobe, he said, "Or any kind of clothes for that matter?" He looked around the room for any diners showing curiosity about Angel, using the redirection of his attention as a good way to end the conversation.

Well-fed and comfortable in her warm, loose-fitting, new clothes, Angel drifted into that state of well-being that precedes sleep. Moses watched her doze off several times before yawning herself awake and smiling in embarrassment at being caught.

"Can't we get a room at the hotel across the street? Ah'm dyin' for sleep."

"Going to a hotel during the day will draw attention. Married folk don't occupy hotel rooms during the day so they'd probably think you're a prostitute and turn us down, which might be remembered if Rush comes looking for us. We need to be on our way. We'll find an isolated place in the country to sleep. I'll rig the tarpaulin against the cart for a lean-to. Let's go."

"Ah done know how fah Ah can walk."

"Let's try walking a little and resting a little and when you can't go any farther, I'll push you in the cart. We should go now."

They went out into the bright sunlit street littered with the trash left by their noisy hecklers now slaving in the steel-mills of the enlightened industrial age. Of the few people about, most were women in drab shapeless clothes, heads bowed, scurrying as though the bundles they carried would melt before reaching their destination. Wearied from the night's escape, Moses and Angel were uncertain if their stiff legs would carry them farther, but they walked out the aches to leave the town behind.

For two days the road led them due west through small, sooty towns and villages, displaying repetitious architectural monotony, particularly in the newer buildings hastily construction for the textile industry, man and machine. Their sameness gave the illusion one was traveling a circuitous route, always returning to their starting place.

Forty miles and four days separated them from Rush when they reached a city at a fork in the highway -- a time and place for rest and the inescapable discussion on duty and expectation. Angel's simple logic was that being saved from Rush made her Moses' woman, and she'd demonstrated her obedience to his decisions on numerous occasions. Remembering an old Chinese proverb "if one saves another's life, it obligates the rescuer to always take care of the rescued" was no comfort to Moses. He'd began by telling her he did not believe any person belonged to another. Then he stress she was now free to start a new life and that she needed to think about her future. He'd follow by showing her how to start planning by making a list of where she wanted to live in the country or in town. She should be sure to include her skills - sewing, cooking, waiting on tables, taking care of the sick – work like that.

"Angel, we've been over this twenty times and we're still not making any headway," Moses said some time later while looking at his notes, which had been crossed out and revised as early understandings were contradicted or modified. "You say you don't like moving from place to place, but that's what you'd be doing if you stay with me. Why anyone would want to tag along with a person who doesn't know where he's going and may never know is beyond me."

"Cause Ah'm used to ya. Ya's easy goin."

"You'd tire of me."

"Naw, ya shows me ways to see things different like and ya don't use me, if ya know what Ah mean."

"But my traveling is not easy," Moses replied, returning to his original reasoning. "It could be too much for you. It could take you nowhere."

"Ya ain't heard me squawk, have ya? An haven't Ah kept up with ya all along?"

"You have, but we've only come a short distance. Always moving about with no home is not right for a woman." Then, giving up trying to reason with her, Moses said, "You told me you were a singer; you like that more than anything. Where would you sing if you followed me? And by the way, I haven't heard one note out of you."

"That's 'cause ya nevah ask me."

"You don't need permission from anyone to sing," Moses replied, getting annoyed. "Sing all you want, any time. Why don't you sing right now," he encouraged, expecting some little ditty hummed in a southern whisper.

Angel's eyes rounded in bewilderment at the thought of singing in broad daylight as pedestrians passed along the street. "Right now?"

"Right now."

She rose to her full height, hair tumbling about her pale face and falling to her shoulders as she pulled off the broad-brimmed hat. She fixed her eyes on some imaginary tableau and with no apparent effort produced a full, rich tone in double high E that turned heads a block away. After holding the note at full volume and without vibrato for an improbable time, she let her voice slide down the scale to sing 'Amazing Grace.'

"My God, where did that come from?"

"Ah learnt it from ma ma. She used go ta tent preachin' afore she died and Ah learnt all them tunes from her. All t'other songs Ah know is dance hall's."

"No, I mean where did you learn to sing like that?"

"No place special, Ah just lissen real good and store it in ma head and one day Ah open ma mouth an it all come out."

"Do you know how few singers, even among the best, can reach that high note?"

"So what's it mean?"

"It means it's the jewel of your voice, a great untrained voice that might make you a famous opera singer."

"What's opera?"

"It's a play with music where everyone sings instead of talking. There's an orchestra with all kinds of instruments and the women wear beautiful gowns. Everyone has to learn a part, but with your memory that should be easy." His enthusiasm was running away with him, leaving her befuddled.

"If Ah don't know about these things, how could Ah do 'em?"

"You'd have a teacher and you'd pick it up quickly the way you remember things. Let me hear you sing something else."

She sang, 'Edie was a lady, although her past was shady,' interpreting the bawdy ballad as a poignant plea for sympathy for a conflicted woman.

"Something else? Do you know 'The Star Spangled Banner?'"

She sang with such fervor, each phrase of patriotism moved Moses as though for his first hearing.

"Angel, you have an exceptional gift. You must not waste it. I will help you make a career in music if you'll let me. Not to encourage you in every way would betray our friendship."

"What do Ah hafta do?"

"Here's a copy of the telegram I sent to Ludwig, Alfredo and my family, and here's their reply. They're looking forward to your arrival and will meet you at the railroad station. You can stay with them as long as you like."

From the first moment Moses had excitedly urged Angel to go east to develop her talent, she was wary about exchanging familiar pitfalls for unimaginable treacheries lurking at each turn. Once Moses found her huddled in a chair, retreating from all about, her head tucked over her breast as though counseling with her heart.

"What if Ah'm no good?"

Persuaded that her talent was extraordinary, she constructed another hurdle. "They may think Ah'm funny lookin' with ma skiddy eye."

"The way you sing nobody's going to notice you," he replied, clumsily trying to reassure her but getting the opposite reaction.

"Ah'm a woman, we likes to be looked at."

And so it went during much of the arrangements for her departure to New York City, engaging in the same give and take which seemed to build her confidence. But he was never able to satisfactorily respond to her confession.

"Ah done wanta leave, Ah love ya, Moses."

Moses was sure from the first time he heard Angel sing, the impresarios to a man would add her brilliance to the diadem of opera greats. Now as he watched her train shrink into the horizon, he wondered if he'd been too impulsive. Her rejection could return her to the hopelessness from which she'd come. Was he beginning to believe his judgment was infallible – and if so, at what cost to others? He looked back to where the train had been. Not even a plume of smoke hinted it had existed.

Chapter 18

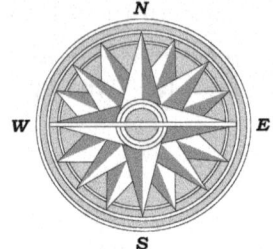

Sleep came fitfully that night to Moses with interruptions of self-incrimination for imprudently urging Angel to plunge into the alien music world. He'd bundled her off to New York, denying her sufficient time for second thoughts, and even worse may have misused her trust in him by dominating the decision. Was his certainty about the future of others counterfeit, or a substitute for doubts about his? Self-assumed infallibility was not a characteristic he sought. He was, however, sure he'd been right to distance themselves from Rush as quickly as possible. The evasion had given Moses a sense of accomplishment, even angry pleasure alarmingly close to hate. But now the stimulation of 'fright and flight' had ebbed, he felt aimless.

Of course there wasn't anything inspiring about lying in the musty bed of a flophouse, symbolic of a town sagging into despair. Through the lone, grimy window he watched dawn bleach the last of night's gray-blue tint and heard the colliding of air as pre-dawn chill collapsed under the day's warming. He rose, prayed – a custom not practiced in recent months – washed in the neglected lavatory, dressed and passed through the seedy lobby to the cheerless street. Except for a lone, outcast dog that slunk away, the neighborhood was empty, its silence violated only by the thump of his push cart on a protruding stone. Near a row of dreary factories defying human occupancy and across a single-track freight siding, a light in the window of a shack bearing the sign 'EATS' beckoned.

Moses' entrance drew no attention from a mute trio of males, their heads bowed either in deference to the hour or the ritual of eating. In an apron tucked into his pants and a checkered shirt, its sleeves rolled up to expose long underwear, a burley man moved in a continuous rhythm from ice box to stove to customer, knowing by heart the preference of each regular. His greeting mirrored the continuous motion of his cooking as he solicited Moses' order with "whatalyahave?" But if he was stingy with speech, he was generous with food. Large portions of eggs, steak, home-fried potatoes and biscuits, washed down with milk, cider and coffee crowded out the bleak ruminations of the night.

The feeling of well-being restored by a full stomach coaxed Moses to linger to watch a dozen or more regular customers enter and receive the owner's nod of recognition. Before choosing a seat, they let their eyes wander over the interior of the shack with no particular purpose as though time was of no concern. Although it was probable at least some were acquainted, no camaraderie animated them, their detached observation treating each as though they were parts of the building's architecture. Each ate to an inner cadence undisturbed by lip smacking, belching or other anatomical anomalies. Completing their meals in exactly the same time daily, they laid out the right payment to the penny for the meal in exchange for a toothpick and left the shack.

This depressing parade of spiritless lives drew Moses' pity until he realized his existence could be viewed as a variation on the same theme. Disquieted by the comparison, he settled the fare with the perpetual motion proprietor and headed his push cart towards the town's outskirts.

Wind came out of the west, peppering his face and bare arms with tiny, flinty grains swept up from the road. The land before him lay empty of buildings; seemingly endless, undulating waves of grasses bestowed no landmarks. No surprises seemed possible along the route -- no turns, no valleys, no rises or brooks meandering across his path to offer variety -- only topographical repetition to the horizon and probably beyond. Infrequent travelers coming towards him nodded and hurried by as though their rush to escape what was behind didn't allow time to talk. During rare moments of calm within the gale, he looked up in wonder at the enormous, open sky, tricked by the illusion he could see over the horizon to lower latitudes than where he stood.

Near day's end he reached a cluster of farm houses at a fork in the road, a geometric conundrum formed by the division of a single route into two, or the combination of two into one, a paradox for future speculation.

In contrast to the inhabitants of the towns left behind, the people in this settlement were as open as the big sky, ready to swap a night's lodging and meals for a day's work; a trade Moses had practiced since his departure from Poland. After the evening meal, by the light of a single candle, not uncommon among frugal plains people, he related his travel through Eastern Europe and his westward trek from New York City.

Their attention unbroken, they measured Moses' account against the stories handed down by kin who'd pioneered in the not-too-distant past. There was never an intrusive question about his presence or where he was going – his unfathomable odyssey remaining undisclosed.

On the morning of the second day, having expressed his gratitude for the farmers' hospitality and listened to their scant information on any distance beyond forty miles, he left uncertain which branch in the road to take.

Lost in his speculation on the prospects of either the southwest or northwest route, he was oblivious to the red-tailed hawk circling above until the bird swooped before him demanding attention, its eerie whistling piercing the sky. Moses stopped and waved his cap in gratitude as the hawk's flight pattern led him to the northwest route. Testing his interpretation of the hawk's direction, Moses started along the southwest branch and was scolded with a raucous reproach directing a change in course to the other branch as it climbed to fly a series of ellipses, each reaching farther to the northwest. By evening the hawk had disappeared, leaving Moses under a lone tree by a spring to eat and sleep.

In the morning as the fog burned off, Moses awoke to find Numbers a few feet away.

Only some occult force could have materialized Numbers, Moses concluded, having no more inclination to question or justify the significance of the donkey now than at his first appearance. Conjecture might be enjoyed by the imagination of the curious; a pure coincidence would be the dismissal of the literal. While Moses never disputed the existence of Numbers, he often wondered if the red-tailed hawk was a precursor to the donkey's appearance or if they were the same intercessor, changing form as demands required.

By the journey's second hour after Numbers returned, they arrived at a juncture of three routes. Moses, characteristically traditional when uncertain, reasoned the middle branch promised the least deviation from their previous course and was immediately challenged by Numbers, who started along the most abrupt, least worn, northwestern path.

"Come along, Numbers," Moses called to the donkey, happy to have him back even if he was being obstinate.

When Numbers ignored several more appeals, Moses raised his voice to a severe command only to be challenged by the donkey planting his hooves to brace against being tugged in the wrong direction.

To an observer this would have been a comic contest, but not to Moses who remembered the similar episode at Molly's where force proved useless. Retiring from battle with his obstinate friend, Moses sat on a log a few feet distant to reconnoiter, plan a strategy and enjoy the warmth of the sun coming through a retreating fog.

Moses awakened with a start, having nodded off while he waited out Numbers' stubbornness. As he scanned the nearby grasslands for the donkey, the cries of a hawk told him of its approach, and looking skyward, he glimpsed the bird as it disappeared into the blinding rays of the sun. Recovering from his temporary blindness, Moses again searched unsuccessfully for Numbers and then turned back to the hawk, which flew in lazy ellipses along the trace Numbers had chosen.

If there was a doubt before, Moses now fully believed in the donkey's and hawk's prescient powers.

With the return of Numbers, the pace of the journey was energized beyond Moses' expectation, and his sense of urgency to find Lightning Lance was reenergized despite the vastness to be searched. Entering the lands of the Algonquians, a linguistically related people of forty to fifty languages with many confederacies and scores of tribes, Moses could have been discouraged by the enormity of the task, but perhaps his ignorance of these cultures saved his quest.

Reaching the first tribal village, he was met by its entire population, from suckling babe to graying elder, all palpably distrustful of the intruder. From the pony paddock to the chief's lodge, a crowd of men, women and children had gathered, leaving a narrow pathway to their leader. Their sullen stares recalled stories of miscreants forced to run the gauntlet line, suffering the punishing blows of a mob. Moses saw a small Indian boy smile at the sight of Numbers, then tug his mother's arm for her attention to the donkey. Her harsh look returned him to suspicion of strangers.

When Moses reached the old chief seated before his lodge in all the regalia of his office, he stopped the cart a respectful distance away, approached the old man, doffed his cap and put his right hand over his heart.

"Peace to you and your peoples."

"We did not expect you," the chief said, apparently deciding to ration his parley to one sentence at a time.

"I know. I did not know who I'd meet," Moses replied, cautiously avoiding admitting he didn't have any idea where he was going.

"Who sent you?" the chief inquired, thinking this was not a man who wasted words like most whites.

"No one. I came of my own free will."

"You speak puzzles."

"I'm sorry. I'm just being honest."

"In my father's time, men who called themselves Mormons pushed carts like yours across our country. They took many wives. Are you looking for a wife?" the chief said, trying another approach to get a sensible answer.

"No. I'm not looking for a woman," Moses said.

"What do you call yourself?" the chief inquired.

"Moses."

"I am Many Arrows," the chief replied, deciding it would reinforce his authority to reveal his identity as the seat of power. "If no one sent you and no one called you to come here, you must be in a wrong place. You are on a fool's errand and need a vision to guide you."

Standing straight to his full height, the chief raised his arm, open palm held high to end the conversation, and entered his tepee, an unspoken instruction for the witnessing Indians that the stranger was of no consequence and should be ignored. Still ignorant of the native's sign language, Moses certainly had no trouble understanding their body language. Returning the chief's slight with courtesy, Moses placed his right hand on his heart and called 'Peace.' It was probably a mistake not to have told the chief he was looking for Lightning Lance, but the old man made clear the newcomer's presence was not welcomed.

"Well, Numbers. What do we do now?"

The donkey, managing a look of long suffering, shook his head in exasperation that Moses could have so easily forgotten the reliability of his path finders, brayed then started pulling the cart.

Moses, realizing he'd slighted his friend, was quick to offer amends. "One thing for sure, you've always given me the direction I need."

Mile after mile they traveled along roads and trails through chest high prairie grasses from one Indian village to the next, never giving up looking for Lightning Lance. At times when Moses would have driven himself to exhaustion, Numbers refused to go farther until they'd rested and could resume the relentless journey.

Along the approaches to the few higher elevations accessible from his route, Moses met tribes leaving their winter lowland quarters for the summer slopes above. The mobility of Indian populations was remarkable; babies cradleboarded on their mothers' backs to grey heads traveled miles with all their worldly goods as regularly as equinoxes mark spring and autumn. Travois, a triangle-shaped conveyance made from webbing attached between two poles dragged by a pony, carried mounds of skins, blankets, clothing, pots, baskets, ceremonial artifacts and weapons to and from each site. Indians rejected Moses' push cart as an inferior transport, openly laughing at its limited container space and its instability in rough terrain.

Unlike his earlier encounter, Moses found the more western tribes increasingly amiable. In the tradition of Indians, there always was an introductory parley in which each party took measure of the other. Moses soon found out the Indians did most of the measuring with child-like prose and penetrating questions. The process repeated with each tribe was time consuming but necessary to gain their welcome, and as Moses would learn later, it was almost as difficult to extricate himself as to be accepted. It seemed few people participated in ceremonies, celebrations and rituals more than Indians, and on occasion each demanded strict obedience to proper protocols. There were rules for feasts, dances, legends, petitions, parleys, the sacred pipe and even a simple invitation to join a campfire. His earlier mistakes had taught him that good manners dictated he ask about Lightning Lance only when he was about to leave, lest it appear the tribes' hospitality took second place in the importance of his visit.

The campfires were comforting; the food ranging from savory to unappetizing to perilous because of the ingredients' origins; the games entertaining and the ritual of passing the pipe transporting. Among the many dances Moses witnessed, there were themes of comic entertainment, creation stories, gratitude for full harvests and petitions for victory over enemies.

In none but the mating dance was Moses free to participate. Regarded by the Indians as a celebration of behavior common to all creatures, this fertility rite was performed most often by unmarried teenage women. The dancers, unclothed beneath their short, loose, leather skirts, performed wild gyrations, twisting, whirling and bending backwards, exposing their genitals to the young bucks in the audience. When the object of a woman's desire responded, he would rise and be led by the woman to his tepee to share his blankets and hopefully offer a marriage proposal. Moses' contrived disinterest did little to deter the boldest of these dancers, and only his petition to the chief that he be excused because his religion demanded celibacy avoided an insult to the tribe.

Legends and heroic tales, the province of a shaman or chief, revered warriors and wise old squaws. Story lines arched from the sublime to the ridiculous, but all were told with respect and rigid consistency, mesmerizing the listener no matter how often heard. In general, the themes of the tales could be categorized as world and human creation; sun, moon and stars; monsters and slayers; war and war codes; love and lust; animals and birds; ghosts and spirit world; and visions. Surprisingly, many tribes though separated from each other related the same legends with only slight deviations. In some secular legends where interpretive excesses could not possibly offend the spirits and jeopardize their future favors, the narrator would employ obscene gestures and animal imitations to heighten the pleasure of the audience.

In his months of wandering from one tribe to the next, Moses gained an insight into the nature of these native peoples and the fundamental beliefs that separated them from other cultures. Theirs was a sacred duty to protect the Earth from all excesses because, like all the animals, they were a part of its resources, true stewards of the Great Spirit's creation.

Each day Moses' search for Lightning Lance seemed no nearer completion than the one before. Ever westward, the ludicrous caravan of Moses, Numbers and the push cart crept across the vast wind-whipped, desolate plains. Reduced to a survival diet of an occasional rabbit, berries of an unknown species and wild grains, Moses' ebbing vigor threatened to halt his mission. Then one moonless night of plunging temperatures as he lay beside Numbers, he awoke to find a band of fierce-looking, mounted Indians bickering in perfect English over his identity.

"It can't be him. The Chief would have told us if he were so measly," said an uncharacteristically rotund brave at one end of the semi-circle formed around Moses.

"You're always so negative, Dismal Clouds. Perhaps he's been fasting to cleanse his spirit," said the largest of them, wearing a war-bonnet of eagle feathers which the wind wrapped around his head before unwinding to trail behind him, floating like a flock of pursuing birds.

"Why did he shrink his pony?" asked a third.

Moses struggled to rise and speak, but could only lie mute.

"He has a fine head of hair. Any brave would be proud having that scalp hanging from his lodge pole," observed another.

"You can't scalp him while he's lying down. It would be unwarrior-like if he wasn't giving you a fight."

"I say we call it a night and leave him here to the wolves," said the youngest, anxious to get back to his blanket and squaw.

"No," said Eager Beaver. "We can't return emptyhanded to the Chief as a failed search party."

"Let's cut off his beard as a trophy. He appears dead-to-the-world."

"It doesn't mean he's dead just because he looks dead. Get off your pony and try to wake him."

"Not me. It's bad medicine to touch the dead if you didn't kill them, particularly strangers. You do it."

Quick to distance himself from the task by assuming an authoritative role, the largest man said, "Who among you will be the bravest of braves and determine if our captive is alive or dead?"

A low murmur of discord spread along the arc of Indians as they tried to shrink from sight into their ponies.

"All right, then," said the largest man, continuing to disqualify himself. "Cast lots to see who the Great Spirit selects to do his work."

"We can't," Dismal Clouds said. "We don't have our lot beads with us."

"You're so unremorseful, Dismal Clouds. Use pebbles from the draw over there," the largest man directed.

"First, we must build a sweat lodge to purify our spirits," someone reminded them.

"Alright, but be quick about it. We don't have all night."

Moses watched in disbelief at how fast the Indians erected an enormous sweat lodge which, when completed, they entered astride their ponies. Shortly, thick clouds of steam pouring from the lodge blocked all trace that it and the Indians ever existed. Then a large, watery-muffled explosion was followed by a sound of sucking and the Indians and the sweat lodge disappeared as the red-tailed hawk returned to drop a map of the way to Lightning Lance.

Chapter 19

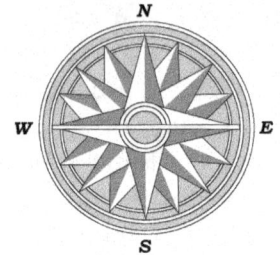

"Welcome to my lodge."

"Peace," Moses replied, placing his right hand over his heart. Were it not for the Indian's voice, strong as ever, the old man, shrunken beyond his age by the engulfing buffalo robe, might not have been recognizable.

"My heart celebrates your arrival. News of you comes on swifter feet than yours. I am told no challenge has been too great for you."

"The journey was longer than I expected--so many delays for rest and enlightenment, some roads were false starts, and I could not pass by those in need of help."

"Many new ways can trick the head, making the known look better than the new path, and you will always find people you must help," Lightning Lance said. "It takes more years to learn which trail is false and which is straight – many miles to rid the journey of the sorcery of false ways." The old man closed the entrance to the tepee and lowered himself to sit cross-legged opposite Moses. "Let us smoke the pipe of thanks for being reunited."

Like sculptures at the entrance to an ancient temple, the men prepared themselves in meditation. Despite the years that had lapsed since his introduction to the ritual, Moses moved deftly through the intricacies of the ceremony. When the pipe had been returned to Lightning Lance, he threw dried sage leaves into the fire for the purification of their smoke. Then he began to speak in a voice that seemed to come from another age.

"I am weathered by years and scarred by futile wars, but memory thieves have not stolen my reason. Many seasons pass waiting to relate this miracle. It is good you be the first to hear my legend."

"Until the days of my father's father's father, our people's lodges remained near the inland sea called Pimlico," Lightning Lance explained, motioning to the southeast. "Our land was fertile – better for growing his cotton and tobacco than our own, the white man said, so he took it. At first he took only as much land as he could work to keep his family. Soon he got greedy and the more land he planted, the more he wanted. When he could not plant and harvest by himself, he stole black people from across the great water. If he could not buy as many black people as he wanted, he'd raid our villages for prisoners to do his work. One day he came and made slaves of my parents when they had not yet come of age. He put them in the fields with the older slaves, and if they could not keep up or understand his orders, he'd beat them. Nothing could be worse, they thought.

"One night the guard was drunk and they ran away to the waters in the Pimlico where big boats took away loads to other places on each side of the great water. Someone told them the black boat with the three masts was sailing to Boston where slavery had been abolished. They went down in the ship's belly and hid many days at sea until hunger made them give up. They were very frightened, but the captain was a good man and fed them for cleaning the galley and crew's quarters. The boat finally landed in Bremen, not Boston, so my mother and father were exiled in a land they didn't know and from a land they could not return to."

Lightning Lance paused to consider how these young people must have suffered, isolated in an alien land.

"For a long time they wandered the streets begging and working where dogs would not go. Always stalked by the city's sickness and violence, they headed east for the open sky. At last the Great Spirit took pity on them and a shoemaker hired my father as a helper while my mother learned to embroider linens with his wife. All their lives they never forgot the ways of our people but knew they never could return to them."

The old Indian stoked the fire to warm his body against the weather's sudden chill, but there was no remedy to comfort his memory of his parents' bleak exile.

"In the fifth year after they escaped from slavery, I was born and my sister three years later. They named her Cries at Dawn because she came with the rising sun. As we grew older, she learned the words and signs of our new country's tongue, while I plotted to return to our people and drive the slavers out. Day and night I practiced throwing my lance until I could spear a rat at thirty paces before it reached its hole. My parents named me Lightning Lance."

Now night had drawn its darkness close on the tepee, its walls capturing the flickering fire-distorted shadows of the Indian and the young man.

"Always I tasted revenge like the bitter pain and sweet pleasure of sucking the blood-red berries of the Bittersweet. My father warned me to put away this hate or be killed by the killing, but I could think of nothing else. I worked at my father's side until I was eighteen when a great sickness came down on the land and took away my parents. The cobbler's wife also died, and he moved his work to a city far away to live with his sons. "Now there was no place to stay for Cries at Dawn and me. Then the Great Spirit told us our parents had left to make room for us and he had sent a man who pushed a cart to sell the cloths my sister embroidered for him. We were welcomed into his family, and Cries at Dawn helped his wife with the children as they came along. I pushed the cart when he went to sell. That seemed strange to me because he was still young and could push the cart by himself, but he said he could go farther and sell two times as much if we worked together.

"I tried to learn their ways like Cries at Dawn, but when the couple's third child came I told them I must go. Cries at Dawn said I was foolish, but she made a medicine pouch to keep me safe and said goodbye. Two years later I reached the land of my father by the water called Pimlico, but our people had been driven from their lodges to a place beyond the great Mississippi. When I found them, their spirit was going out like an abandoned campfire turning to ashes.

"I spent my days trying to rekindle pride in my people, but many had grown timid and turned away from me. Then a government man from Washington told us to move again, but we did not and they sent soldiers who torched our lodges. Many women and children were killed. I led our braves on the warpath, and we killed all the soldiers who had done this evil thing. The people made me chief, and we fought many battles with those who would rob us of the land that fed us. Our enemy never stopped coming. The more we killed, the more they sent and in each battle more braves were lost until there were none to fight for our tribe. I could no longer make war. I had to learn the ways of peace to save what was left of our people."

The old Indian's voice grew hoarse as he remembered the humiliation of defeat. For a moment he bowed his head as though submitting to the victor's ax.

"Twenty-two years ago a man from the mission brought me a letter from the push cart peddler across the sea. The man read it to me and then I burned it, so if you did not come no one would ever know what I tell you now. All the years since I left his family, Cries at Dawn stayed to help raise the children he and his wife had. When the seventh baby came the mother died. Now Cries at Dawn was needed more than ever and after a season's turn she married the husband. After another turn of all the seasons she had a son but never lived to know him. You are her son."

Moses' body and mind grew rigid. He sat as though in a stupor. It could only be legend, not fact.

Confused by the incredible tale, Moses carelessly blurted out, "You mean I'm part Indian?"

"No, part Jewish," Lightning Lance replied.

Chapter 20

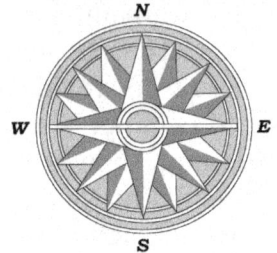

Moses' night had been one of fitful slumber, his thoughts ricocheting in confusing fragments. The revelation was so disturbing all common sense was lost in a myriad of questions that surfaced and vanished unanswered. Exhausted by pursuing the elusive transfiguration of identity, at last he slipped into a deep sleep.

The piping and crackling of the old man singing a prayer of thanksgiving for Moses' safe deliverance filled the tepee before the first rays of the sun. Moses slowly came awake to hear no joy in the chant, which if he understood it was supposed to celebrate a happy occasion. He lay still as though asleep lest he demean the solemn ritual. His limited understanding of the native tongue hindered a literal translation of the monotonous intonation, but some familiar phrases revealed its basic theme:

> I have waited
> He is my sister's son
> This is his lodge
> He will know the way

When Lightning Lance had finished the incantation, he removed and laid aside his eagle-feathered war bonnet of authority and threw dried sage leaves on the fire.

"You slept like a man plagued by many devils," the old man said, "We should go to the sweat lodge."

"First, I have things to discuss with you. This is a much different destination than I had imagined," Moses replied. "There seems to be no reason for me to be here."

"You have bad visions if you look and cannot see. Your tribe is wasting away."

"It's not my tribe. I've just arrived. These are your people. You're their leader."

"Are you blind to my ebbing power? I've laid my eagle feathers aside. I'm no longer their chief."

"They don't know that. You just took your war bonnet off."

"They know that. That's why they drift not knowing what do to. No ears but yours have heard you are my sister's son. If you stay no others should hear this until the tribe accepts you."

"I cannot promise to stay," Moses replied, "but I will honor your wish. If I stay, what reason will you give the tribe?"

"I will say you are a man of peace I brought here to counsel with our braves."

Moses' thoughts had been so scattered earlier that he failed to ask Lightning Lance if he had a son who could be his successor. Now his question roused the old man who locked eyes with him to draw him into the tragedy he was about to recount.

"Only three years ago this tepee was a place of good spirits for my wife and son. My woman was faithful and beautiful to behold. He was a son above all others in the tribe. At thirteen he captured his own mustang to ride with the braves. He could shoot a quiver of arrows into the sky before the first returned to earth. He fought by my side in one battle when sixteen, then put away war paint saying it was hopeless to fight the whites. One year after he stopped fighting he married the most sought-after maiden in the tribe. She is called Doe Eyes."

The Indian paused as though not wanting to enter the rest of his narrative.

"After one season of snows and blossoms the white man's smallpox poisoned my wife and thirty members of our tribe. They lie on the rise east," he said, raising an arm against the fatigue of sorrow to point to the place.

"Then my son idled from hunting buffalo because few escaped the white man's slaughter, became a slave to firewater and was stabbed to death over a bottle of whiskey. Until I found you I was alone and only wanted to die."

The tragic story of alcohol's destruction was one Moses had heard many times before from other tribes and at each telling he wondered why he, a white man at least in appearance, was not hated by the Indians.

At one Indian camp along the way, he asked a chief after hearing about the massacre of his people, "Why don't you hate me for what the whites have done?"

"We do not hate our enemies because then they will control our heads and we will become their prisoners."

When Lightning Lance had put aside his melancholy, Moses said, "You still have Doe Eyes to comfort you when you're feeling lonely."

"She chooses not to share my tepee because she thinks bad luck has followed her to this lodge."

"That doesn't make sense. It's superstitious," Moses said.

"White people see only superstition because they look at what is obvious. Indians look behind for hidden meaning," Lightning Lance replied.

"I will stay with you for a while to see if it is right for us," Moses said

The first sounds of the Indian village coming awake were the voices of women and children punctuated by dogs barking. Moses noted the exchange between women was flat and dispirited, the universally irrepressible decibels of children at play missing. He wondered if the rising sun would enliven them.

Slowly the futility of his quest overtook him. Was this what he'd traveled five thousand miles and given five years of his life to reach -- a place of hopelessness as bad as that he'd left, a bogus prize won with hardship and perseverance, sometimes at the risk of his life? Even Lightning Lance was an illusion -- an impotent figurehead who had masqueraded as an in-the-flesh commanding presence.

Had he been cheated by inner voices falsely commanding him like Abraham's God, to 'leave your country, your people, your father's household and go to the land I will show you'? Grasping for relief from his predicament, he contrived the possibility this was not his destination, only another way station, but the drive to renew his pilgrimage was gone.

Moses' despair was abruptly driven out by a woman's scream. Shirtless, he leapt through the tepee flap to see a drunken army cavalryman, like a cowboy cutting a cow from the herd, wheeling his horse in decreasing circles around a young Indian woman all the while shooting his revolver over her head and threatening he'd brand her with the hot iron in his pants.

"Stop! Stop in the name of the law," Moses yelled, running towards the rider to snatch the horse's bridle.

The rider laughed and kicked Moses with a spurred boot, to sprawl in the dirt.

"Stop! You're breaking the government's treaty to protect these people," Moses yelled, grabbing the rider's leg to unseat him.

"Get outa my way, you lousy Indian lover," the cavalryman screamed, still in pursuit of the woman.

Moses looked to the Indian bystanders for help, but even the men young enough to come to the rescue put up no resistance. As the victim neared exhaustion, Moses pulled a long pole from a dismantled tepee and swung it along a sweeping arc, knocking the rider senseless from his horse. In a few minutes the cavalryman regained consciousness and lay clutching his bloody jaw, gasping for breath between curses and threats. The riderless horse stood over him, pitching its head, uncertain what had happened, while Moses with purposeful exaggeration unloaded the soldier's pistol and stuck it in the saddle's holster.

"We could have killed you and thrown your body to the wolves. You are a peace breaker. Say nothing of what happened and never come back or you will not live to see the war you start. I will help you mount your horse. Then leave us and do not reload your gun until you are off our lands."

The solder, once more astride his horse and groaning in pain from the bounces of the animal's trot, still directed a string of curses at Moses. The Indians who'd assembled to witness the incident made way for the retreating bully, then clustered in threes and fours to squabble over the consequences of the confrontation with the soldier.

"You'll see," said one old squaw. "Ten more will be back to burn our village. I say hand over the bearded one."

"What's he doing here? He's not of us," said another.

"He was right to help her. None of our braves would. They have forgotten how to fight like men," said a young Indian girl.

"She should have gone with the soldier, all he wanted was a little fun," said the young boy standing next to the girl who'd just spoken.

"She brings only trouble to our tribe. She don't belong here."

"Get rid of the bearded one before it's too late," said the old squaw. "Hand him over to the soldiers and be rid of the problem."

"We can't do that," the girl insisted. "He saved our sister from rape."

"Soldier too full of firewater to get into a woman. He just having fun," rationalized one of the young braves who'd stood by and watched the attack.

"No matter," said another brave. "He cause big trouble here."

Moses, no longer able to contain his anger at the villagers' cowardly betrayal of the young woman, strode into the midst of them shouting, "Listen to me, you heartless people. Do you care so little for your sister, your daughter, each other, no abuse, no torture, even rape will not unite you to resist? There were many of you but only one drunken soldier, yet you stood and watched him torment the woman as you would not treat an animal."

Moses, growing more agitated by their indifference to being rebuked, raised his voice to shout a bitter denouncement to each. He stood before them one by one so none could hide from his condemnation in the anonymity of the group, calling out their names for all the rest to hear his charge of cowardice.

"You stand silent and witness the anguish of a helpless neighbor or if you speak only quarrel among yourselves. That's what your enemy wants you to do. You become irresolute, weakened, easier to control. You are becoming evil because you do not resist evil."

The villagers made no move to walk away from this man whose powerful talk held them in obedience.

"I risked my life for one of you -- a people I don't know. I came here in peace to be with people I thought lived in peace, but you live in slavery. Your ancestors were a tribe to be reckoned with, yet they lived in peace until the soldiers took their land.

"Your fathers chose to fight the soldiers, for that was the old way, but there were many and they kept coming. Now they have taken much of your land. You think you can live in peace, but fear is making you slaves. Don't you know you can resist without killing?"

There was a stirring of some who muttered comments so indistinguishable their feelings towards Moses were obscured.

"Next time, and there will be a next time, someone will come to degrade one of you. Who will stand up to him? Will any stand up to him, or have you surrendered your spirit?"

Moses made his way back through the befuddled tribe to his tepee, pausing before going in to call out, "Remember if you return to the old way and kill, you'll surely be killed by the soldiers' guns; remain as I found you and the spirit of each will die. You must find a new way."

The emotional mixture of the Indians' guilt, anger and pessimism fired by Moses' scolding broke them into boisterous factions.

"Who is this who dares to speak this way?"

"He speaks the truth we hide from."

"My mind is made up; he should leave. We should turn him in."

"He speaks of another way. Why not hear him?"

"We are weak up against the whites."

"You say that because you think only of the old way of warriors."

"He's right. If we stay as we are, the spirit in all of us will rot till we are nothing."

"Turn him over to soldiers. They will reward us as friends."

"You pathetic one. Your spirit is already beginning to pass away."

And so never reaching unanimity, they argued all day and into the night until the last lodge fire burned out.

When the sun passed the meridian's zenith on the third day after Moses' arrival, Lightning Lance returned to his tepee from a long vigil of sweats and mortification. Though permanently scarred of spirit and figure, his presence now awakened memories of a greatness that had been his. The voice, although compromised by years, still captured attention with the content of all he rasped.

"Your tongue carries the sting of a whip," he said to Moses.

"Some obvious truths are not easy to bear because there is no escape," Moses replied.

"Do you always speak the truth or what you want to believe?"

"I know I spoke the truth when I censured the villagers who stood idle while a young woman was tormented like an animal."

"You have caused a great dissension among the people," Lightning Lance charged.

"There was dissension before I arrived. No one had made them face their wretched decadence."

"How will you help your people find a new way?" Lightning Lance asked.

"I'm not getting involved with a people who won't even help their own," Moses replied.

"You are already. You exposed their disloyalty."

"Now you are trying to make me feel guilty if I don't stay."

"I do nothing to you, but what you did to the tribe will lead you to find your own reason to stay or leave."

"We'll see. We'll see," Moses said, having finished dressing and eager to leave the tepee and end the discussion.

He wandered haphazardly through the concentric circles of tepees, passively registering the villagers' reactions to him. Little children playing on the grassless ground showed no unusual awareness of his existence. Adults gave him guarded smiles or turned their backs. At a noticeable distance beyond the outside ring of tepees, and closer to the paddock where Numbers was tethered with the Indians' ponies, a young woman who seemed to match the one he'd protected from the soldier was startled by his approach and hastily retreated into her lodge.

Making his way to the paddock, Moses found Numbers stubbornly trying to undo the tether that restrained him from socializing with a mare.

"I don't think the owner of this pony would appreciate having a mule for a mount," Moses said as he curried his donkey. The beast tossed his head a couple of times as though irritated with Moses for tightening the tether, then settled for grazing as second best to reproduction.

"Eat your fill, my friend. The grass may not be as lush where we're going."

Moses' three day respite from harsh travel began to restore his vitality, and having promised Lightning Lance to stay for a while, he concentrated on learning the tribe's ways. He built his own tepee, made and set traps for game, tracked buffalo and rode a pony bareback, drawing a scornful look from Numbers. At night by the campfires of those few lodges where he was welcomed, Moses memorized elders' supplications and legends. Early on it was difficult to distinguish Indian imperturbability from malice, but Moses' patient observation was rewarded by discovering the subtle differences between the two attitudes.

Knowing relationships with strangers often come easier through their children, he appealed to their young curiosities by working on crafts outside his tepee. With scraps of wood, sinew and leather he made marionettes for the youngsters, drew pictures with campfire charcoal and discarded skins for the adults, and formed and baked a checkerboard and disks from clay to introduce a new diversion to the tribe.

On one of Moses' daily trips to inspect Numbers at the paddock, he passed the young reclusive woman carrying a pot of water to her tepee.

Taken by surprise, she tried to flee to her lodge but her trailing skirt caught on a stake, sending her sprawling naked and soaked from the waist down.

"Go," she screamed, trying unsuccessfully to get free without exposing more of her body. "Go! Go! I take care of me."

"I wouldn't say you've done very well so far," Moses volunteered, suppressing a smile. "Your skirt has trapped you against the side of the tepee."

"I want you go. Trouble traps me when you near."

"You've got that as wrong as possible. This is the second time you've needed me to get you out of trouble, and you've never thanked me for the first rescue," Moses said, beginning to enjoy the banter.

"Go, take care your donkey," she snapped.

"I'd be better off. He isn't half as stubborn as you. If I leave you here, you'll never get loose, so I've decided to help you this one last time."

"No near me."

"Now here's what I'm going to do," Moses explained as the woman started screaming unintelligible Indian curses. "I'll cover you with my coat."

"No touch. I no want touch," she protested, attempting to wriggle the coat off her rump before thinking better of it.

"Next I'll kick the stake toward you to loosen the skirt."

"No near me," she repeated less forcefully.

"Here we go. Your skirt is free and I'm looking away from you."

The woman was on her feet and in her tepee as fast as a loosed animal makes it to its hole.

"Sorry I haven't a towel to dry you," Moses said in jest as he left for the paddock.

Twice the woman had been alarmed by confronting him. Now, Moses decided, was the time to learn the reason for her peculiar behavior. On his way back from Numbers, Moses called out as he approached the entrance to her tepee.

"Woman, I've come for my coat."

She opened the entrance flap just enough to pass the coat out to him.

"Come out and hand it to me," he ordered.

Her response was to shake the coat, indicating she'd do nothing more than hand it to him.

"If you don't come out, I'll come in," Moses said, grasping her arm firmly. Slowly, head lowered as though shamed by revealing herself, she slipped through the opened flap to the outside.

"I'll not harm you. Don't you remember I saved you from the soldier? Why should I hurt you now?"

"You fight for me. You could make me your woman," she said, still hiding her face.

"I only want to talk with you. I am Moses."

The woman raised her head, guarded but somewhat assured he would not treat her badly.

"I know you are. You one Lightning Lance waits for."
"Who are you?"

"I wife of chief's son. No more."

"My God! You are Doe Eyes," Moses said, bending low to see the face of a woman whose beauty could not be masked by the ashes of shame. "Why do you disfigure yourself? Don't you believe the Great Spirit decreed you to be a beautiful woman?"

"Husband disgraced lodge of father. Not live to bear suffer. I atone his wicked ways while Lightning Lance lives."

"Bad counsel has jolted your brains. It was your husband's wrongdoing, not yours. You're wasting your life with false customs instead of being responsible for what you do as the Great Spirit intended."

Doe Eyes stood silent, considering words of a different way she'd not heard before. Returning to the moment, she realized her wrist was still captive to his grip.

"Let wrist go, hurts."

"I'm sorry," Moses replied, releasing her. "I was so determined to learn why you ran from me, I forgot I was holding your arm."

She shook her wrist to restore circulation. "Tribe say I bad medicine, bring trouble of bad husband. I leave Lightning Lance lodge. Now you leave. Others see us do you harm."

"Their words cannot hurt me," Moses said.

"I scorned; you stay, be scorned. They make many falsehoods of you, me. Only bad come of our meeting. I warn you," Doe Eyes said, entering her tepee.

Mellowed temporarily by a gentle summer, little effort was made by the tribe's factions to reconcile the dissension that enfeebled its people. Moses neither lost nor gained supporters for his call to revitalize unity. Lightning Lance, after a brief, unexplained rally of his faculties to a level nearing his legendary days, went into a steady decline. He sought more of Moses' presence, but the young man's decision to stay or leave was never mentioned. Ever since Doe Eyes' identity had been revealed, Moses vacillated on whether to call down the old Indian for keeping him ignorant, but he decided to let it go for it would serve no purpose.

Numbers provided an excuse for an occasional meeting with which an outcast might risk. Her questions about the unfamiliar animal gave Moses the chance to ease her from reticence, and she was attentive to each story of Numbers' origin and the nomadic lands of the Far East where Arabs used Numbers' breed as commonly as Indians used ponies.

When asked if he'd acquired Numbers while living in one of the exotic countries described, Moses replied, "I've only read about them."

"If not there, how you get beast?" Doe Eyes asked.

Uncertain how to answer the anticipated question, Moses hesitated so long, Doe Eyes pressed. "You make up story?"

"No, but you may think I did when you hear what I'm about to tell you."

He related how Nitti revived him from a coma, his care of her through a fatal illness, her dog's uncanny sense of approaching death and her parrot's flight into the old woman's cremation. Doe Eyes listened intently, her expressive face reflecting a child-like wonder.

"You great storyteller," she said. "Definitely have Indian blood, but no tell about the donkey. You think I no notice?"

"The story of the donkey is filled with adventure stories, good omens. After I left the fire that burned until there were no remains of bodies, of the cabin, of anything, I walked out of the woodland to an area of open field with just one tree, a large spruce, bigger than any trees around your village. There standing beneath the tree was a donkey I named Numbers."

"You name donkey Numbers? What mean?"

"It's just a name for a book in the Bible which has the story of a wise donkey."

She frowned in confusion.

"Let me start over," Moses said. "The Jews, my people, have many old stories they wrote in books."

"Legends?"

"Yes. The first book they called Genesis, 'the beginning;' the second, Exodus, and on till Numbers, which is about counting all the people in the tribe."

"Donkey count people?"

"No, no. The donkey is another part of the Numbers book. It's the story of a donkey that was wiser than its master who was a shaman. Each path the shaman chose was dangerous, and the donkey refused to go, so its master beat him. Finally when the donkey complained, the Great Spirit showed himself to the shaman and made him a better master."

"Beaten your donkey?" she asked with Indian bluntness.

"No, but sometimes I've wanted to. Numbers helped lead me here, never going the wrong way."

"Do all legends possible?"

"No, but we Jews -- "

She interrupted him to correct his inaccuracy. "You half Jew. Do whole Jews believe stories?"

"I don't know, but you will find some people believe there are hidden meanings to learn from in legends, while others think they are bad medicine."

Having been no threat to Doe Eyes, Moses stopped almost daily for visits, and with time, growing confidence allowed her to venture beyond the tepee's entrance. All others shunned her, making exaggerated detours around the lodge to proclaim her exile. When her weight loss became apparent to Moses, she reluctantly admitted the council, declaring her an undesirable, reduced her widow's food ration even in the season of plenty. From then on Moses spent more time fishing and hunting to share a larger catch with her.

As Moses' provisions restored her vitality, Doe Eyes' confidence grew and their conversations became less guarded. She related how her family, captured in a battle between their tribe and the villagers, now lived little better than slaves. Despised by some, she had been granted qualified acceptance as the wife of the chief's son, but with her husband's disgrace and death, she was isolated as a carrier of bad medicine.

Late one afternoon when Moses returned from the traps, Doe Eyes invited him to enter the tepee to eat a meal she had prepared. Both knew it would be a celebration of friendship, a response to his generosity, and a confirmation of their mutual trust, but neither anticipated her phoenix-like revival. Accidently, Moses spilled a jar of water over Doe Eyes' head as she unexpectedly turned to straighten up from cooking. Instinctively, he took his neckerchief and dried her head and face, removing the penance of unjust ashes. The stunning restorative power of washing away the stigmata gave back her full beauty of mind and form. Moses, as much in wonder at her transfiguration as Doe Eyes, stood mute. He watched her slowly examine her hands before lifting them to feel her mouth, chin, brow and hair to assure herself she was alive. She moved deliberately to a large pot of water catching light from the fire, and lowered her head toward her reflection as though unsure she could bear the pain of a disappointing image. Sobs of bewilderment and joy shook her as she turned to look at Moses. Slowly approaching Doe Eyes, he cradled her temples in cupped hands and kissed each cheek before withdrawing from her presence.

Throughout the night Moses pondered the meaning of the phenomenon he'd just lived, but he could arrive at no satisfactory explanation. Could anyone who'd washed away the ashes of unjust punishment experience the same transmutation? Rebuking himself for indulging in the possibility he had such liberating power or any positive effect on the lives of others, he rationalized his intimacy with Molly simply a lustful gratification.

Doe Eyes, in true Indian innocence, accepted the occurrence as the will of the Great Spirit.

And for a time each kept secret counsel until the catalytic enigma joined them in love.

Chapter 21

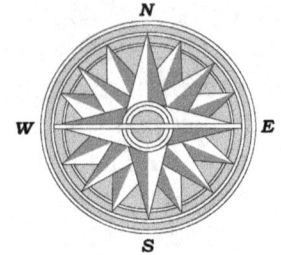

D oe Eyes attributed her sense of release from dark places to the laying on of Moses' hands and hoped his powerful medicine would extend to a conversion of the village bigots into charitable neighbors, but vicious gossip and hostile acts continued. Dead, rotting animals lying upwind from her tepee at first seemed to be accidents of nature, but as quickly as she removed them others appeared.

She chose not to tell Moses of this heckling, and the abuse continued until one night as he left her lodge he surprised two old squaws depositing the putrid remains. He upbraided them and for a while there were no more incidents.

Then one day on her way to the spring two young braves leapt from the cover of the brush along the path screeching like ferocious animals. Startled, Doe Eyes dropped her clay water pot, breaking it in shards.

When Moses learned this, he called on the most tractable villagers to punish the troublemakers, but as a minority they feared those who outnumbered them and no action was taken.

Then all the badgering ceased and the tribal council decreed Doe Eyes to be a sorcerer whose bad medicine weakened the people and incited neighbors to fight. Finally they judged her guilty of bewitching Moses with her evil spirit.

Outraged, Moses confronted Lightning Lance and demanded he force the council to recant the accusations and guarantee Doe Eyes protection from molestation.

"The council has spoken and I cannot go against them."

"But Doe Eyes is an innocent daughter-in-law," Moses replied angrily.

"There are many wise men on the council. I cannot beg them to cast aside their own law. I cannot grovel for favored treatment."

"Then I will go to them. I will not stand silent while they persecute a guiltless woman," Moses said.

"What will you do?" Lightning Lance asked in a voice made feeble by the strain of the dilemma in which he was caught.

"I will resist," Moses shouted, not knowing what else to say as a clap of thunder loosed a cloudburst of bullet-like hail on the village.

Moses strode across the tepee-encircling bare ground, fast becoming a quagmire, his water-soaked garments tight as skin, his hair and beard plastered against his skull, his a carved-stone countenance of a fierce warrior.

Throwing open the flap of the council tepee, he burst in to face the tribe's ruling elders in the solemnity of the pipe-passing rite.

His entrance, as rude a disturbance as the thunder to the council's silence, caused anger amongst its members.

"Get out, you have trespassed on the lodge of the ruling elders," one said.

"How can you sit in council with your most illustrious member absent? You are not a council without Lightning Lance. You have broken the circle of law," Moses challenged.

"Get out. You are not permitted to speak here unless brought before us."

"As long as a member is absent your council is invalid. You have taken unlawful action against Doe Eyes with your false charges," Moses yelled.

The council sat in anger, humiliated by Moses' bold indictment. Only the relentless rain and hail thumping on the tepee's skin broke the silence.

"I come to correct this wrong," Moses shouted against the storm, followed instantly by lightning stabbing its blinding bolts over the village. "I come with the truth."

"This is not the time to make your petition," a chief said.

"This is exactly the time. You have accused Doe Eyes of falsehoods – bad medicine that makes the people's minds weak; lodge mistrusts lodge now, brothers shun each other. You misplace blame recklessly and cause blood feuds."

"You dare speak to the council with such words?"

"There is more and you shall hear it all," Moses snapped back. "You have imposed suffering on an innocent woman for the errors of her husband because you shrink from admitting one of your braves, the son of Lightning Lance, was a fool. When the white soldier broke the treaty and attacked Doe Eyes, you abandoned her to be abused by the blue coat and excused your cowardice by branding her as evil. You cheat her of food rightfully hers and taunt her with rotting animals at her lodge. You have tried to drive her into exile, and when I befriended Doe Eyes, you accused her of filling me with evil spirits. She has done nothing evil," Moses cried out, his voice rising above the deafening storm. "Look into your hearts for evil. Ask the Great Spirit to cleanse and heal you."

As Moses turned within the circle of chiefs, sachems and shamen to challenge each face to face, a thunderous bolt of lightning shot down the tepee's vent hole and exploded in the council fire. The acrid eruption enveloped him from head to foot in a fiery cocoon, stripping his face clean of a beard, straightening his hair and catching it in jet-black, shoulder-length braids.

For an instant he felt dazed but unharmed by the phenomenon; then returning to time and place by a wall of heat from the burning tepee encircling him, he regained full consciousness.

Inanimate except for their shallow breathing, the elders sat struck dumb, imprisoned in a stupor, defenseless to escape.

He grabbed a tomahawk, slashed through the skin of the tepee and one by one dragged the unconscious Indians out to the open air.

For five days and nights Moses fasted and kept vigil for the lifeless council, all crouching in their exact positions at the time of the lightning strike, expressionless as though mummified. On the sixth day the sun burned away the vaporous grey shrouds and all the faculties of the elders but speech returned.

Moses spoke to them of truth, tolerance, forgiveness, and demonstrated the strength of unity by easily breaking a single arrow in his bare hands then the impossibility of destroying arrows when they were bundled together. His memory never faltering, Moses called each Indian by name and asked to be a brother. He moved about them clasping their arms in the fashion of Indian friendship before leading them out of the barren place once occupied by the council tepee to the sweat lodge for prayers and healing. Each found his voice and was amazed.

When they emerged from the seclusion of the sweat ceremony fully restored, they told the assembled villagers, "We have been spared and returned to life. Only the Great Spirit could have done such works through one of us."

Then they brought Moses from the crowd for all to see

"You are Moses, Spirit Messenger."

A spontaneous cheer from the people affirmed their excitement that the Great Spirit had made one of them a healer of whom legends would be told.

"You must lead our people so they can return to greatness," one said.

"We can be a people to be reckoned with," said another.

"From now on you will be called Moses Spirit Messenger, our great chief."

"Spirit Messenger! Spirit Messenger," the people cried out, working themselves into a frenzy as they danced in a circle around Moses.

As though long desired for this moment of deliverance from woe, a war-bonnet of eagle feathers materialized to be placed on Moses' head and a white buffalo robe draped his shoulders, signifying authority.

Reconciliation had begun.

Feasts and dances celebrating the cleansing of the people's aimlessness, frustration and dissension lasted till next day's light replaced the curling, skyward smoke of the last camp fire. Voices stilled by the call of sleep and birds not yet acknowledging the coming dawn created a space of peace.

Moses, submitting to his body's demand for rest, drifted away while considering the miracle that connected him to Lightning Lance who someday he would succeed.

He would counsel with this wise old man before the chief's insight grew feeble.

Cool air of a coming dawn carried the familiar screech of a red-tailed hawk.

Moses would go to Lightning Lance before the sun set once more.

Chapter 22

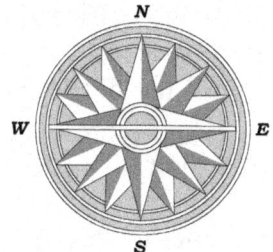

"Time grows short. It is well that we talk," Lightning Lance said, looking up from his abstraction with an ant struggling to dislodge a straw that blocked the entrance to its hill. "Even ants teach us it is better to toil to remain in our ancestor's home than to be moved to a strange place."

"Greetings and peace," Moses said, settling in a place near the chief. "I come beholden and with respect."

"You wear well the white buffalo robe once granted me."

"Lightning Lance will always be known by the greatness of the mantle though it passes on."

"Remember, unlike a tattoo it can be removed from the bearer who serves it ill."

"Or the one whose work is done well and lays it aside for another to fulfill his duty."

"Your wisdom can be a deliverance for the people," Lightning Lance observed. "Hear the message of an ancient chant for it is wisdom," the old Indian added and began to sing,

> 'The old men say
> the earth only endures
> you spoke truly
> you are right.'

"Mine should be among many voices for the robe is big enough to be shared. I will strive to make room for all," Moses assured the elder.

Both men entered the silence of thoughtfulness to absorb the covenant they were shaping.

"See, the ant has removed the barrier to its home and goes in and out freely," Lightning Lance observed.

Moses waited quietly until the old Indian was ready to return to their deliberations.

"You will be alone for a long time serving our people. Have you thought how you will live?"

"I have my own lodge, good in both foul and fair weather."

"It seems too big for one alone," Lightning Lance said, fishing for a clue to Moses' plans for marriage.

"I think my tepee could hold several people with comfort," Moses replied and then, deciding not to tease the old man, added, "There is a matter I need to discuss with you."

"I know," Lightning Lance replied.

"I want Doe Eyes to be my wife."

"Have you told her so?"

"No, but she knows I will look out for her welfare."

"Friends look out for one another's welfare but don't need to marry."

"Yes, but it's more than that. I'm whole, fulfilled when we are together. I find my truth in her. She is the truth I've searched for."

"And she?"

"I think she loves me."

"Has she told you? It is a woman's way to speak about such things only when she is asked, for she will have to hold her tongue as a chief's wife."

"We have only hinted of such things. When we're together words don't seem necessary," Moses replied.

"Love is more than sharing a blanket. Open your hearts to free the words."

"I come because she is like a daughter to you. She was the wife of your son."

"I have no son but you. Tell Doe Eyes we have talked of these things, then both come to me if you will marry."

Lightning Lance drew into his blanket, seeking restorative warmth. With detectable restraint he refrained from asking Moses to refuel the fire and struggled to add even aged, brittle wood to the embers. Leaning back, he watched with satisfaction the varicolored, dancing flames, pleased with the added whoosh and blue jet of escaping burning air. Then he forced himself to sit upright, chin tilted in defiance of his infirmities, and sang Sitting Bull's chant.

> 'A warrior I have been
> now it is all over
> a hard time I have'

"The time approaches when you should kill me," he told Moses.

Moses shrank back from the horrifying words, incapable of committing such an act.

"My body is tortured by demons day and night. My flesh has no defense against their barbed arrows. They tear at my belly. My eyes are pulled back in my head to see devil spirits blinding me with venom. They cut at me with red-hot hunting knives while seeking new untortured parts of my body. My enemies overtake me but will not kill me, for they find pleasure in my perpetual misery. An Indian chief may not end his own life. You must bring me peace."

When speech returned to Moses, his voice was barely audible. "Your agony lays waste to my senses. To only witness is not to walk in another's moccasins. As much as I would, I cannot own even a part of your suffering, and my imagination's terrors will never equal your reality." He paused as though to drive away the messenger of death.

"If I do as you ask, the miseries of your dying will cease to be as you will, but my memory of taking a life will never be forgotten. When your torment ends, my torment will begin. I can do nothing else but pledge to stay with you along your journey."

"I ask for the most heroic act of your life," the chief said.

"Let me be called cruel, cowardly, pitiless, all manner of vilification, but never assassin. I would die for you, but I will never kill you," Moses said.

"You are a man of true courage. Let us smoke a pipe to ask the Great Spirit for concord as each fights his own battle."

At the prescribed moment of incantation, Lightning Lance held the pipe skyward with trembling hands in the gesture of an offering before taking a measured number of puffs and passing it to Moses. The tranquility of the ceremonial smoke enveloped Moses with the same sense of calm he'd experienced the first time he and Lightning Lance celebrated their bond. His thoughts came unhurried and well-ordered. Earlier irreconcilable differences with Lightning Lance seemed solvable. Finishing his inhalation, the younger celebrant reached to return the pipe to the old Indian whose trembling hands almost dropped it. Moses prevented the ceremonial piece from hitting the ground.

The great chief, seated in prayer, lifted his eyes to Moses and said, "You are rightful heir," then fell over dead.

After spreading ceremonial sage ashes around the fallen chief, Moses began a fast of grief that lasted night and day until some feared for his well-being. His cries that escaped the lodge were so distraught none dared approach him. When mourning had at last purged him of his devils, Doe Eyes led him into the sunlight.

In the month when corn's green sprouts show above the earth, Lightning Lance's life and passing to another world were memorialized with chants and dances. On the open plains where there was no interruption of sight to the horizon in any direction, Lightning Lance was buried facing west to welcome the fiery thunderbolts that came from there to affirm his name. The head and tail of his favorite pony hung on poles before and behind the chief's body to carry him through the fair hunting grounds of the skies. When the chants and dances ceased, the Indians returned to their village in single file, trailing Moses, their new chief, chanting 'Moses Spirit Messenger.'

Though the village elders had restored Doe Eyes' food to full ration, Moses continued to supply her with game and took pleasure in the intimacy of watching her prepare their meals. The sensual command of her body as she moved at work within the tepee aroused him as never before. Still, because of his awareness of the possible lingering nightmare of her marriage and the soldier's attack, Moses curbed his impulses and always approached her with gentleness.

At first Moses and Doe Eyes guarded their thoughts, then discovering each other, their hunger to know and be known propelled them through hours for freely given and eagerly received confidences. Doe Eyes told of her family's origins in another tribe and their defeat in a battle with the warriors of this village. She related how they were brought here as captives, their status soon declining to that of slaves, which was not remedied until Lightning Lance became chief. When her parents died and Lightning Lance was often absent fighting white land grabbers, her status reversed to again become the target of abuse. Being the young orphan she was grateful for the attention of Lightning Lance's son, but without parental guidance, she was unable to detect the young man's flaws that led to a disastrous end.

Doe-Eyes ended the tale with her husband's descent and death, branding her as cursed. With no one to defend her, she was marked with her husband's disgrace.

Though limited in each other's language, they explored and grasped the subtleties of complex subjects. Once Moses said he prayed the approaching winter would not be too severe for the villagers, to which Doe-Eyes replied "as no one can control the weather, the Indian prays the Great Spirit will make him able to cope with whatever comes."

She spoke of the Indian living in harmony with Nature, heeding each new moon in their endless cycles as pleasurable reminders of things to be enjoyed, while the white man's obsession of trying to control time with ticking objects steals away his life.

Moses quietly reflected on all she had told him before relating the twisting, sometimes indistinct trail he'd followed from his first to his last meeting with Lightning Lance.

"I think all my life I've been looking for something I couldn't describe. Every person on my path gave me of their wisdom, but at each juncture the question of my life's purpose remained unanswered. In some mystical way I felt bound to Lightning Lance at our first meeting, but my reunion with him here did not put my discontent to rest."

Moses, recalling the words of Lightning Lance at their last talk, suddenly realized his quest might be fulfilled at this village.

"Just before Lightning Lance died, he asked if I would marry. I told him you would make me happy, complete, if you would be my wife. He persisted in making me think how that would happen, never satisfied until at last I told him I found truth in you, truth for which I'd always looked without the vision of your eyes.

"You, Doe-Eyes, have shown me there is no greater truth than love. Without love there is no truth. Lightning Lance put the words on my tongue. You have put the meaning in my heart. Stay with me as my wife so I may honor you with my life."

"Let me bring only peace and joy to you, my husband."

On an evening when the day's last meal was finished, Moses and Doe Eyes walked to the edge of the village to move Numbers to a new pasture. As the couple approached, the donkey saluted Moses as usual by stomping his feet, then added a loud bray conveying delight that Doe-Eyes had joined his master. When the chore was completed and Numbers surrendered his allegiance to the couple in favor of tender young grasses, Doe-Eyes suggested they stroll along the creek swollen to overflowing by heavy spring rains.

Downstream a mile or more from the village, the creek's current had undercut its banks before emptying into a small lake. Unaware of the hazard, Moses in his impatience to reach the lake walked on the overhanging bank, which gave way to plunge him into the frigid torrent.

Unable to gain a foothold or steady himself on a tree root, he tumbled head over heals to Doe-Eyes' amusement until she realized Moses couldn't swim.

She jumped into the swirling, wet blackness, and though dragged down by her sodden deerskin garments, towed him to a place where he could be dragged onto the creek bank.

Between fits of coughing he gasped, "You saved me. You are truly my woman."

"Must hurry," she said. "You shake. Get to tepee fire."

Moses awakened to the setting of the moon and guessed seven hours had passed since he nearly drowned. Lying on his side, he had no success looking for his woman from that angle, but rolling over was rewarded to find her buried under the buffalo robe beside him. Held by the intimacy of lying together, only their nakedness separate, he watched the rhythmic rise and fall of her breathing, memorizing the beauty of her face in repose. Her body, dwarfed by the mammoth covering, seemed incapable of pulling him from the water's turbulence and half carrying him a mile to the lodge. *What unconditional love,* he thought.

He returned to studying the harmony of his desire -- the pleasing contours of her cheekbones, the arched brows, sculpted forehead, cameo face, raven black hair now released from braids to frame the beauty of her features like a primitive headdress.

He resisted the temptation to wake her and fell asleep to dream.

At Moses' first council, in deference to the elders, he purposely sat removed from them to visibly demonstrate his intentions were respectful and moderate. Signaling he presented no challenge before all their testimonies had been given, he committed to memory the appearance, gestures and words of each esteemed warrior.

One council member was heard to say, "Moses Spirit Messenger will find it easier to complain about the tribe's mistakes than to do something about them."

Not surprisingly, most of the elders' suggestions for solving the tribe's territorial problems were only a slightly different version of the same failed endeavors.

When all had spoken, a sachem sitting cross-legged and so bent from age that he seemed to be addressing his knees raised his hand and lowered his voice to a whisper, perhaps more for attention than from infirmity. "Moses Spirit Messenger, we would hear your words."

"I ask you to ponder this," Moses began. "The smart warrior taking a path to his lodge that leads him to nowhere tries others until one leads him home. The stubborn warrior follows the same trail again and again going nowhere and may not survive to warm himself at his campfire."

Moses paused long enough for the council members to reflect on how the moral of his fable would apply to the tribe's unsuccessful dealings with the white treaty breakers. Then he spoke again.

"No one better than you can number the times your peaceful existence has been violated since the moon rose from the same place at the same time. Think now how many times you've taken the same tomahawk against the same threat without success."

Unable to refute the failure and offering no new stratagems, the elders held their tongues in awkward silence.

Then a young brave, breaking the tradition of deferring his words until all the elders had been heard, blurted out, "What would you do?"

"Let us meet with other tribes of the Sioux and forge an agreement among all with the same purpose so that one voice is heard by the whites. Let us with our brothers who represent many, not just one tribe, demand the treaties be honored."

"Where will you find a leader of the whites who can make his people obey the treaties?"

"In Washington," Moses replied, "where the great chief of the whites lives."

"Our young chief can do this?" one elder whispered, bending close to the ear of another.

"He is Moses Spirit Messenger. Let him show us," was the response.

Moses, hearing this and other similar exchanges, wondered if he'd carelessly trapped himself. Surely the outcome could differ in the mind's eye of each council member.

In the days that followed, Moses and three young braves, chosen by elders, prepared to set out to persuade other Sioux tribes to form a coalition to demand an end to lawless aggression. Doe Eyes, learning the delegation might be away as long as five months, asked to go with Moses.

"I cannot take you with me and deny my companions the same privilege. If their squaws make the journey, the men will be so satisfied they will forget the urgency of our mission," Moses explained.

"You right. I stay. Pray you return every rising sun. Tonight I make you count moons until you return," Doe Eyes said. "Close eyes. Open I say yes."

Moses sat cross-legged, deprived of sight, dependent on other senses. The dark of night, silent as a trespasser, crept in from the walls of the tepee so only the warmth of the fire confirmed he was still alive. Moses' heightened awareness of silence belied that his breathing was thunderous.

About the time Doe-Eyes' withdrawal seemed a departure, Moses heard a rustling as faint as a hummingbird's hovering, while a slight stirring of air carried the fragrance of wild flowers. Then blossoms caressed his neck, his forehead, nose, mouth and bare chest.

Doe Eyes unexpectedly made her presence known. "Rise!" she commanded.

In one deft motion, she stripped him of his leggings to bath him in cool, mint-soaked water, his skin tingling even after she dried him. It was overwhelmingly reminiscent of her saving him from drowning, and he wondered if Doe Eyes experienced the same symbolism and purposely added it to her love ritual.

Anticipated his impatience to look, she said, "No see yet," and began to slowly circle him, ever closer, whispering a love song more seductive than any potion. The warmth of her body and the fragrance of her hair teased him with her nearness.

"Now see," she said, releasing him from blindness.

In the last light of the fire she stood girdled with snowy egret feathers that cloaked and revealed her nakedness as she moved toward

Moses in slow rhythmic submission, making the enchantment complete.

Moses swept Doe Eyes into his arms and carried her to their bed of buffalo robes. When he reached for her, she loosed the feather girdle and slid under his belly to lock her legs around him. She tied her long hair around his neck, drawing his face close to hers.

"I make you come back," she predicted.

"I will always return to you," he replied.

Chapter 23

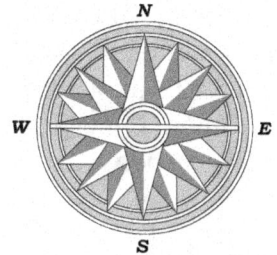

From the departure of the tribe's delegation, Moses was aware the ultimate success of forging an alliance of Indian nations across the country for a showdown in Washington was dependent on first winning the support of the Sioux tribes. Even then it was not unexpected that corrupt government officials and ruthless private interests would seek to destroy a United States/Indian agreement in any way possible.

Though conscious of the novel Indian psyche, Moses was unprepared for the exhausting frustrations and circuitous negotiations of trying to build a consensus of councils. Back and forth he traveled from tribe to tribe to bolster the weak-willed and repair the damage of erosion subtly employed by opportunists. Two tribes rejected Moses as counterfeit and declared their lands off limits to his delegation, requiring him to make long time-consuming detours to reach other tribes.

Because powwows with every Sioux tribe had taken twice a long as originally estimated, Moses believed any further delay in starting for Washington would jeopardize the mission. To reduce this risk, he dispatched a scout to tell his villagers of his difficult decision, while other braves rode to all the tribes who'd pledged support to instruct them to start the journey to Washington along well-defined routes appropriate to pony-riding plains people. To minimize stragglers and keep the retinue compact, the main body of Indians planned to stop about every fifty miles and let others catch up.

As the growing caravan reached larger white settlements, the probability for racial confrontation increased, risking the legitimacy of the movement's purpose. Hoping to avoid or minimize troublesome incidents, representatives from all the tribes had devised rules and punishment for violators.Braves would be paired, with each responsible for the other's actions. Two braves could never be separated longer than an arrow's flight from each other. There would be no contact with white women. Other women must leave the camp before dawn. Any disagreement between members of the same tribe would be settled by their chief. Any disagreement between members of different tribes will be settled by their chiefs and Moses. Fighting and stealing would be severely punished. First time offenders of the rules would be punished by public humiliation and running the gauntlet. Second time offenders would be cast out in exile from the coalition without their ponies.

Each time as the caravan approached concentrations of whites, Moses and the chiefs counseled to devise an orderly passage. Before entering or passing a white settlement, Moses and his three braves would go forward to inform leaders of the community the reason for the large assembly of Indians and then select a mutually acceptable place to camp. Never underestimating the persuasion of a friendly recital of the law, Moses quoted United States regulations on Indian and settlers' conduct and concluded by saying the same respect for the law should be observed by both races.

Preparation and moderation was rewarded with no incidents until the cavalcade reached a water hole a few miles west of Fort Dodge. The riders had only dismounted to water and graze their mounts when the acute ears of the Indians detected the hoofbeats of many horses galloping towards them. Within seconds the sharp notes of a bugle preceded a company of blue coats sweeping down from the crest of a long, barren rise towards the resting tribes. The mounted soldiers, reins in one hand, uncased rifles in the other ready for the order to attack, approached at a canter to halt one hundred yards from the leaders of the tribes. With a simple hand motion from the unit's commanding officer, a young lieutenant, the troopers moved from a compact formation to spread in a long semi-circle facing the Indians.

With considerable ceremony designed to capture attention, the lieutenant removed his bleached, deerskin, elbow-length gloves and tucked them under his belt, signifying his wish to be open-handed, then sat resting his palms on the saddle's pommel, searching for his counterpart.

Slowly Moses and three chiefs rode towards the lieutenant. Fifty yards distant from the officer, the three braves halted while Moses rode on alone close enough to see the colorless scar of a bullet wound on the lieutenant's cheek.

Moses silently searched the measure of the soldier, but a few years his senior, noting his neatly barbered hair and mustache, the well-tailored uniform and spit-polish shine of the boots. When the officer spoke, Moses sensed it was to end being scrutinized or to establish control of the meeting.

"If ya speak English, tell me where ya from."

"From the watershed of the Belle Fourche and Wounded Knee Rivers."

"What ya doin' here?"

"We are going to Washington to reinforce your government's territorial treaty with the Sioux."

"Ya gotta return to ya reservation or ya'll be breakin' the treaty."

"How can there be any treaty when the whites have already broken it?"

"Makes no difference, ya gotta go back where ya come from," the lieutenant said.

"We are peacefully assembled and only going to the authorities to redeem the lands your government gave us forever. We have no reservation that you people have not entered. We have the right to ask Washington for help.

"Do not stand in our way. What we have been promised has been taken away. Let us proceed to work it out with your people. Our tomahawks have been put aside. Don't force our braves to take them out to sharpen," Moses said, knowing the lieutenant was aware he'd met more than his match in debate and battle manpower.

Without authority and adequate forces, the lieutenant could now only attempt to save face by seeming to be permissive for the moment. Putting on his gloves with pomp to match their removal, he tried to bluff a threat.

"Ya can stay the night, but I'll be back in the mornin'," he said, wheeling his horse to lead his troops back to the fort.

Morning came and went as did the following and three more without any sign of United States troops. When the Indians' restlessness seemed patience might be at an end, Moses and the chiefs decided to break camp and resume their march to Washington. But on cresting a hill to their east to reach open plain, they heard a bugle call from the fort giving notice they'd been detected.

Within minutes, the young lieutenant and two corporals rode out to accompany Moses and the braves to the fort for a parley with the commandant.

Explaining the reason for the delay to the tribes' chiefs, Moses instructed them to stay on guard. Then he followed the troopers to the fort.

As Moses and his braves rode through the fort's gateway, the massive log doors of the stockade were slammed shut with a reverberating bang, reminding them they were temporary prisoners.

Dismounting to cross a bare earth parade ground spawning short-lived dust devils, the troopers led the way into a small building so empty of furnishings it appeared unused. The main room was absent of pictures, charts, files, mementos, of everything but two straight-backed chairs and a table made from a door and two sawhorses to support the improvised top. It was placed in front of a lone window facing out to the parade ground.

One chair, occupied by a colonel, commandant of the fort, rested precisely sixteen inches behind the middle of the table's back edge, the other against a back wall. When the colonel was interviewing anyone and chose to offer him a chair the bright light from the parade ground would be directly in the person's eyes.

In typical Spartan deprivation, the colonel's uniform was buttoned up to the throat against the cold, daring the winter make him use the fireplace.

"Which of you is the leader of this Indian migration?" the colonel demanded, peering through wire-framed glasses.

Moses and three chiefs nodded affirmatively.

"There can't be four leaders," the colonel replied in annoyance. "Who speaks for your people?"

"I do, colonel, because I'm fluent in English."

"Where do you think you're going?" the colonel asked imperiously.

"I explained this all to the lieutenant," Moses responded.

"Explain it to me," the colonel ordered, showing no civility.

"We're going to Washington to get the terms of our tribes' treaties with the United States government enforced."

"And by what authority do you propose to do this?"

"By the authority of the Sioux as a sovereign nation and the United States government's pledge to honor its agreement."

"The Sioux is not recognized as a sovereign government," the colonel scoffed. "It's a group of tribes. You must return to your reservation."

"We have no lands that whites don't trespass. They make every place their own. You've already allowed settlers in our hunting grounds. Soon you'll tell us we don't belong there. Now you tell us we don't belong here. How long will it be before you say we don't belong anywhere?"

"We are prepared with force to make you return if you don't leave peacefully," the colonel threatened.

"Don't make us fight you. Our braves outnumber your troops and they will defeat you. You and I can prevent another senseless killing that will only lead to more battles between our peoples," Moses said.

The colonel, sensing the meeting could quickly become an embarrassment for him, searched for a proposal that would avert the possible defeat of his troops while not appearing to compromise his authority.

"If your tribes return to their villages, I will later allow a small delegation to pass this way to Washington," the colonel bargained.

"I will have council with all the chiefs first, but they will want at least twenty chiefs to accompany me," Moses countered.

"Only ten," the colonel insisted.

"Ten chiefs and three of your officers who will accompany us. We will leave from here when our tribes turn back."

"You're asking me to give you three officers as a hostage?" the colonel snorted.

"No, as a sign we are on an authorized mission," Moses said with finality.

Returning to the Indian encampment, Moses gathered a council of chiefs from all the tribes to relate in detail the meeting with the blue-coats.

"Now listen to what your chiefs who went with me heard," he said.

The accounts of all were nearly identical with only slight variations in the individual's rhetoric. The same questions were raised and the same answers given over and over as Moses had come to expect from inter-tribal powwows.

When the anger and venting slowed and ceased, Moses spoke. "We have two choices, war or peace, fight or negotiate. If we fight, Washington will not believe we want to live in peace. If we fight now we may win this battle, but more blue-coats will be sent until we are no more a nation.

"We have already won a small victory," Moses continued. "Eleven of us and three blue-coats will be allowed to leave here for Washington at the same time your tribes start home. I think we should take the path of peace but always be prepared for trickery."

And so a good-faith compact having been made, the delegation departed for Washington and the tribes turned westward toward their villages.

In a light snow foretelling winter's approach three days after their departure from Fort Dodge, Moses, his chiefs and the three soldiers passed a detachment of blue-coats going in the opposite direction. Later that day and all the next when larger army units passed Moses was convinced these troop movements were not military exercises but major deployments that might affect the tribes' return.

The fifth day Moses' party came upon the U.S. 7th Cavalry, a unit rebuilt to combat strength after Custer's defeat at Little Big Horn. The troopers, at first on guard at the sight of Indians, were eased when told the three soldiers were accompanying the delegation to Washington.

"Where are all the troops goin'?" one of the soldiers with Moses asked.

"First, show us some 'dentification," a sergeant from the 7th demanded.

The soldier handed over identification papers and orders putting him and his comrades on detached service to accompany Moses' party to a meeting with the Secretary of the Interior.

"These Injuns must be mighty important," a trooper from the 7th ventured.

"It would appear so," the soldier replied. "Anyway, what's goin' on?"

"All I know from the grapevine is we're headin' out to Sioux country. They're expectin' a big Injun uprising."

For an hour Moses' party continued eastward in silence, their apprehension growing with each mile. False or true, the rumor could cause an incident and start a war, or it could be meaningless army gossip and dissipate. It was probable this would be their last chance to confront responsible government officials and persuade them to uphold the treaty. But should they not be with their tribes in crises?

Unwilling to prolong the indecision, Moses halted the delegation to parley. To a man, the Indians were vehemently opposed to being separated from their tribes at a time of crisis and they turned their mounts to backtrack west.

With little rest except to water and graze their mounts, they rode until some fell asleep on their ponies. Two days after they turned back, they reached Fort Dodge and the soldiers rejoined their unit.

"Ya really think what ya's doing is best for ya people, don't ya?" one of the soldiers in the delegation asked.

"Yes. Do you?"

"Let's hope next time we meet we ain't enemies," the soldier said and snapped a smart salute.

In three more days of long rides they reached the tail-end of the homeward bound Sioux who showed distress over Moses' incomplete mission and the increasing numbers of blue-coats. As each chief came abreast of his own tribe, he left the delegation to calm his people, but anxieties continued to be voiced in the Oglala chant.

> The Black Hills
> Is my land
> And I love it
> And whoever interferes
> Will hear this gun.

The delegation dwindled until Moses rode alone plagued by the uncertain omen of the Army's actions -- a reorganization of commands, a massive training maneuver of all western units, or the dreaded eradication of tribal settlements and culture. As he drew ahead of the returning Indian parties, he questioned each to learn the extent of tribal unrest. Nearing the pathfinders of the entire procession, he saw among them an Indian dressed in leather leggings, a faded, blue-coat shirt and black stove-pipe hat, regalia often worn by Army scouts. On closer inspection he saw the man rode with his hands tied to the pommel of his saddle and a brave riding behind to his rear leashed him with a tether.

"Why is that man tied?" Moses asked the brave.

"He's a breed. They cannot be trusted. They spy for the blue coats."

"Do you have proof he does what you say?"

"It's enough to know he's a breed. Only breeds spy for blue-coats and ride horses with saddles. The blue-coats are the only ones who want them. He tells them how many braves we have. He counts out our ponies and guns on the fingers of his hands."

"How do you know this? Were you with him?"

"I go no place with this dog. Only guard him. Before, we saw him watching us, then he go so we don't see him. Then he return. This time we capture him so he can't tell the blue coats again."

"Did you ever ask if he could stay with your tribe?"

"If his tribe shun him, why would we take in him?"

"I will speak with him. Untie his hands and put the tether on his horse," Moses ordered, exercising the authority of his headdress. "I will be responsible."

"What are you called?" Moses asked as he rode alongside the breed.

"Broken Bow," the prisoner replied in accented English.

"I am Moses Spirit Messenger."

"I have heard of you when the great chiefs of the Sioux are spoken of."

"Is it true you spy for the Army?"

"I have scouted for the cavalry."

"Do you count our warriors and ponies and guns for the cavalry or any other blue coats?" Moses asked, narrowing the question to block evasion.

"Not now, only one time when I was a scout for the 7th cavalry at the battle of Little Big Horn."

"But our tribe's lookouts say you still ride with the troopers."

"I go to the blue-coats each time I see them come to scout trails, but they turn me away."

"Still you wear blue-coat's shirt and white man's hat like other Indians who have gone over to their side. How is one to know you would not betray a brother?"

"I'm a half-breed, not red not white. I have no people, not Indian, not white man. My mother was a squaw and the tribe drove her out.

My father a soldier, I don't belong to anyone. I have no family. Tribal people spit on me. They call me trash."

The prisoner repeated much of what he'd already said as though it would gain him credibility.

"The soldiers say they are friends and I can join them when they want something. As soon as they get what they want they talk different and drive me out."

"Maybe they think you'll cheat them," Moses said.

"White men don't drive other white men out before they cheat. It's because I'm a breed. You don't know what it's like to be a breed."

Moses slowed till the brave securing the tethered breed caught up to him.

"I am Moses Spirit Messenger. I will take charge of the prisoner and keep him in the village of my tribe."

The guard looked slightly confused by anyone wanting to accompany such an undesirable, but quickly handed over the tether, glad to be rid of Broken Bow.

"You will take me to your people?" Broken Bow asked in disbelief.

"Remember, I carry no weapon," Moses said as he and Broken Bow turned away from the cavalcade to head southwest. "You must make your way in our tribe without a gun. Our tribe must learn not to fear but trust you. If you betray them there is nothing I can do to save you from their punishment. Come, we are only a half day's ride to my lodge."

News of Moses' return to the village preceded him, but none had spoken of the odd, top-hatted breed who rode at their chief's side.

Doe-Eyes stood at the entrance to their tepee watching the villagers hail the return of their Moses Spirit Messenger. The people pressed close to touch and question Moses as he dismounted, for the moment ignoring Broken Bow.

"I did not reach Washington. My heart told me I was needed here. The Army spreads rumors our people will rise against them. I see no lawbreakers among you or any other of the Sioux. I have brought Broken Bow to live with us so the tribes cannot say he has gone over to the side of the blue coats. He comes as neither an enemy nor a friend, but a stranger. Let him prove which he will be. Now, I go to my squaw for I have not seen her for two seasons."

As Doe-Eyes lay in his arms later that night feeling the stirring within her, she turned her head to touch Moses' lips with hers.

"I carry your child," she whispered. It is good that you have returned before this moon departs and another arrives with our baby."

"I was troubled that I failed to reach Washington, but you have made my return joyful," Moses said.

"You will always come to me for I will make your heart dance," Doe-Eyes replied, drifting into a peaceful sleep.

Because it was the command of Moses Spirit Messenger, the villagers treated Broken Bow as a stranger, waiting to see if he'd be an enemy or friend. No one objected to his choice of location for a tepee nor access to their trapping grounds, but neither Broken Bow nor the villagers risked the uncertainty of the first move to become friends. The stalemate lengthened to weeks before Broken Bow's lengthy, solitary excursions away from the village were rumored to be not for trapping, but for meetings with the bluecoats.

"Some villagers spread lies about me scouting for the Army," Broken Bow complained to Moses. "They say I do not go to trap but to tell about the tribe's plans."

"You must be patient, Broken Bow. Those who tell lies will be shunned and no one will hear. Take those who doubt your intentions trapping with you and say nothing.. Sooner or later any who talk falsely will come before me."

When heavier snow began to fall, accounts of the blue coats mobilizing greater numbers near Pine Ridge reached all the tribes of the Sioux nation. Like prairie fires, stories swept from one tribe of the nation to the other. Sachems prayed that this large assembly of troops was the beginning of an exodus and a return of the land to the Indians. Ghost dancers tried to assure the peoples with their animated rituals offering hope the white man would go before the next greening of grass.

Then the assassination of Sitting Bull sounded an alarm across the plains, and once again the tomahawk swung on the warriors' girdles. At the time of the Moon When Deer Shed Their Antlers, Moses received word Indians were gathering with Chief Red Cloud at Pine Ridge and the U.S. War Department had ordered the imprisonment of Big Foot 'for causing disturbances.' Hearing he would be arrested, Big Foot surrendered to Major Samuel Whiteside, commander of the 7th Cavalry, in an effort to avoid bloodshed.

Each time a report arrived, sketchy as many were, Moses moved among his people trying to calm the fearful and cool warriors' tempers. On the day following the news of Big Foot's arrest, a brave arrived stating Colonel James Forsyth had taken over the unit's command from Major Whiteside and ordered the disarmament of Indians. When Forsyth was not satisfied with the weapons turned over, he directed his men to search the tepees and tear any bundles apart that might conceal axes and knives. Angered that no weapons had been found, he stripsearched one hundred and twenty men and women and children in the freezing weather of mid-December.

For several days no news reached Moses as he agonized over what action, if any, to take. Finally, he decided he must go to the 7th Cavalry encampment to work out a fair and peaceful settlement directly with Colonel Forsyth.

"I will take two braves and Broken Bow who also speaks English," he told the villagers. "While I am gone obey the words of the council."

"Hurry back to me and our child. It will soon be time," Doe Eyes said, making believe Moses had only gone to feed Numbers and would soon be back.

At each tribal village Moses' party passed, Ghost Dancers performed their rites to exhaustion, certain such medicine would force the white man to withdraw before the waxing of the new moon. A short distance from Pine Ridge, the territory's white agent, fearful this frenzied dancing was a signal for the Indians to attack, notified the 7th Cavalry. Blue coat troopers quickly located and surrounded a band of Indians who engaged in a peace-seeking ceremony and surrendered without resistance.

When Moses came on the scene, the troopers were using physical force to herd the Indians into a large hollow between two hills.

Moses identified the unit commander, a large, red-faced, disheveled man wearing captain's insignia who kept racing his horse around the Indians to pack them together. When he saw Moses' party a hundred yards distant watching, he turned over the round-up to a sergeant and rode up to his intruders.

At his approach, Moses and party raised their hands to show no weapons were concealed under their blankets.

"Who are ya?" the captain demanded.

"Chief Moses Spirit Messenger. What are you doing with these people?"

"My orders is to move them closer to Wounded Knee till I hear different."

"It's too cold to march them in this weather. They show no sign of rebellion. Let them return to their campfires at Belle Fourche," Moses suggested.

"Who did ya say ya was?" the captain asked again.

"I am Moses Spirit Messenger, one of their chiefs."

"Ya speak better English than any Injun I ever knowed. Go see if they'll lay down any hidden arms for a night outta the cold."

"I will tell them your terms," Moses said, then interpreting the offer to his two braves who understood no English, he began to lead his party to the captive Indians.

"You go alone," the captain ordered, before cocking his rifle to motion the braves and Broken Bow to a place by his side to keep his view clear.

"Ya some kinda Injun with that get up ya wearin," the captain said, mocking Broken Bow.

Broken Bow remained silent, looking straight ahead.

"Ya understand English?"

Broken Bow nodded his head affirmatively.

"Some kinda scout or somethin'. Ain't I seed you before? Now I know, ya scouted out the Little Big Horn. Some of the troopers said ya give us bad information."

"I gave you the best, but your officers wouldn't listen and they broke their promise to make me a trooper."

"Ya a trooper?" the officer snorted.

Broken Bow wished Moses would hurry up and ride back the hundred yards that separated the blue coats and the Indians captives.

"Ya a trooper? That's a good one," the officer laughed, enjoying his joke. "Why the Injuns can't trust ya. Why ya think we'd know what side ya' be on?"

"You could trust me," Broken Bow said, almost pleading not to be baited.

Moses turned in his saddle and waved as though indicating the proposal might be accepted.

"Ya just a breed. How ya goin' show me ya can be trusted?"

"Right now you think Moses will get them to lay down their guns, but they'll attack when you least expect it. I'll show you whose side I'm on," Broken Bow cried, maniacally pulling the rifle from the officer's hands and, with a single shot through the head, felled Moses to lie dead at the feet of his mount.

In the blurred chaos of the explosive after-moment, one of the braves with crushing strength choked Broken Bow to death, knocking him to the ground to be trampled by the other brave's pony. Instantly blue coats started firing their rifles, killing or wounding most of the men, women and children. Those still standing were blasted with Hotchkiss cannons. Only a few of those struck down were able to crawl away to escape freezing to death and later compare this slaughter with the horrors of the Wounded Knee massacre.

Some have said it was as dreadful as Wounded Knee.

Grieving for one brighter than a cloudless day, constant as the returning seasons, first among the many legends and true as the Great Spirit's message, Doe-Eyes was washed with tears till no more could be shed. Now a stirring within her Doe-Eyes reminded her to put away the sadness of death and rejoice for the coming of one to whom they'd given life.

On the day the sun began its eternal ascending from the low of its orbit, a babe cried in hope, emerging from its mother into light.

"What will the child be called?" asked a squaw come to celebrate.

"I will give the child her father's name when he came to us."

"Moses?"

"No, Morganstern, but she will bear the name in Indian tongue – Star of the Morning – star of the morning when a new day full of hope is given to us."

And no one witnessed Numbers break his tether and follow the red-tailed hawk to aid others on their journey.

www.ingramcontent.com/pod-product-compliance
Lightning Source LLC
Chambersburg PA
CBHW072208170626
46813CB00003B/847